DARKEST NIGHT

MEGAN ERICKSON

Piatkus
An imprint of
Little, Brown Book Group
Carmelite House
50 Victoria Embankment
London EC4Y 0DZ

An Hachette UK Company
www.hachette.co.uk

www.piatkus.co.uk

PIATKUS

First published in the US in 2018 by Forever,
an imprint of Grand Central Publishing, a division of Hachette Book Group, Inc

First published in Great Britain in 2018 by Piatkus

1 3 5 7 9 10 8 6 4 2

Copyright © 2018 by Megan Erickson
Excerpt from *Zero Hour* © 2018 by Megan Erickson

The moral right of the author has been asserted.

A CIP catalogue record for this book
is available from the British Library.

ISBN 978-0-349-41961-9

Printed and bound in Great Britain by
Clays Ltd, Elcograf S.p.A.

Papers used by Piatkus are from well-managed forests
and other responsible sources.

Megan Erickson is a *USA Today* bestselling author of romance that sizzles. Her books have a touch of nerd, a dash of humor and always have a happily ever after. A former journalist, she switched to fiction when she decided she likes writing her own endings better.

She lives in Pennsylvania with her very own nerdy husband and two kids. Although rather fun-sized, she's been told she has a full-sized personality. When Megan isn't writing, she's either lounging with her two cats named after John Hughes characters or . . . thinking about writing.

Learn more at:

meganerickson.org
@MeganErickson_
Facebook.com/meganjerickson

ALSO BY MEGAN ERICKSON

Zero Hour

To being your own hero

ACKNOWLEDGMENTS

Thank you so much to my readers for embracing this series like they have. I'm so thankful at the response to *Zero Hour*, and I can't wait to bring you more of my crew!

Huge thanks to Marisa Corvisiero for sticking with me and this series and finding a wonderful home for it at Grand Central/Forever. Thanks to Alex Logan for your insightful edits. I look forward to your Friday emails every week! Huge thanks to Estelle Hallick for being a wonderful, hard-working, friendly, supportive—and many other adjectives—publicist. You did so much for *Zero Hour*, and I'm so grateful!

Thanks to my husband for putting up with my annoying computer questions. You are the real MVP of this series. Big thanks to Keyanna Butler for holding the fort down as my assistant.

As always, a massive thank you to the members of Meg's Mob. What would I do without you all? Also the bookstagrammers who are out there taking amazing photos of books. Thank you!

Thanks to my family, especially my mom who always buys my books even if I tell her that one of them might be a bit too racy for her. She supports me no matter what!

And last but not least, Andi, you'll never be one of the little people.

DARKEST
NIGHT

PROLOGUE

AS soon as Fiona reached into her small mailbox and closed her fingers around the mail, she knew. She knew by the crinkle of the bubble mailer, the feel of the smooth paper. She just knew.

She walked to her apartment robotically, not paying attention to those she passed in the hallway—like little Yvonne in 5B who just had her birthday party and always had a smile or Terry in 8E who was finishing out his seventies but still had a wink for her every time she saw him.

She ignored them all. Because she'd be moving soon. The bubble mailer proved that. She wasn't sure why she moved anymore. They always found her, but maybe it gave her some satisfaction that they'd have to spend time finding her again, and for a few weeks, sometimes months, she had a brief, false sense of security.

Her numb fingers had trouble holding her keys, but she managed to get into her apartment on the fifth try. She dumped all the junk mail on the floor, right inside her door. Then she ripped open the package.

She looked every time. She wasn't sure why, but she did. She kept everything they mailed to her in a shoebox and that shoebox went with her everywhere she moved.

What woman traveled with her own skeletons? Oh right, she did.

Three photos this time. The scared, strung-out Fiona Madden who stared back at her was a different woman. Maybe that was why she could now look at the photos with a certain sense of detachment. Because that woman was someone who had lived the nightmare. The Fiona Madden she was now was the woman who had survived it.

She flipped through the photos. Two of her face. One of her being violated, the man in the image always blurred out. Didn't matter. She remembered their faces.

No threats this time, just the photos. To remind her that they could get to her at all times. It was a sick power game that she had never, ever consented to play.

She ripped up the envelope, stuffed it in her trash, and went right to her closet. She pulled down the shoebox from the top shelf—an orange Nike sneaker box—and dropped the photos on top of the pile of notes, flash drives, and other photos. She wasn't sure why she kept everything, but she did. Every. Single. Thing. They were hers now, and sometimes she took comfort in the fact that they were giving something back, even if they didn't realize it. The proof of what had been done to her was sometimes the only way she stayed sane. It hadn't been just a bad dream or a figment of her cracked mind. It'd happened, truly, and she was still standing.

She put the lid back on the box, looked around her apartment, and sighed. Florida had been nice, and it'd been a mild winter. She'd miss it. With heavy footsteps, she retreated to her bedroom, pulled out her suitcase, and began to pack.

They'd find her again. And again. But staying alive was her single greatest *fuck you*. So she intended to live as long as possible.

CHAPTER ONE

SHE'D nodded at him one time.

He remembered it—the way her blue eyes slid up to his, narrowed a minute, assessing, before her chin had dipped quickly. Her running shorts had made a *swish swish* sound as her long legs ate up the length of the apartment hallway, and a bead of sweat dripped toward her belly button from her sports bra. As she'd passed him, she'd tucked a stray piece of blond hair behind her ear.

It was a fuckup. She was never supposed to see him, but he'd had to run to his P.O. box to pick up some equipment. She'd changed her schedule that day. Thrown him off. Jamison "Jock" Bosh didn't like to be thrown off. That had been a week ago, and he still couldn't get that nod out of his mind.

He rubbed the back of his neck, wincing at the cramp in his muscles as he squinted at the lines of code on the computer screen inches from his face. *What time was it?* He glanced at his watch. Six in the morning. He blinked at the digital letters and scratched the days-old stubble on his jaw. Another sleepless night, but at least it was also another night of Fiona Madden still breathing.

That was why he was here, camped out in an apartment

rented under one of his aliases, surrounded by empty take-out containers and the hum of PCs. There was a bed in the corner but he hadn't slept much.

He'd sleep when he was dead.

A week of living in this Brooklyn apartment and he'd successfully tapped into just about every part of Fiona's life and made it secure—anything he could do to make her existence invisible to those trying to find her.

Two months ago he'd joined up with Roarke Brennan to avenge the murder of Roarke's brother. While searching for the killers they'd uncovered an underground sex ring that had landed them on the radar of the most notorious, dangerous hacker there was—Maximus. Maximus's connection to Fiona and the sex ring was murky, as were most things with the skilled hacker, but he'd made his threat to her clear. She was a loose end. Fiona had been victimized once, almost ten years ago in college, when she'd been drugged and abused. Like hell would it happen again.

There'd been a lot of people Jock hadn't been able to save, including the most important person in his life. So he'd forgo sleep and stare at this computer until he went nearly blind. Fiona would go on to live a happy life and would never know she was being threatened again, if he could help it.

Her life seemed good. At least, good in a way that he could be happy. But also not good in a way that he knew wasn't healthy for a thirty-year-old woman who looked like Fiona. She didn't leave her apartment much—she was a freelance writer—and she never had friends visit. She also had a big mutt she called Sundance who barked at goddamn everyone. Sundance was a German shepherd mix—at least, that was what he looked like to Jock—who guarded Fiona like she was a queen. Jock considered him a silent partner.

Most of Jock's work was done. He'd placed Fiona's apartment security on a separate server because that had been faster than making the entire building more secure. He'd stopped short of installing a camera in her apartment and worried every day that his discretion would turn out to be a mistake. Anyone else and he would have done it, but spying on her when she thought she was alone, after the way she'd been violated already...he couldn't bring himself to do it. So he worked day and night making every other area of her life safe.

The lack of rest was catching up to him. The rumpled sheets on his bed called to him. He couldn't sleep yet, though. Fiona always woke up early and took Sundance out into the small apartment courtyard around seven. He could see her clearly from his window, and while he'd started watching for her safety he couldn't deny that he looked forward to seeing her there every day. Some days, it was the only time she left her apartment. Everything she needed, she got delivered to her door. He knew because he ran background checks on the delivery employees of the few businesses she used. If a new driver was sent, he ran checks on them, too, and he would go as far as to hide out in her hallway if he wasn't able to get a check finished on the delivery driver.

A buzzing sound filled the small apartment, and his foggy brain took a minute to catch up that his cell phone was going off. After a quick glance at the caller ID, he picked up. "Yeah."

"Jock." Roarke's voice was low and calm in his ear. "How's it going?"

"Going," he answered as he powered down his computer. He stood up, stretched, and took a sip of cold coffee.

"Anything?"

"No hits on her cell records, bank account, or apartment security."

Roarke's voice was muffled as he repeated Jock's words, probably to Wren, his girlfriend. Back in college Wren and Fiona had been friends, and both had been taken by the bastards. Wren had escaped quickly. Fiona didn't get away until weeks later.

Wren's voice filtered through the phone, and then Roarke was back. "Wren, uh, wants to know Fiona's mood or attitude. Is she happy?"

Roarke sounded as uncomfortable asking the question as Jock felt answering it. "Fuck if I know." He couldn't read women that well, even if he'd known them for years. He'd only been observing Fiona for two weeks. Except sometimes he did notice the nervous habit she had of biting her nails, the way she kept her hand tucked into her purse when she did leave the house, and the brisk way she walked. "Always on alert," he added.

"How so?"

"Takes stock of her surroundings, hates something at her six," Jock answered. "Equipment in her apartment shows some history of self-defense classes. She works out, stays in shape. Runs on her treadmill." He liked that about her. Tracking her while she ran outside sounded like a nightmare.

"Okay, that's good. Sorry, we can't risk Wren calling her so…"

"It's fine."

"We can relieve you if you want. Marisol's from the Bronx—"

"Got it handled," Jock said quickly. The thought of someone else—even a member of their crew—taking over this job didn't sit well with him. He knew the lay of the land. He knew Fiona and her schedule. He'd lived a long time learning the person he could trust the most was himself.

"Okay," Roarke said slowly. "Any problems, hit us up. You're doing us a favor."

Roarke didn't realize how much this job wasn't about the crew anymore. This wasn't for Wren or Roarke or anything. This was a job that Jock had volunteered for and one he'd see through to the bitter end. He was committed now. "Alerts are all on, so gonna get some sleep."

"You do that. Later, Jock."

He hung up the phone and glanced at the time. Almost seven. She'd be out soon. He stood near his window, where his blinds were drawn but left open just enough for him to see outside.

The sun wasn't high in the sky yet, and the air had that hazy, humid look to it. It'd be hot today.

The staircase door opened and Sundance exited first, nose down on the pavement. Fiona stepped out behind him and blinked up at the sun. She wore a pair of loose cotton shorts and a thin tank top. Thin enough that he could see the outline of her dark bra underneath. She wore her hair in a messy knot on top of her head, but strands escaped, falling in tendrils around her face.

Objectively, she was a beautiful woman. Subjectively, he was attracted to her. And personally, he'd once allowed himself to wonder what it would be like to touch her. The time she'd nodded at him. Then he'd locked it all down, cut off the feeling, and focused on the job.

As far as he could tell, she didn't date. She had no dating profile on any dating sites. Her apartment was stocked for her and her alone. He'd searched it when he'd first arrived for any bugs, and found nothing. Although he had found a variety of vibrators in the drawer of her bedside table. He'd worked really hard to forget about that, but clearly he hadn't. He was tasked to keep her safe, even if that meant from him, too.

She let the leash go, and Sundance wandered around the small courtyard as he usually did, sniffing plants and small bushes, doing his business and marking everything he could.

Fiona sat down on a small stone bench, pulled a paperback out of the back of her waistband, and began to read.

Jock didn't move, only watched her. The way she bit her lip and ran her fingers over the edge of the cover, the way her head turned as she read from page to page. She read romance and mystery novels. She alternated. The last couple of days she had been reading a romance novel, and she was almost finished with it.

She read another twenty pages—he counted—and then she turned the last page. Her shoulders heaved with a sigh, and she closed the book, setting it gently in her lap. Her head came up, and her eyes looked wet. Unless he was imagining it, or it was allergies. She ran her hand under her nose and stared at the apartments around her. Her eyes passed over the window where he looked out, and for a moment he swore that she saw him, locking eyes, before her head turned.

He sucked in a breath at the expression on her face. Wistful? See, now Wren had him worrying about emotions. He didn't know what to name emotions. His spanned a whole spectrum of three—calm, annoyed, and angry.

Then she whistled softly. Sundance picked up the end of his lead and trotted after her as she walked back into the building. When the door shut behind her, Jock closed his eyes. That was it. That was the last he'd see of her until the next day. He hated it a bit, that he couldn't keep an eye on her all the time, but he was used to it now after two weeks.

She'd taken Sundance to the dog park yesterday—the park being one of the rare places she went to when she left her apartment—and she only went three days a week, so he had some time to sleep now.

After checking to make sure all his alarms were working to alert him to any breaches in his security, he stripped down to his boxers and slid into bed. He didn't even remember his head hitting the pillow.

* * *

The humidity was so thick Fiona could barely breathe. Add to that the ever-present Brooklyn smell of the nearby restaurants' meat and spices, plus the exhaust from way too many vehicles, and she was about done.

She hadn't brought Sundance. As she ducked her head and speed-walked up the street to her Bushwick apartment, she felt naked without her constant canine companion. This had been stupid, but the grocery order she'd placed had come in and her usual delivery person hadn't been available. She hadn't wanted a stranger at the door so she'd gone to pick it up. Juggling groceries and her dog had seemed like a difficult task when she'd decided to go. Now she wished she'd brought him. At least she had her weapons in her purse.

She thanked her workout routine for her arms, but even this short of a walk was taxing as she regripped her heavy bag, hitched her purse up higher on her shoulder, and continued on. Despite the neighborhood's low crime rate—having decreased in the last decade despite Bushwick's reputation—she didn't feel safe. She hadn't felt safe for over ten years. She'd probably never feel safe again.

"Calm your shit, Fi," she whispered to herself as she blinked sweat out of her eyes and squinted at the glare of the evening sun. She'd give just about anything to head to the park down the street and read her book there on a bench without a care in the world, but she didn't remember what that was like. Maybe she'd try it with Sundance soon.

She passed an alley and a chain link fence rattled. Her steps faltered and her stomach cramped with nerves. *No, no, no.* No way would she be caught out here like this, on a hot night with a clear sky, carrying produce. Had she really needed fresh vegetables that badly? She couldn't have lived on the canned goods for a while?

She picked up the pace, and by the time she turned the corner two blocks away she was winded and all her senses were on alert. The instinct she hadn't had ten years ago, but the one she had now, was in full-alarm mode, blaring in her brain, coursing through her bloodstream like a shot of adrenaline.

She tried to calm herself, thinking about the book she'd just read, but even an eighteenth-century widow finding love with an outlaw gunslinger wasn't enough to take her mind off whatever the hell was moving in the corner of her vision.

Something was there—alive. And that something could range from a rat to a kid to an adult person intent on doing her harm.

Another block. Close to home. People here kept to themselves, and the last thing she needed was attention. A cat screeched and sprinted out of the hallway, just as a human-shaped shadow melted back into the alley.

Nope, that was enough.

She drew her gun, silencer attached, and pointed it at the dark hallway. Overkill, but no way would she be caught vulnerable again. "Who's there?"

No answer. Not even a breeze. But something had scared the cat, and she'd seen the shadow. "I have a gun. Tell me who you are before I start shooting."

A rustle followed her words, a scuff sound of shoes on macadam, stepping on trash, and then a figure emerged from the alley. Her eyes adjusted to take in a massive man—tall, broad-shouldered, and scowling, and that was all she needed to know.

She pulled the trigger.

The bullet whizzed by the man's head and he jerked to the side, his hand coming up quickly to cup his ear. "Fuck, woman!" He pulled his lips back in a grimace, and she knew she should feel bad but it'd only been a warning shot. She hadn't hit him.

He dropped his hand and dark red blood dripped from his earlobe. Okay, *oops*? She'd tried to miss. Still, she didn't drop the gun. What normal person skulked around in an alley? "What do you want?" she asked, trying to control the shaking in her voice. "Next time I won't miss."

He held his hands out to his sides, palms facing her, and his expression looked bored. "Put the gun away."

"You're not in a position to make demands."

"You just shot me in broad daylight."

"I'd call this dusk, to be honest."

His eyes narrowed slightly, and she wondered why he didn't look more scared. Oh shit, were there more of him? More big-ass dudes lurking in the shadows? She took her eyes off him for a minute and glanced around.

Big mistake. *Huge.*

For such a large man, he moved with a quickness that

took her off guard. He had the gun out of her hands and his beefy arms wrapped around her body within seconds, incapacitating her.

Her heart beat against her ribcage like the bones were prison bars, which only made her feel more trapped as she was pressed against the man's body, her back to his front, and well within the shadows of the alley.

Her purse had a Taser and pepper spray but she couldn't get to it now, not with the man squeezing her. She wouldn't cry. Not now. Tears would get her nowhere. Hell, they had never even gotten her out of a speeding ticket.

"Fiona." His voice was deep, and the rumble in his chest vibrated against her back. He knew her name, and the only answer that gave her was that she was fucked. She closed her eyes and swallowed, taking the time to gather some strength before she went full-on wildcat to get out of his grip. He took a deep breath. "I'm friends with Wren."

Her eyes flew open and she stared out into the street. Those were not the four words she'd thought he'd say. She tried not to react, not to show that she knew Wren, in case he was feeling her out. "What?"

"Wren Lee, Korean-American. Parents live in Erie. Brother's name is Erick. You and her went to school to-gether."

She wasn't prepared for this kind of conversation. She'd assumed if they ever sent someone after her, they'd kill her on the spot. "I'm sorry, what?"

Another sigh. "Not going to hurt you. Will you promise to stay put if I let you go?"

She snorted. "No." Then she clacked her jaw shut. Shit, she was stupid. She couldn't have just said yes?

He paused for a minute and then made a huffing sound that might have been a laugh. "You shot my ear. Think you owe me five minutes without running. Not. Going. To. Hurt. You. Okay?"

His arms loosened and blood rushed back into her hands. She curled her fingers into fists and waited until the heat of his body left her back. Then she whirled around and clutched her purse to her body. She had her pepper spray pulled out and pointed at him just as he pulled a cell phone from his pocket.

He arched a blond eyebrow at her, but otherwise didn't make a big deal about the pepper spray pointed at his face.

He pressed a button and waited, never taking his eyes off her. "Put Wren on," were the first words he said into the receiver. Then after ten seconds, all he said was, "Made contact." Then handed the phone out to her.

She looked at it, then at him, and then back to the phone.

"Probably have to put the pepper spray away to talk on the phone," he said slowly, as if she were a scared deer.

She shoved the canister back into her purse and snatched the phone from him. "Hello?" she said into the receiver.

"Fiona."

The word was a gasp, and Fiona blinked at the brick wall, processing the fact that she hadn't heard her friend's voice in nearly a decade. "Wren?"

"I don't even know what to say right now. I wasn't prepared...what happened? Did someone try to hurt you?"

"Uh, I shot some guy." That was all she managed to say as she stared at the man in front of her, standing with his hands on his hips, blood dripping from his ear.

"You shot someone?" Wren asked.

"The guy who handed me the phone?"

"You shot Jock?"

"I don't know. He didn't introduce himself. He was hiding in an alley like a creepy person, and I freaked out and shot him!"

"Is he okay?" Wren's voice was reaching screech levels.

"Fine." The man, who Fiona assumed was Jock, muttered loud enough for the phone to pick up.

"It's like...his ear, I think. I meant to miss, honestly."

"I'm kind of proud of you. I like knowing you're up there, capable of defending yourself." There was a smile in Wren's voice, and Fiona's heart ached. She missed girls' nights out. Girl talk. All the things that came from talking woman-to-woman with someone who knew you better than anyone else. She'd had that at one time with Wren.

But that was before...before everything.

She cleared her throat. "So can you tell me...?"

"Oh right," Wren cleared her throat. "So that's Jock, and you can trust him. He's been there for about a week watching out for you..." Her voice changed, and Fiona braced. "I can explain, or Jock can, but we have reason to believe they are looking for you. *Actively* looking."

Fiona's throat constricted, and a panic attack like she hadn't had in years—that Sundance had seemed to placate—threatened to drown her. She flared her nostrils, seeking more oxygen just as the edges of her vision began to blur. *Fuck, fuck, all of this just for some fucking kale...*

His arms were around her again, but this time they weren't contracting. There was something else about them, something that didn't elevate the panic attack but certainly didn't make it better. Wren was still talking, her voice sounding more frantic. Then the phone was out of her hand, and a deep voice murmured. She couldn't concentrate on the words.

Fiona's legs buckled and she wanted to cry for being this weak, for being unable to handle this news. She'd feared this for so long and had known it could happen, but the actual truth was too much.

She never hit the ground, though, despite her body giving out. She was airborne, and although that deep voice was no longer in her ear, a warm body cradled hers. Her fingers slipped into coarse hair and she held on, not sure where she was being taken, but Wren's words telling her she could trust this giant of a man were on a repeat in her mind.

Trust him. When was the last time she'd trusted anyone but herself?

CHAPTER TWO

JOCK hadn't expected this. He prided himself on always thinking of all possible outcomes, but he'd never imagined Fiona would shoot him and then nearly collapse in a panic attack.

He couldn't stop thinking about the look in her eyes as she'd aimed the gun at him, the determination and strength even as her hands shook. He was lucky she hadn't taken his head off.

He held her in his arms and grabbed her grocery bag. She was dazed but aware, her breathing short and sweat beading at her temples, matting her hair to her forehead. She mumbled something about being able to walk so he placed her down gently and, with a firm hand on her bicep, directed her up the street and to her apartment. If she'd been more alert, she probably would have wondered how he knew where she lived and which key on her key ring unlocked her deadbolt.

Paws skittered on the other side of the door and a deep *woof* seemed to shake Fiona out of her daze. When Jock opened the door Sundance immediately bounded into his owner, sniffing her hands, checking out her body. When he spotted Jock his ears went flat, and his lips curled back to reveal his teeth. A deep growl rumbled from the dog's chest. He reminded Jock a bit of the dog he'd had as a kid so he held out his palm for the dog to smell while keeping a firm hand on Fiona.

Sundance sniffed his hand tentatively and stopped growling but didn't take his eyes off the intruder.

Jock nodded to Fiona to walk toward her kitchen. She stared at him in confusion. "Groceries," he said, gesturing to the bag in her arms.

After a moment, his words penetrated. "Oh right, thanks for grabbing them."

Of course. Like he'd leave her food on the street.

She led the way and he set her bag on the counter while Sundance stuck to Fiona's side. Jock began to put away her groceries—vegetables in the crisper, eggs on the top shelf, milk in the door.

When he straightened up, Fiona was watching him. Her breathing seemed normal, and her eyes were less panicked. He poured a glass of water and handed it to her silently. She took it with a hesitant hand. "So, you're Jock."

He nodded.

"And you've..." She bit her lip. "Been watching me?"

He nodded again.

"Are you going to speak?"

"I can speak when I have to, but you've been asking yes or no questions."

She took a sip of her water. "Okay, so can you tell me *how* you've been watching me without me knowing? Wren said to trust you, but this isn't easy for me."

He folded his arms across his chest and leaned back against the refrigerator. "Got an apartment here for the last two weeks. Secured your online accounts so it's harder to trace you. Ran background checks on every delivery person that comes to your door. Also checked this apartment for bugs."

She choked on her water. "I'm sorry? You checked my apartment?"

He wasn't going to apologize for keeping her safe. "Yes."

Her eyes widened. "When? How?"

"Two weeks ago. I didn't install cameras or anything, just checked to make sure your apartment was clear. You were at the dog park at the time. If it makes you feel better, Wren told me to do it." He didn't want to be cruel but he was blunt and honest. He didn't know how to be anything different. He could understand if she was pissed, but he figured she'd be more pissed if she were dead.

She blinked at him and then chugged the rest of her water while staring off into the rest of her apartment. It was a comforting space—the kitchen was painted a bright yellow with blue tile, her living room was a soft green, and a purple blanket rested along the back of her beige couch. The floor was old, scarred hardwood and creaked a bit under his boots.

"I don't know what to say right now," she said softly. "I don't know you. And it's been a long time since I've known anyone, really. No one comes into my apartment, and now you're here." Her gaze traveled down his body and back up, and he was surprised at the heat that flushed through him at her perusal. "Taking up a lot of space."

"I do that," he said.

She cocked her head. "Can you please tell me who you are? How you know Wren? I'm still trying to process..."

Talking about himself hadn't been in the job description. "Do you want me to call her back?"

"Maybe later," Fiona answered. "But you're the one here

right now, standing next to me, supposedly watching over me. So I'd like to hear you talk."

He didn't say anything for a moment, unsure where to start.

"How about you tell me if your name is really Jock?"

Okay, that was easy. "No, it's a nickname. Hacker term for using brute force."

Understanding dawned. "You're friends with Erick and Roarke, then. Wren told me what they did."

"Met Roarke years ago. Owed him a favor and helped him out with a mission recently."

"Do you still owe him a favor?"

He frowned at her. "Sorry?"

"Is this, with me..." She pointed at herself. "Is this another favor?"

He shook his head.

"Then why are you here? You don't know me. Why do you care what happens to me?"

It was a good question. "I didn't two weeks ago. Watched you and now I feel responsible. When I feel responsible for something, that's it. I'm all in."

Again, her gaze perused him. "Are you ex-military?"

He wondered how she'd guessed that. "Retired."

She nodded. "You have that... vibe."

"Vibe?"

"The taking orders, honor code, *hoo-ah* vibe. I bet you have some sort of military tattoos beneath that tight tee, right?"

He liked how perceptive she was. "Yep."

She jolted. "Oh shit, that reminds me. I, uh, shot you? We should probably look at your ear."

He ran his fingers along the ragged rim of his ear. She'd taken a chunk of cartilage, but he didn't need it anyhow. Plus, the blood had clotted. "It's all right."

She opened a cabinet near the sink and pulled out a small white plastic box that said First Aid in red block letters. "Please, let me at least clean it."

He didn't move, and they stood in the kitchen awkwardly, with him leaning against the fridge and her standing with the first aid kit clutched in her hands. She pointed to the small table at the edge of her kitchen. "How about you sit down, and I'll take a look?"

Fine. He'd do this, even if he'd rather just look at it on his own. He strode toward the chair and sank down in it, waiting for her to attend to him. Sundance, tongue lolling out of his mouth, trotted over and sat down beside Jock.

Fiona placed the first aid kit on the table, flipped it open, and pulled out a disinfectant wipe. She stood at his side, so close that her tits brushed his shoulder, and he closed his eyes. He didn't want to be attracted to her, and for two weeks he'd been able to ignore his growing interest. But now he knew her, heard her voice, saw the anger and fear and strength and everything else that lurked in her blue eyes. He liked *her* now, and his protective instincts were in overdrive.

It would have been better if she weren't a nice person. If she'd shot him and then hadn't tried to clean him up or get him to talk to her. If her voice wasn't so soothing and her skin so soft.

Fuck.

The antiseptic wipe stung a bit, but he'd been hurt worse so he didn't move. He let Fiona clean his ear and apply a bandage to it. Her breath blew over his scalp, and her fingers handled his injury as if he were made of porcelain. When she was finished, she swiped at his shoulder. "There's blood on your shirt."

He opened his eyes to see Sundance still watching him.

Fiona was so close he could smell her, some citrusy scent that he'd never forget now. "It's fine."

"I can wash it for you, if you'd like."

He tilted his head to eye her. "I have five others just like this. It's fine."

"But still, if you want to leave it with me—"

He stood up abruptly, towering over her smaller frame. Sometimes he forgot how large he was, but next to her in this small apartment, he felt huge. "Fiona, do you really want me to take off my shirt right now?"

Her eyes were huge and round as she stared up at him. Her hand had been on his shoulder, and as he stood up it slipped down to rest on his chest. The heat of her fingers burned through his thin T-shirt, lighting up his body like fireworks. He clenched his jaw and she backed up, the hot weight of her hand leaving him as she cleared her throat. "Right, I, uh, can get it from you some other time."

He didn't know her history with men, if she'd had a man's hands on her since the assault. It'd been ten years so maybe she'd been able to recover enough to be touched. But he wasn't about to put her in a position where she was uncomfortable with a half-naked man in a small space. He'd never hurt her but he understood trauma—it fucked with your head, twisted shit and turned everything ugly.

With a whine, Sundance nudged Fiona's hand, and she briefly rubbed his nose before pointing to her door. "He needs to go out."

A red leash hung on a hook near the door. Her apartment was so small that he was there in a second. He clipped it to the dog's collar, who sat patiently, and then he wrapped the leash around his wrist. "Let's go."

She didn't move for a minute, as if she hadn't expected him to go along.

"You want me to stay here?"

She bit her lip and then shook her head with a couple of quick jerks.

He opened the door and motioned for her to go on ahead. He followed her out with a happy dog.

* * *

Fiona walked the route down to the courtyard on autopilot as her mind spun to catch up with all that had happened. First of all, Sundance had been fine with Jock. How was that possible? Her dog hated everyone but her. Was the man some sort of dog whisperer, too?

And why was it that she herself felt so comfortable in his presence? He was just so...big. She glanced over her shoulder at him. His gaze continually took in their sur-roundings, his jaw set, full lips in a straight line. Yeah, she felt safe. Despite his size. She'd avoided large men for years. While she worked out and built up her strength, she couldn't change the fact that she was short and petite. A large man could still overpower her. When she had tried online dating—which hadn't been for years—she'd always asked about height before agreeing. Which was probably neurotic, but then she *was* neurotic.

And now she was willingly placing herself in a small space with a man who could and already did overpower her. Wren had said to trust him, and even though it'd been a while since Fiona had seen her friend, she knew Wren had always cared and looked out for her.

When they reached the courtyard, Jock dropped the leash and Sundance dutifully trotted around, sniffing at flowers and digging up some dirt. She sat on a stone bench, still warm from the daytime sun.

Jock didn't sit. He stood at the end of the bench, thick arms across his chest, looming over her. It was weird. After five minutes of said looming, she was over it. "Can you sit down?"

He looked down at her with that frustratingly blank expression. Was he part cyborg? Maybe that was how they made hackers now. Half machines themselves. "Sit?" he asked.

"Yeah, you're ... looming."

"'Looming'?"

"Yes, looming. It's making me nervous."

He sat promptly, as if those were magic words. His body took up three-quarters of the bench as he spread his massive thighs and leaned his elbows on his knees, head still up as he scanned the courtyard.

"Thank you," she mumbled, but he didn't react.

There were worse things, she figured, than a silent bodyguard. What if he hummed? People who hummed nonstop were the worst. She ran her finger over a small hole in the knee of her jeans. "So, what happens now?"

Again he had one eyebrow raised. "What do you mean?"

"I mean ..." She gestured vaguely. "Are you going to go back to lurking invisibly? Are you leaving? What?"

"I'm not leaving," he said like that was the stupidest suggestion ever. "Made a commitment to your safety and intend to see it through."

"Okayyyy, but—"

He straightened and twisted at the waist to face her. "How much you see me is up to you. Got an apartment where I sleep and work, so no need to crash your place. You want someone to run your errands? I'm here. Want someone to watch over you at the dog park?" He jerked a thumb at his chest. "Me."

This was all so weird. Who was this guy? "I don't get it. I can't pay you—"

He made a disgusted sound in his throat.

"I'm just saying, I'm confused how this is possible for you—"

"I have plenty of money. More than I need. Can't take it with you when you die."

Must be nice. She was in constant danger of her electric being shut off. "Don't you have family, friends—"

"Nope."

She smacked her thigh to draw his attention. "Can you stop interrupting me?"

He jerked at her raised voice and then bowed his head slightly. "Sorry."

"I get the impression you don't like to talk or answer questions, but you have to understand I need answers. My instincts have gotten me this far. I can't ignore them when they question why I'm going to trust a strange man."

Shit, the telltale prickle of tears burned her eyes. She didn't want to cry, but this was a lot in one day. She'd learned that horrible event in her past was resurfacing, and she now had a six-foot-something bodyguard. Sundance trotted over like he sensed her distress, and nudged her hand. She rubbed his ears and he panted, his moist breath blasting her leg.

Beside her, Jock sighed heavily. "This isn't normal for me. I prefer the anonymity of working from behind the computer. Letting you see me was a mistake, and I'm not trained to...to..."

"Deal with humans?" she finished with a slight smile. The man was trying; she had to hand it to him.

"Yes." He blew out a relieved breath.

"But you can protect me physically, too?"

This time he met her gaze square-on. "I can protect you in every way."

The intensity in his eyes was too much for her. She looked away, focusing on Sundance, even as the words sunk into her bones like a drug. He could protect her. He *would* protect her. He'd had the chance to kill her or kidnap her about five times now, and he obviously hadn't. "I don't know why you're doing this for me, but thank you."

He didn't respond, only reached out and ruffled Sundance's ears.

"So, what do you know about me?" she asked.

"You write freelance, mostly listicles and quizzes. You like romance and mystery books that you either read on your Kindle app or buy from the used paperback store over on King. You take Sundance to the dog park every three days, and when you're not looking he likes to flirt with that golden retriever."

For some reason, she latched on to the last thing and ignored everything else. "I knew it," she hissed dramatically. She glared at Sundance. "You hussy."

Jock's lips tilted up at the corners, the first semblance of a smile she'd seen from him. "You burn grilled cheese but make great omelets."

"How the hell do you know that? Do you have cameras in my apartment?" The thought that he'd been watching her...

He shook his head and tapped his nose. "I can smell everything you burn."

"You can smell it?" What kind of cyborg was he?

Then he laughed, a rusty sound that rumbled up his chest and burst from his mouth. "I'm kidding. You wrote it in an article that I read."

She snapped her jaw shut and slumped on the bench with relief. "Don't freak me out like that again."

He rubbed his palms together, his gaze on his hands. "I couldn't put cameras on you. To spy. Thought you'd been through enough."

Her hulking bodyguard had a conscience. And it occurred to her now that he knew. He knew everything about her and her past. Her stomach twisted painfully. "So you know. What happened to me."

He looked at her sharply. "It didn't just happen to you. *They* did that to you. Blame is on them. And as soon as we get any sort of idea how to find who's behind this, I'll be first in line to make them hurt. Understand?"

She'd never met a man this intense. His words, when he finally did speak, dripped with determination and confidence. Something fluttered in her stomach, a feeling she hadn't experienced in a long time. Sexual attraction. To a real human being sitting in front of her, not harmless porn on her phone in the dark.

She nodded and looked back at Sundance, thankful he was the perfect distraction. Attraction to Jock was stupid. This was a job to him, another duty in a long line of them, she was sure. She was merely a body he meant to protect, and he wanted to take down the men who were criminals. Pure and simple. This wasn't personal for him. Not like it was for her.

He was a bodyguard to keep her safe. *Don't make it a thing, Fiona*, she thought to herself.

Jock stood next to her. "Up," he said, like she was a dog, and she didn't even bother to argue. Maybe tomorrow she'd establish better boundaries. Right now, she was too tired. The sun had set so the only light in the courtyard came from a couple of yellow pole lights. She stood up and grabbed Sundance's leash, walking ahead of Jock.

She had to admit that not having to look over her shoulder all the time, to have him back there doing it for her, was a relief.

But what would happen once he left? He wasn't going to stay with her forever. That was crazy. When it was just her and Sundance again, would her instincts still be as sharp? Would she forget how to watch her back?

She'd never relied on anyone. Her parents had only gotten married when her mother got pregnant, and they'd divorced before she entered elementary school. Her father quickly remarried and started another family while Fiona's mother—who'd never been a pleasant woman—worked nonstop. Fiona learned at a young age how to do just about every household chore herself, from cooking to cleaning. She'd grown up like this, so relying on someone else was foreign to her.

By the time they made it back to her apartment, a headache had her feeling like her head was crushed in a vise.

Jock closed the door of her apartment but didn't stray far from it while she poured fresh water for Sundance. She downed a couple of Advil dry before turning to Jock.

"I'm up on the fifth floor. 5H. If you need me. Number's already programmed in your phone." He handed it to her with no explanation of how he'd gotten it or when he'd had the time to type in his number. She didn't bother asking. Maybe one day she'd get him to spill more secrets.

"Thanks," she muttered.

With a nod and one more lingering look he walked out, closing the door behind him. She stared after him, feeling, for the first time in a long time, not alone.

CHAPTER THREE

HER hands scorched up his back, nails digging into his skin, and he grunted, wanting more pressure, wanting her marks.

"Jamison," Fiona panted in his ear as her tight heat clamped around his cock. "Fuck me."

He rolled onto his back and thrust up into her. She moaned as he held tight to her hair, wrapping it around his fingers. The softness brushed his chest, his neck, his face. He was surrounded by her scent and the sound of their bodies colliding. He tried to speak, to tell her how perfect she was, how fucking amazing she felt sprawled on top of him, skin to skin. Her body trembled and her nails dug into his shoulders as she braced herself above him. He was almost there, the feeling of his impending orgasm speeding down his spine like a bullet.

Her hips stuttered. "Jamison," she said on a moan, continuing to thrust. His real name on her lips was fucking heaven to his ears.

He tried to speak again, but then something wet trickled down his chest. He glanced down to see red rivulets of blood from where she'd pierced him with her nails. The drops turned into spurts, hot gushes of fresh blood, *coating his chest, slipping down his sides to wet the sheets.*

"Jamison!" The urgency in her voice had him jerking his head to face her. Her eyes were wild, unfocused, her mouth dropping open as she continued to ride his cock in frenzied thrusts.

The pain hit him then, daggers in his shoulders, from her nails digging into his flesh, muscle, scraping his bone.

"Fiona!" he finally shouted, his voice sandpaper rough.

"Jock!" she screamed as mascara-tinted tears streamed down her face, mixing with the blood on his chest. Fuck, his vision blurred as he tried to figure out what was going on.

Something was tugging her off him and she clung harder, her hands coated in his blood. "Save me!" she cried.

He tried to hold Fiona to him even as something was yanking her away. He wrapped his arms around her naked body but his skin was slick with blood and he was weak, so weak. Why so much blood? His vision darkened. "Fiona!" He blinked rapidly. Where was his gun?

"J!" she shouted, and then she was gone, her body pulled into the darkness, out of his arms.

"Fiona!" he shouted, his bloody hands grasping at nothing but air.

Jock bolted upright on his mattress, clutching his chest, swiping at the blood but only finding clean, dry skin. He breathed deep, heart racing, whipping his head around his darkened apartment, looking for Fiona.

He blinked, his brain slowly filtering out his dream from reality. He peered at his shoulders, rubbing them but not finding any wounds, no blood. Nothing. He was, however, hard as a fucking rock, his cock an iron bar in his boxers.

A dream. A dream that turned into a nightmare. But it

wasn't real. Not real. Jesus, would this be how the mission went? Him dreaming of fucking his charge? Because that was not okay. For fuck's sake, why did his unconscious have to be a horny bastard? He hadn't had sex dreams since he was a teenager.

Save me. Fiona's voice echoed to him in the dark. He scrambled on the floor for his phone and pressed a button. It rang three times before a soft voice said, "Hello?"

"You okay?" he asked, trying hard to keep his voice calm.

"Jock?"

"Who else? You okay?"

There was a rustle, like she was turning in her sheets. He swallowed hard as his cock throbbed.

"Um..." She yawned. "It's two a.m."

"Didn't ask the time, asked if you were okay."

"Right." There was a smile to her voice. "Well then yes, I'm okay."

"Did I wake you?"

"Uh, not really. I sleep in fits a lot."

He didn't like that. She should be getting a solid eight hours. "'Kay, get some rest."

"Is that an order?" Her bedroom voice was killing him.

"Yeah."

"'Kay, will do, Jock."

"Later."

He hung up and tossed his phone on the floor and then fell back onto the bed with a groan, rubbing the heels of his palms into his eyes. His dick could fucking deal. He wouldn't be getting anywhere between the legs of Fiona Madden, and that was that.

Now if he could just tell his subconscious that, maybe he'd make it through this mission without losing his goddamn mind.

* * *

The first half of the night Fiona hadn't slept well. Sundance was fine, snoring in his bed beside hers, but she tossed and turned, thinking about Jock. Would she see him every day? She still had to work. It wasn't like she could sit and talk with him in her apartment all day. Then the image of Jock's big body sitting in her kitchen while they drank tea and chit-chatted made her smile. Yeah, she didn't think she'd have to worry about him trying to take up her time with conversation.

Then Jock had called to check on her, which was weird, yet his order for her to get some sleep was something her body obeyed. She'd hung up the phone and fallen asleep.

When the sun came up and she was awake again, she felt like she could have slept a whole extra day. Her shoulders hurt from firing her gun and she was still shaky from yesterday's panic attack. Which...she didn't really want to think about that. The way that her throat had closed and her mind spun had been fucking terrifying, and no training could have prepared her or stopped her body's natural reaction.

She'd been so confident that she was prepared for what could happen, but her meeting with Jock proved her one-woman show wasn't as strong as she thought it'd been.

When the sun rose she stared at the ceiling until Sundance got up, stretched, and began to nudge her. She let him lick her fingers with his long tongue. She ruffled his ears, and he sat on his haunches and let out a soft *woof*.

"I know, I know, you have to go out."

She rolled out of bed and pulled on a pair of leggings and

a hoodie. She let her hair down, not bothering to fuss with it. A long time ago it'd been a source of vanity to her; now she contemplated chopping it off just about every day.

By the time she'd let Sundance do his business and then climbed the stairs back to her apartment, she was yawning and irritable. And oh shit, she just remembered she didn't have enough coffee. She'd meant to get some yesterday with her groceries.

A movement by her door had her jerking her head up but it was only Jock, standing with his arms across his chest, leaning against the wall outside her door. He had on the same shirt he'd worn yesterday, minus the stain.

Her eyes remained glued to his chest because she wasn't sure anyone who was attracted to men could look away from a chest like that. "You really do own several of the same shirt, huh?"

He didn't answer her, probably because he was wearing the answer. She almost asked him to be a little considerate and buy a bigger size, but she kept that to herself. His damn pecs were distracting, not to mention his biceps.

He straightened from the wall and picked up several plastic bags at his feet. She frowned at them. "What's in there?"

"Supplies."

"Supplies for what?"

"You."

She'd been the recipient of random acts of kindness over the years, like that time she'd gone to the grocery store but forgotten her wallet. She'd only wanted some peanut butter and jelly to tide her over until her next paycheck. The woman behind her had paid for her groceries, no questions asked.

But this...this wasn't a random act of kindness. This

was a man doing things for her, things that would probably make her feel indebted to him. Did she want that? "Is this a thing where you're going to say I owe you?"

He gave her that look again, like he was disgusted. "Owe you?"

"Yeah, you're buying me supplies, basically working for me, and I don't—"

"Open your door."

"You're interrupting me again."

"Not having this conversation in the hallway, babe. Open the door."

Her eyeballs bulged. She actually felt them swell in her skull. "Did you just call me 'babe'?"

He inhaled deeply, his eyes sliding shut for a moment, before he exhaled with a flare of his nostrils. "Open. Your door."

They were going to have words, but those words would be said inside because she did have nosey neighbors. She imagined Marlene was across the hall with her ear to the door right now.

So Fiona flung open the door and marched inside. After pouring Sundance's food into his dish and fetching him fresh water, she rounded on the man who'd crashed into her life. He was unpacking his *supplies* on her counter while she fumed five feet away.

Her kitchen was now littered with a smoke detector, surge protector, new router, and several other odds and ends she couldn't identify. Finally Jock leaned his hands on the counter and looked up at her. "There is no owing in this. None. This is my job to watch over you, and I take it seriously. You don't have to like me or be kind to me. I don't really give a fuck. But one thing you won't do is assume I think you owe me."

He held her gaze for a long time as she processed what he'd said. Of course she wouldn't be unkind to him. No matter if it was his job or not, he was here for her benefit. Something she was thankful for. "I'm sorry. I've been alone for a long time, and one thing that's nice about that is never feeling like you're indebted to someone."

He nodded. "I get that."

"And I do appreciate what you're doing. I..." She looked away, the memory from yesterday threatening to swamp her. "I thought I was strong, and then yesterday, when you told me they were looking for me, I..."

He didn't speak for a long time, and she fought not to cry or break down in front of this man. That might be too many emotions for him.

Finally he took a step closer to her. "You are strong. You shot me, remember? And when the panic attack hit you, Wren had already told you that you could trust me. I think your mind knew it and let you react like you did."

She tilted her head at him because what he said...made sense. "Really?"

"Really." He turned away, surge protector in hand. The conversation was over, since Jock deemed it to be. He was already next to her TV, pulling out plugs from the extension cords she'd rigged up. The more he worked, the angrier his actions seemed. Yeah, she knew that what she had set up was a fire hazard, and she had had every intention of fixing it but hadn't gotten around to it yet. *Oops.*

Finally he turned to look at her, eyes narrowed. "Rest of your rooms look like this?"

She twisted her lips to the side. "Uh, maybe my bedroom?"

He growled.

"Look, can you ease up on the electronic shaming? I

haven't had my breakfast, or coffee, and I'm out, so I need to run to the bodega."

He pointed at a bag at the corner of the counter that he hadn't unpacked yet. Just pointed and then resumed what he was doing. His avoidance of speech was both annoying and endearing.

She shuffled over to the bag and peered inside. In it were a can of coffee—the same brand she had on her counter-top that was now empty—some fresh fruit, a small carton of eggs, and bagels with cream cheese.

And she was going to cry. Just bawl her eyes out right there in front of God and Jock and Sundance. He'd bought her coffee. And food. And was right now over in the corner of her apartment preventing fires like a boss.

She rubbed her chest, blinking rapidly as she pulled the coffee out of the bag, and began to make it. Her hands needed to be busy—even if her mind was going a mile a minute. Getting used to this care was dangerous. It wasn't even about depending on someone else...now it was about depending on Jock. Big, silent, protective, attractive Jock. Jock who made sure she was safe, and noticed her coffee was low—*he'd fucking noticed!*—and thought to bring her a fresh breakfast, since she'd been subsisting on oatmeal in the morning for months.

She glanced at him. Had he eaten? A man the size of a grizzly needed to eat a lot, right? That muscle mass had to burn about five thousand calories a day.

"Can I make you breakfast?" she said, unsure what she'd make, but she could think of something.

He straightened and began to walk toward her smoke detector by her front door. "Already ate."

"Okay, but second breakfasts are all the rage, you know."

He stopped and turned to look at her. His eyes did that thing, the body scan most men did that usually left her feeling cold and objectified, but when Jock did it, she felt...protected, as if just his perusal was enough to cage her in a force field.

Even so, it struck her she wasn't wearing much— leggings and a shirt that only came to her waist. She wasn't wearing a bra either, just a tank top. Her nipples pebbled beneath her shirt and goose bumps broke out on her arms.

From a simple look. Okay, so maybe it was a force field, but since Jock had made it, he could penetrate it.

He turned away before she could read his expression. "I'll eat whatever you make."

While he proceeded to take down her old smoke detector, she turned on her heel to face her stove. Right, food. She hadn't made breakfast for someone other than herself in a long time. And when had she last made eggs? She had bagels, fruit, and some cheese in the fridge. Egg sandwiches. That was pretty much a luxury.

The coffee sputtered next to her, filling the room with its delicious scent, and feeling a bit lighter than she had in a long time, she pulled out a skillet and began to cook.

* * *

Jock tested the smoke detector, happy when the device beeped, loud and shrill in the small apartment. Her other one had been old enough that her landlord should have replaced it.

Jock was pleased with his handiwork so far. She had a new router and surge protector, and those damn extension cords were going in the trash. He'd deal with her bedroom later.

Now that he'd finished the tasks at hand, he had nowhere to look but at Fiona. She stood at the stove, stirring scrambled eggs in a pan, a steaming mug of coffee on the counter next to her. She took a sip, closing her eyes momentarily, and then set the mug down with a small smile on her face.

His heart beat loudly in his ears, and he willed himself to look away as she turned on a small radio by the sink and began to swing her hips to some pop song. Her pants were skin tight—obscene really—and her heart-shaped ass was right there. Protecting people wasn't new to him; he'd done it before. He prided himself on focusing on the job, not the person. Getting attached didn't work. It complicated things, forced bad decisions. Fiona Madden wasn't the first beautiful woman he'd crossed paths with or worked to protect, so why was he so intrigued by her?

He'd never been a man who was controlled by his sexual desire for women. He could go without sex for a long time, and usually did. Getting into bed with someone, no matter who, took a level of trust he rarely felt. Maybe that wasn't what most would consider the norm but he liked it that way. He was okay with his brand of normal.

So this thing with Fiona...he was unsettled. Visions from last night's dream came to him in a rush—Fiona in his arms, Fiona under him, Fiona on top of him. Fiona calling his name in pleasure. And Fiona screaming his name in terror. That had been a mindfuck.

Fiona turned around and caught him staring at her. She didn't say anything, only masked her reaction with a tight smile as she held up two plates. "Breakfast is ready."

Angry with himself for being caught staring—and for staring in the first place—he grabbed a mug of coffee and took a seat at the small table across from her. Sundance lay on the floor near his food bowl, eyes closed and ignoring them.

She'd made them bagel, egg, and cheese sandwiches. Jock had only scarfed down a quick protein bar earlier so this hot meal smelled like heaven. She'd cut up fruit, too, and placed it in a small bowl on his plate.

"Thank you." He popped a piece of melon into his mouth. "Didn't have to make me anything."

She shrugged as she picked up her sandwich. "I wanted to."

The eggs were flavored with some type of spice he couldn't place, but they were delicious. He'd eaten the entire sandwich before she finished half of hers. When he wiped his mouth with a napkin, he looked up to see her staring at him. "What?"

"You ate that in, like, less than a minute."

"Did you time me?"

"No, but I'm good at estimation."

He liked her rapid-fire answers when he questioned her. He smiled and took a sip of his coffee. "It was good. Thanks."

"Glad you liked it." She slipped a strawberry slice between her lips and he had to will himself not to react. "Have you ever done an eating competition? I bet you're good at it."

"I think I did a wing-eating one sometime when I was active."

She leaned back in her chair and deepened her voice. "'I could eat fifty eggs.'"

He blinked at her, surprised at the movie quote. "*Cool Hand Luke*, huh?"

"Classic," she grinned. "I'm just saying, you're a big guy, you could probably win the Nathan's hot dog one."

"Not really into being on TV and shoving hot dogs in my mouth for ten minutes."

She laughed, the sound pretty and soothing. "Yeah, I can't really see you doing that."

He drank the rest of his coffee while she finished her sandwich. When her plate was empty, he took the dishes to the sink and washed them. She didn't say a word, but he felt her eyes on his back. When he turned around Sundance was up, sitting at Fiona's feet while she ruffled his ears.

"Thought we could call Wren today," he said. "She can give you more background on what's going on. If you want to."

She nodded. "I would like that, yeah. Can I see her? Video chat?"

"Sure."

He took her phone and dialed Roarke. When Roarke picked up he was rubbing his eyes and squinting at the screen. His black hair was falling in his face, and Jock could see he was sitting in a bedroom. Jock wasn't sure where Roarke was now—maybe a tropical island or somewhere in Europe. A soft female voice murmured something in the background, and Roarke said something over his shoulder before focusing back on the phone. "Jock? Man, it's early. Everything okay?"

"Yup. Fiona wants to talk to Wren."

He held the phone out to her without waiting for a response from Roarke. Fiona took the phone, her slender fingers brushing his, and he bent to pet Sundance to hide the flush of heat creeping up his neck.

"Um, hi," Fiona said into the phone.

"Hey there, I'm Roarke."

"I guess you know who I am," she said with a smile.

"I do. Everything okay? Jock using his words?"

She laughed, and Jock decided he was okay being the

butt of the joke if it meant he got to hear her laugh like that. "He is. I'm glad he's here."

That made him feel warmer than it should have.

"He's good, the best. Here's Wren. Nice to meet you."

"Nice to meet you, too."

"Fiona!" Wren's voice echoed through the apartment then. "I was worried about you, but Jock texted you were okay."

"Yeah, I'm okay."

Fiona turned from him, walking back toward her bedroom. Jock followed, and when she reached her bedroom door she turned around, frowning at him. "Can I talk to Wren alone?"

Oh right, he was following her—him and Sundance, her human and canine shadows.

"Girl talk," she said, as her apology.

"Right, of course. I'll just..." He gestured back down the hallway. "Got stuff to do."

She smiled and shut the door. Her voice was muffled behind it, and Jock glanced down at Sundance, who panted up at him. Jock shrugged. "Guess we're kicked out."

Sundance didn't say anything.

Jock went back into the kitchen to clean up a bit. He knew Wren would explain what they'd been doing the last month or so. After Roarke's brother, Flynn, was killed, Roarke suspected that Flynn had been silenced because he had uncovered his boss's criminal activity. With Wren's help, Roarke, Jock, and their crew of hackers had ended up uncovering a black market sale that put millions of people's personal data at risk. During all of that, Roarke and Wren had fought feelings for each other...until they stopped fighting.

The crew they'd cobbled together to avenge Flynn's

death had disbanded and were all getting back to their sep-arate lives when Maximus found them, and they'd realized what they'd gotten into went much higher and involved Fiona. One of the men they'd taken down—Darren Saltner—had been involved in the kidnapping and selling of women, including Fiona. Maximus, they suspected, had helped bankroll the operation and wasn't happy when Darren was arrested. When Maximus had threatened Fiona as a way to keep them all in line, Jock volunteered to watch over her.

Even now, as he stared down into the courtyard, sur-rounded by her things and aching over his feelings for her, he didn't regret coming here. He didn't trust anyone else with her safety. The problem? With the jobs he'd had, he hadn't gotten away without enemies. They'd already hurt everyone close to him and cauterized that part of his heart, so that it was impossible to hurt him that way again. Their last task was to take him out...if they could find him. He'd had a bounty on his head for years—a long time, so long that the threat felt as if it had gone stagnant. Jock thought the men who wanted him dead either no longer cared or were biding their time. Didn't matter to him. As long as the bounty was still there, he had to fly under the radar.

Finding out who was a threat to Fiona's life was impor-tant. Then he would move on and get the fuck away from her before the people who wanted him dead thought they could use her to get to him.

His feelings for the woman in this apartment were new, and unwanted. Worse? He would never want to take ad-vantage of her vulnerability. If he ever made his attraction known, if he ever made an advance on her, he worried that she would only reciprocate out of fear that he'd pull his support from her if she rejected him. Gaining her trust now was the most important goal, not how he felt.

"Shut it down, Jock," he whispered to himself. "And focus."

About ten minutes later Fiona walked out of the bedroom. She wore a distracted smile when she handed the phone back to him. "Thanks. It's been a long time since I talked to Wren. After everything..." She waved her hand and turned away, biting her lip. "I lost touch with a lot of people."

He knew she didn't have family, really. Her parents had divorced when she was young. She'd never been close with her father, and he'd passed away from a heart attack when she was a teenager. Then her estranged mother had died from a stroke when Fiona was in her twenties. No siblings. No extended family she knew. Just her and this dog.

"After all this is over, I can take you to her," Jock said, feeling around for something that would make Fiona feel better.

The offer must have worked because she flashed him a smile with watery eyes. "Yeah, I'd like that. We were close once." She swallowed and blinked. "Anyway, I have work to do. I have a deadline coming up—"

Yeah, he needed to get out of here. "Sure, I'll leave. You need me, just call."

She nodded. "Right. Thank you. This morning was nice."

It had been nice. Too nice.

CHAPTER FOUR

HIT still active? Jock typed.

Yeah, came the reply.

Any activity?

No one wants to touch it, you know that.

Jock tapped his booted foot on the floor below his computer desk in agitation. While he was grateful no one was stupid enough to try to earn the bounty on his head, he didn't like that the hit was still open. Well, actually, he hadn't cared for a long time, confident no one would fuck with him. But now he had...Fiona. He didn't want any of his heat to blow back on her. She had enough of her own.

I want it canceled.

Sure you do, doesn't mean it'll happen. Also doesn't mean anyone'll take it.

Jock curled his lips into a smile. Hitman ethics. What Jock's enemies didn't know was that when they'd ordered a hit on him, they'd ordered a hit on a mercenary for hire that no one wanted to fuck with. He was respected and well-liked within a community with blood lust. He had a dozen eyes and ears, including Tarr's, who he was currently messaging with.

He had dirt on all of them—their real identities, their

families...everything. If he died, all of that information would be exposed. They all had a vested interest in keeping him alive.

Tarr was a bit different. Tarr owed him. Tarr was not quite a friend, but the closest thing to one Jock still had from his former life. Tarr—a hitman himself, like Jock had once been—was one of the few who Jock trusted to watch out for him.

I'm keeping an eye on it. Always, Tarr typed.

Good, Jock typed back, and signed off.

His phone beeped with a text, and he frowned at it, his fingers stalled in their rapid tapping across the keyboard. He picked up his cell.

I'm making lunch. Roasted chicken salad. If you're hungry.

He was hungry. Well, he was always hungry, and although he wasn't actually sure what roasted chicken salad was, he was eager to eat anything Fiona cooked. In the last couple of days since he'd made contact with Fiona, he'd noted she was a good cook, even though she rarely had the money for decent ingredients. It grated on him how she lived, but she never seemed to complain about the simplicity of her life. It was just...her norm.

He had money. He hadn't had money growing up—his mom wasn't so great at holding down a job—but Jock lived simply as an adult. He didn't really have a home base. He had a couple of properties for investment purposes that a property manager looked after, but no place he called home. He was always working, and nearly every cent he earned went right into the bank for savings or went into investments. By now, at age thirty-eight, he had a nest egg that could take him well into the golden years of his life. It was why he had volunteered for this job. He wasn't getting paid for it, but he had the time, and if he wasn't working...well, then he had nothing. No friends, no family. Just his thoughts and his memories, and he didn't want to spend time with any of that.

He locked his computer, slipped his phone into his pocket, and left his apartment. He was at Fiona's door in a few minutes and rapped loudly. The door across the hall opened a crack, and he turned and glanced at it over his shoulder. The door shut quickly, and he frowned at it.

She had neighbors. Neighbors who might be curious why Fiona all of a sudden had a man visiting her apartment when she'd never had visitors before. Neighbors who would take note and ask questions.

He registered Fiona opening her own door just as he swiveled his head back to face her. He'd seen her a couple of times in the last few days, but didn't want to overwhelm her with his presence so he tried to keep a bit of distance. He'd figured they both needed a break.

Now she stood in her doorway wearing shorts and a T-shirt dampened by her still-wet hair. Her eyes widened as she took him in. "Oh, I thought you weren't coming. You didn't text back."

He hadn't realized he'd had to text back. "I'm here."

Her lips twitched. "Yes, I see that." She stepped back. "Well, come in."

He walked inside and immediately smelled roasted chicken. His stomach growled. Breakfast had been...wow, hours ago, and even that hadn't been nearly enough.

Fiona walked past him on her way to the kitchen. "Chicken salad gets you out from that apartment of yours?"

"Any food, really." He followed her into the kitchen and took a seat when she waved him over to a chair. She dropped a plate onto the table in front of him, and he stared at the sandwich. Chunks of chicken in a mayonnaise mixture, with pecans and grapes, all on a Kaiser roll with lettuce and tomato. A side of chips. Fuck, he was hungry. He waited until she made another sandwich for herself and sat down before he dug in. He had it polished off in under a minute and was munching on the chips as she stared at him.

"Do you want another sandwich?"

He could probably eat five, but he just shook his head.

"I take it you liked it?"

"It was fucking great. Thanks."

She beamed and plucked a grape from her sandwich, sticking it into her mouth. He looked away as her lips closed over her fingers. Sometimes she did something so pretty, and a little bit sexy, and it hurt to look at her.

Sundance sighed heavily in the corner, his eyes drooping.

"Why'd you name him that?" Jock asked.

"Sundance?"

"Yeah."

Fiona glanced over her shoulder at her dog and then back toward Jock. "I was alone a lot as a kid. Not just at home but at school, too. I was shy. Wren was one of the first real friends I ever had." She snorted. "Sad, right?"

He didn't laugh. "Pretty sure you get I'm not a social type."

She smiled. "Yeah, I guess you understand then. Anyway, I always wanted a friend, a partner. Ride or die, you know? Like Butch Cassidy and the Sundance Kid. So I named him Sundance because the name makes me happy."

Jock nodded. "I like it."

Fiona's eyes were soft. "I'm glad."

Jock cleared his throat. "Anyway, we need to talk."

She paused as she raised her glass of water to her lips. "Oh."

"Sorry to bring it up, but I want to know if you've had threats before, why you moved, how they contact you, all of that."

She pushed away her plate. "Yeah, I guessed this discussion was coming."

"Apologies."

She shrugged. "Not your fault." She propped her elbow up on the table and dropped her chin into her hand. "So where should I start? Well first, I never bothered changing my name. Fiona is my middle name, and the name I always go by, but my documentation is all Sara F. Madden."

He knew that but stayed silent.

"I didn't have the money or the street smarts to change identities or go into hiding. So I try to use cash whenever I can and keep to myself. They find me, though; they always do. They send me..." Her eyes dropped to the table. "Photos of myself. That's usually when I move. Even though I know they'll find me again, I move. I've had no choice, no way to protect myself. All I could do was change where I lived under the illusion that I was hiding from them and keeping myself safe."

That was a harsh life, to be waiting for them to find her again.

"Do they ever call? Email?"

"Only mail," she said. "I think they like me to know they have my address."

"And what are their threats, specifically?"

"To keep quiet. They remind me that I promised to tell no one what happened to me, and if I did, they'd take me again and..." She swallowed and looked away. "They'd do worse this time."

He'd kill every fucking last one of them.

She shifted in her chair and tucked her knees under her

chin, clearly uncomfortable. "I hate talking about this. I hate it. It's embarrassing—"

"You have nothing to be embarrassed about," he barked, maybe a little too loudly because she flinched. He inhaled sharply. "They are predators and sick fucks, and I'm goddamn impressed you've built a life for yourself knowing they're watching you. You're still standing, and I'm sure, every time they look at you, they know you're stronger than them. It probably eats at them that they didn't break you."

She stared at him, her mouth open. She blinked rapidly and her throat worked. "I—thank you, Jock."

He nodded, the muscles in his shoulders tight with the anxious desire to fuck up these men. "Have you ever felt like they are following you physically? Have you ever felt watched?"

She shook her head. "Not really. I look over my shoulder all the time, but that's habit. I've always known they could come for me anytime. Even though they told me they'd leave me alone. I don't trust it."

"Yet, you live," he said.

She wrapped her arms around her legs and rocked slightly, chin on her knees. "What choice do I have? I want to stay alive. I know that with a bone-deep certainty. Sometimes it's the only thing I'm certain of. My life isn't perfect. I'm scared more than I'm not. But I don't mind my job. I like living here, and my dog is great. I've been here a year now, and I hope to stay here."

"I will get that for you," he said.

Her head jerked back. "You're just watching me for now to make sure the threat is empty, right?"

The job had changed. "I ensure your safety, then I'll take out the men responsible."

Her eyes widened. "Wait, what? *Take out?*"

"Take. Out."

She didn't speak for a long time as she studied his face. He wanted to fidget and squirm, but training kept him still, letting her look her fill. Finally she stood up and gathered their empty plates, body tense.

He spoke. "Fiona—"

"It's probably an empty threat from this...Maximus." She placed the dishes in the dishwasher and didn't look at Jock. "He wanted to punish Wren and Roarke, and he wants to hold me over their heads, but I'm nothing. I'm an insignificant woman that they drugged, raped on video, and sold to a bidder." The emptiness of her voice chilled him. "I'm used to my life. The photos they send don't bother me anymore, and their threats are always the same. I keep my head down, I live my life, and it's okay. You don't need to *take out* anyone for me."

She could say that, but that didn't change what he intended to do. So he stayed silent.

She sighed and stared out her back window. "You have your mind made up, then?"

"Yes."

Her eyes closed briefly. "What if that puts me in more danger?"

"It won't."

"You sound so certain."

"I'm very good at my job."

She swung her head to face him, and the fatigue in her expression pierced him. He stood up and walked over to her. Fuck she smelled good—sweet from whatever soap she used in the shower. His fingers ached to touch her hair but he kept his hands at his sides. "You don't have to worry about anything for a while. For now, I stay in New York, and I watch over you, and I ensure the threat is as meaningless as you believe it is. Okay?"

She sighed. "Will you promise me you'll tell me when you leave New York and change the trajectory of this mission from protection to revenge?"

He could do that. "I promise."

She exhaled and turned away. "Great. Now get out of my kitchen and go find something to do. I have brownies to make, and you're going to sit and eat them with me. But I get the corners. All four of them."

He reached up and allowed himself one touch. He clasped his hand around the back of her neck, and her body stilled beneath his palm. Her eyes lifted to his, and his heart beat rapidly in his chest. He wanted to tell her he wouldn't be leaving, not ever. That when he did leave, she'd be coming with him where he could always make sure she was safe. But that was ridiculous and made his palms sweat. So all he said was, "Corners are yours."

Then he walked away to check on her front door locks. He felt her eyes on his back the whole way.

* * *

Maybe it was Jock's presence that was giving Fiona the confidence that she'd long ago lost. Or maybe she wanted to prove to him—and herself—that she could handle life while this threat loomed over her.

While Fiona wasn't sure yet that this threat would lead to anything, she was under no illusions that the men who'd tormented her would ever go away. But maybe she could start to live less in shadow. So with that, she'd announced that if Jock would go with her, she wanted to attend a weekend festival that night. A few streets away, the heavily Dominican neighborhood shut down the streets and flooded them with food, dancing, music, and laughter. She wanted to go. She wanted to eat and dance and feel like an actual person.

When she'd asked Jock he'd been silent for a long time, so quiet she thought he'd say no. But then he'd nodded.

So here she was in her bedroom, standing in front of her one full-length mirror, smoothing the fabric of her dress over her hips. It was a warm, humid night so she'd gone with a simple cotton dress in a light blue that complemented her eyes. She'd left her hair down—a rare occurrence lately—and brushed it until it shone. Hell, she even wore makeup even though she was a little concerned about the age of her mascara and hoped it wouldn't give her an infection.

She was nervous, not just about attending the festival, but to be in Jock's presence in a way that didn't have to do with feeding him or standing by while he checked her smoke detectors.

There was a knock at her door, and after a swipe of lip gloss to her lips she ran to answer it. A deep voice said, "It's me," before she even got a chance to look in the peephole.

She threw open the door, expecting to see Jock in his ever-present camo pants and black shirt, but she sucked in a breath at the sight of him. He wore a pair of dark jeans, worn at the pockets and knees, snug on his lean hips and thick thighs. His broad chest was covered by a dark gray button-up. His hair was even semi-styled, and he'd trimmed his beard. Good God, he was dressed up as if this was a date.

For a moment, his blue eyes raked over her, taking in her appearance with a heat that seared straight to her marrow. In a blink, he was back to all business, but her body was warmed to the core.

This felt like a date. She hadn't been on a date in...well, she couldn't really remember. She did, however, remember what it felt like—the butterflies in her stomach, the excitement of the night stretched before her, unsure what it would hold. She didn't need a spoken compliment from Jock—that look had been enough.

When he spoke, he said softly, "Babe, you need shoes."

She glanced down at her bare feet and wiggled her toes. "Oh right, I forgot." She whirled away to go find a pair of sandals that would work. She heard the door close, and when she came hopping down the hallway while slipping her feet into her shoes, she found Jock waiting for her in her living room.

Jock's eyes had lost some of their harshness, and as she straightened before him, once again smoothing her skirt, he reached out to finger a strand of her hair before dropping it back where it draped over her breast. "I like your hair down."

Oh God, he'd verbalized a compliment. Her entire body flushed hot. She decided right then she going to wear her hair down more often. Every day. "Thank you. You look so nice. I didn't realize you owned these clothes."

"Didn't. Bought 'em today."

She smiled.

His eyes dropped to her mouth for a moment before he announced. "This is a date."

Her body jolted. "What?"

He pointed across the hall. "Neighbor?"

"What?"

"Who's your neighbor, Fiona?"

"Oh, uh, Marlene."

"What's she like?"

What did Marlene have to do with him saying they were

on a date? And why were they on a date? Still, she answered his question. "Marlene is in her seventies, lives alone."

"She nosey?"

"Uh, yeah, she's a seventy-year-old woman who lives alone. She's maternal and watches out for me."

"So this is a date," he said again.

Okay, what in the world? "I'm sorry?"

"Neighbors are nosey, neighbors talk. I do not want talking. To explain my presence, I'm your boyfriend. That means we act like it. That means I cannot show up here with you looking like that to take you out on a date wearing camo. I gotta wear this. Because a man with you on his arm is going to make a fucking effort."

Fiona stared at him. There might have been a few more compliments in there, but she couldn't be sure. "So wait, you just decided this and I go along with it?"

"Not asking you to suck my dick in the hallway, Fiona. I'm asking you to pretend I'm your boyfriend in case your neighbors ask because having a bodyguard is not fucking normal."

Visions of herself on her knees at his feet filtered through Fiona's mind in a way that should have freaked her out in a scary way, but instead freaked her out in a good way, while his face darkened and he muttered "fuck."

That drew her from her pervy visions. "What?"

"Forgot, uh, flowers, or some shit."

"Oh, in case Marlene saw?"

"Marlene?"

She gestured toward the direction of Marlene's apartment. "Yeah, the whole fake-boyfriend thing."

He scowled. "Nothing to do with that. Just thought you'd like flowers." He picked at his shirt. "And while this is also for the illusion of a date, also had to step up my game so you weren't embarrassed to walk out there with me. Haven't been out in a while, or maybe ever, so I wanted tonight to be good for you."

That told her a couple of things. Yes, Jock was playing a part, but there were a couple of things that he hadn't had to do. Flowers, clothes, and mainly, that look he'd given her when she opened up the door—he'd done those for her benefit. No one, not even Marlene, needed to know he'd looked at her with that heat in his eyes. Fiona wasn't sure what to do with all this information.

She forgot Jock didn't play games. He knew going out on a date wasn't something she did ever. She wasn't comfortable with it, and hadn't been. Probably wouldn't be again if Jock wasn't here. But he was now, and maybe, just maybe, she could get there on her own.

"I don't need flowers," she said softly. "And I don't care what you wear. But you do look nice, and I appreciate the effort more than you know."

He absorbed the words, she could see, and his chest inflated slightly. "Good. You ready?"

She grabbed her purse from a hook near the door on the way out. "Yeah. I'm hungry, too. I can pretty much smell the meat cooking. Can't you?"

"Yep, I'm starved, too."

She didn't even think much of it. When they stepped out onto the sidewalk, she linked her arm in his. The warmth of his body against hers fueled her confidence, and she leaned her head back, inhaling the night air full of city smells. Some weren't that great, but luckily the scents of the food from the festival overpowered the bad ones.

She closed her eyes, and when she opened them she grinned at the sliver of the moon. She turned her head to say something to Jock, but whatever she had meant to say fled as soon as she met his eyes. He was staring at her with an expression she had trouble figuring out. Longing? No, that couldn't be. Maybe he missed his family or his friends. Maybe he wished he was here with another woman. But he was directing that look at her. Her. Fiona Madden. A man hadn't looked at her like that...well, she wasn't quite sure how long it had been. She'd grown to be an expert at blending into the background.

"What?" she asked, when he didn't say anything.

He shook his head and looked away. "You're happy, so I'm good."

And that was that. She knew deep down he meant every word. "You're the best bodyguard ever," she breathed.

He laughed, a sound that surprised her, a hearty laugh that made him look altogether like a different person. She'd been funny once. Her family had told her so, her friends. She and Wren used to be hilarious together. A two-woman show. Maybe she could get back to that. Find that inner humor she must have left behind. She needed to hear Jock laugh like that more.

The sounds of music and voices grew louder the closer they walked toward the festival. She smiled a bit, wondering what the neighborhood would think of Jock. He was like a giant blond Viking. She bet he'd totally rock a *Game of Thrones* costume for Halloween.

But as they entered the crowd, Jock blended in well. Other than his size, he didn't stand out as much as she'd expected. He took her arm out of his, and she was sad for a split second until he grasped her hand, twining their fingers together. Right, he still wanted to keep her with him, but he probably had more control this way.

She led him right to a stand that sold pork on a stick, and she ordered one while Jock ordered four. Four. And he ate each one in two bites while Fiona nibbled on hers as she browsed some jewelry stands.

She loved the handmade beadwork of the necklaces sold by one woman. The price tags, although high, were perfect for the beauty and amount of time each piece must have taken to make. She fretted over one, a pretty black and coral-colored one. She could afford it, but she might have to go without some of her favorite fresh produce.

The necklace was pulled from her hands and she turned to yell at whoever had taken it from her but found the necklace intertwined in Jock's thick fingers. He checked the price tag and then handed it to the woman along with a wad of cash.

"Gorgeous," the woman said, trying to sell it even though it'd already been sold. "This will look beautiful on your neck. Want another? I'll discount the second."

Jock shook his head and took the necklace. He took a moment to run it over his palm, studying the stones before twirling his finger at Fiona, a silent order for her to turn around. "You didn't have to get that," she protested. "I was going to."

"You want it on or not?" he asked.

She swallowed. "I guess...on."

"Turn around," he said.

She did, her eyes closing briefly as he gathered her thick hair and pushed it to the side then slipped the necklace over her chest. He fiddled with the clasp at the nape of her neck and draped her hair down her back again.

She fingered the beads at her throat, the weight comforting. It was a simple necklace, not that expensive, but she felt like a million bucks. "Thank you," she said.

He nodded, gripped her hand, and kept walking.

She couldn't stop touching the necklace, not as they

passed stands with hand-woven scarfs, not as vendors hollered out their goods. She only dropped his hand when they reached a stand that was selling a sweet fried dough.

Jock ordered enough for both of them—well, enough for an army, to be honest—and by the time she was finished, her stomach was full and she was drowsy.

Something felt different, and it took her a minute, with her hand linked in Jock's, to discover that she was . . . happy. Relaxed. The normal tension she carried in her shoulders and in her neck was gone. She appreciated the way Jock remained alert to their surroundings in his effort to protect her, and maybe that was why she was able to let her guard down.

She'd downed a water as well as some sort of frozen concoction, so the urge to relieve herself was strong. "Hey, I need to go to the bathroom." She pointed to a pizza store where the doors stood open. "I'm just going to run in there."

Jock led her over to the restaurant and glanced around. He didn't let go of her hand, and she shifted restlessly. "Is that okay? Do you need to come in with me? Hold my dress up?"

He didn't roll his eyes at her but his expression conveyed the same emotion. With a squeeze, he dropped her hand. "I'll wait right here."

She ran inside and used the bathroom. She glanced in the mirror and didn't even recognize the woman who'd left her apartment an hour or so ago. The eyes that stared back at her were bright, her face flushed with happiness. God, she looked younger. She wasn't even thirty, although she sure felt double her age some days. Amazing what a little freedom did for her skin.

She washed her hands, and as she made her way to the front of the store she saw bodies pressed to the glass. A band was parading down the center of the street, and most of the patrons were crowding the sidewalks. Trumpet wails and drum beats filled the air. She didn't see Jock, but she was sure he wasn't far.

The sound grew louder as she reached the front of the pizza store, and a small fissure of fear slid down her spine. The crowd was immense now. So many people packed together. She took a step out onto the sidewalk just as loud cracks of sound rang out.

Bang. Bang Bang Bang.

Gunshots. That had to be gunshots. Oh God, where was Jock? What was happening? She whirled around but all she saw were faces of strangers. Just a sea of strangers and no one she knew, not one. She didn't want to see blood, or hear the moans of the injured.

Bang. Bang Bang Bang Bang Bang.

She began to scream, covering her ears with her hands and crouching into a huddled ball. She waited for the bullets to pierce her flesh. And she hoped no one else was caught in the cross-fire. If any bystanders were hurt... This was all her fault. She knew it. They were after her. She'd left her apartment, and this was all her fault...

Hands gripped her shoulders and hauled her to her feet. "Fiona." Her name sounded a mile away. Someone shook her. "Fiona!" The voice was more insistent now. Her screams dropped to whimpers. Where was the pain? Was anyone hurt?

She blinked her eyes open to see Jock staring down at her, blue eyes filled with fury. She glanced around to see that a crowd had gathered, curious eyes staring at her. There was no blood. No one was panicking.

She began to shake, her body going into flight mode. "What—?"

"Fireworks," Jock said sharply. "Just some mother-fuckers with fireworks."

And she'd...she'd fucking lost it. On the street, in front of these people just trying to enjoy their festival, and she'd lost her mind. Tears filled her eyes. She wasn't past this. How could she have thought that Jock's confidence would rub off on her? She was fucked up. Tainted.

Jock picked her up with a swift curse as the first sob racked her body. She clung to his shoulders, crying into his brand new shirt as he walked the short distance back to her apartment. Back to where she felt safe and protected. Her own prison.

CHAPTER FIVE

FIONA sat on the stone bench in her small courtyard, watching Sundance sniff around. There was a book on her lap but she hadn't opened it yet. She had an article due, a list of the best nudist beaches—she couldn't have been assigned something to write about that was further from her actual life—and it'd been a bitch to focus.

It'd been a week since she'd lost her shit at the festival. A week of Jock watching her warily, like she was fragile, like she was going to break any minute. She hated it. For a short amount of time, she'd once again felt like a normal, desirable woman. And now she was back to feeling like a scared deer. This man awakened feelings in her she hadn't thought possible, but now he treated her as if she was a child. Why would he treat her any differently? She was a job to him—he wasn't actually trying to date her. Ugh.

The memories flooded back now, assaulting her, dredging up images she only visited sometimes in her nightmares. The dirty rooms, being tied to a bed, the drugs they'd jammed into her arm to keep her compliant. The men. The red light of the camera. The hands on her skin.

She didn't dare close her eyes because she knew that would make the pictures in her mind multiply, filling her skull until she thought her head would explode from the force of it all.

Sundance lifted his head, sensing her distress, and he trotted over. He nudged his nose under her hand, forcing her fingers into the fur on top of his head. She rubbed his ears, thankful for her companion.

Here in Brooklyn, she'd felt safe for a while, blending in to the bustling New York City life. Until Jock showed up. Until she'd spoken to Wren. Until everything she had tried to forget was once again in the forefront of her thoughts.

Sundance whined and she shook herself. She needed to get inside, feed the dog, and then herself. As she stood up and walked to the door of the apartments, she wondered what Jock was doing. Would he eat with her? Meals with him were...nice. She'd forgotten how pleasant it was to eat a meal with someone. She'd given up dating years ago, and although she had a neighbor or two she'd befriended over the years, she didn't make it a habit to invite anyone over for dinner.

As she walked up the stairs to her apartment, she heard a voice. It was Marlene. She was an older Jewish woman who loved to feed Fiona and ask her questions. Fiona didn't really want to answer questions but she did love Marlene's food, and the woman seemed lonely. Her son visited sometimes, but he didn't live in New York City so Marlene was alone a lot. Like Fiona.

Marlene's door was open, which was unusual. Fiona slowed as she neared it and then peered inside.

She couldn't see Marlene because Jock was taking up most of the small foyer. He wore a pair of jeans, boots, and a black T-shirt. Marlene was still talking. "I asked you a question," she said, her voice demanding in that way old women had when they had nothing to lose.

"All due respect, ma'am, you shouldn't open your door to strange men," Jock answered. His *ma'am* made Fiona smile.

Marlene scoffed. "I can take care of myself. But I'd like to know why you're sniffing around my Fiona. She's lived across from me for a year, and I've never once seen a man who wasn't a delivery driver hanging around her door."

Jock didn't answer, probably because he didn't get a chance. Marlene's pale bony fingers wrapped as far as they could around Jock's massive bicep before she pulled him farther into her home. Or at least, she tried. Jock's boots didn't move.

"Come on, young man," Marlene was saying. "We'll talk over some tea."

As much as Fiona would have paid to watch Jock sit with Marlene over tea, she needed to end the man's misery. "Marlene," she called.

Jock's head turned at the sound of her voice. He did that head-to-toe scan thing and then angled his body toward hers to reveal petite Marlene behind him. She wore a blue and yellow housecoat and slippers. Her hair was neatly curled, and she had on dark lipstick. "Fiona," she said with a smile. "Just interrogating Jamison here. Please tell me his attentions are invited or I'll call up my son. He's FBI, you know."

Marlene loved to talk about her FBI agent son. Also, Jock's real name was Jamison? *Huh.* Fiona focused on Marlene's question. This was when she had to play her part. "Yes, his attentions are ... invited."

Marlene narrowed her eyes, and Fiona hated lying to her but this wasn't a game. Fiona stepped forward, Sundance at her side, and slipped her fingers into Jock's. He stiffened for a brief moment before he squeezed her hand back. Fiona pressed into his side, placing a hand on his stomach. She was not prepared for the rock-hard abs beneath her palms. Good God, this man was jacked. "He's my boyfriend," Fiona added. "It's new."

Marlene's gaze shifted from Fiona to Jock and then back to Fiona. "Hmmmm, pictured your type a little different. Not so...big. He good to you?"

This was so awkward. "Yes, Marlene."

"Guess no one messes with you, if you take him out by your side, huh?"

Fiona smiled. "Yes."

Marlene held up her hands. "Fine, fine. As long as you're safe. I worry about you, Fiona. Over there all alone."

"I'm fine. You're over here alone, too!"

"But I'm an old woman. No one cares about me. You? You're a pretty young woman."

"I have Sundance, too," Fiona said.

Marlene pressed her lips together. "Let me feed you two."

Jock looked alarmed. "That's not—"

"I have some brisket. I made too much for me so you both will join me." She waved them inside. Fiona felt Jock's boots drag on the floor with reluctance before he allowed Fiona to tug him inside past a beaming Marlene. The older woman then scooted around Jock to shut her door. Fiona could feel Jock's gaze boring into the side of her head, imploring her to get them out of this situation, but Fiona knew there was no getting out. Marlene wanted to feed them, and feed them she would.

So Fiona turned to Jock with a bright smile. "How nice! A home-cooked meal."

Jock's gaze dipped to her mouth before his shoulders slumped slightly. Ah, defeat. Fiona grinned wider, and Jock's eyes narrowed slightly.

"Come," Marlene said, leading them into the kitchen.

"Jamison?" Fiona whispered.

"Told ya Jock wasn't my real name."

He had. She just hadn't thought about what his real name would be. Jamison. She liked it.

They entered the kitchen to find Marlene puttering around a huge pot. "Jamison, be a dear and grab the pinot noir down from my wine rack."

Jock's eyes cut to Fiona. "Get you back for this," he muttered.

"What was that?" Marlene asked.

Fiona held back her laughter. "Thanks again for the invite, Marlene. Jamison said he loves brisket!"

Marlene clapped her hands, Jock glared, and Fiona knew this would be the best meal she'd had in years.

* * *

Jock decided that the old woman's questions were tolerable if it meant he got to see Fiona like this.

Her cheeks were flushed pink from the wine, and her laughter was long and loud. She came alive with her belly full of brisket and her head full of good conversation. Well, he assumed it was good conversation. He didn't really know what that entailed, but Fiona and Marlene seemed to be enjoying it. They chatted about the corner bodega, the recent changes to the local park, and the weather.

The brisket was fucking delicious. Jock hadn't eaten this well in weeks. The meat was so soft that it fell apart on his plate. The sauce was tangy and full of flavor, with large chunks of onions, carrots, and heavy on the garlic. Also eating kept his mouth full, so then he wasn't called to participate in the conversation.

"So how did you two meet?" Marlene asked as she pushed her empty plate away.

Fiona paused with her second glass of wine halfway to her mouth. Her gaze shot to him, and he had just swallowed. It would have looked awkward to eat more just to avoid talking.

"I was dog sitting for a friend of mine," he said. "Saw Fiona at the dog park and thought she was beautiful. I heard her laugh once, at something Sundance did, and I decided I wanted to hear her laugh more often." That last sentence was true, but she didn't need to know that. She stared at him now, her wine glass still clutched in her hand, eyes round in her flushed face. She wore jeans and a T-shirt, the neck wide so it hung off her shoulder, exposing a tank strap. Even wearing those casual clothes, she was a fucking vision.

"I was done dog sitting but I kept asking my friend if I could take his dog to the dog park just to get an excuse to see Fiona. Finally asked her out, and she said yes." He met Fiona's gaze steadily. "Now I get the privilege of hearing her laugh whenever I want."

For a moment, a brief moment, he wanted that to be true. He wanted their lives to be that simple, for them to be other people who could meet at a dog park and date. Get married, and have kids and a normal life.

But they didn't. Neither of them did. He didn't think they ever would. Too late for that now.

Marlene was quiet for a moment, and then finally she stood and began to pick up their empty plates. "That's good. That's really good. Fiona should laugh."

Jock didn't take his eyes off Fiona as Marlene carried the plates to the sink. He wanted to get up and help Marlene but couldn't look away from the woman staring at him from across the table. Maybe there was too much truth in what he'd said. The thing was, he hadn't said enough. There was so much more he wanted to say—that he loved seeing Fiona smile, relax, and look over her shoulder less. That she seemed better rested since he'd made his presence known to her.

But he didn't say those things because this was a job to him and he couldn't be falling for her. He didn't love anymore. He maybe liked and sometimes gave a shit, but more often than not, he just worked.

Fiona slowly set her glass down on the table just as Marlene began to hum from the kitchen sink, where she rinsed the plates and put them in the dishwasher. "Your laugh isn't so bad either, Jamison," she said softly.

He never used his real name and had surprised even himself when he'd blurted it out to Marlene. Now hearing it from Fiona's lips was making him uncomfortable. Uncomfortable in a way that he had to fight from getting hard. Jesus, she was so goddamn beautiful, and he'd never in his life met a woman like her. He wouldn't again. So he knew in that moment he'd lay down his life to make sure she kept on laughing.

Marlene returned with three plates, each holding a slice of cake. "Honey cake," she declared. "Just made it this afternoon. I guess I have a sixth sense for company."

"Marlene, this is so much. You don't have to feed us all this." Despite her words, Fiona stared at the cake like she definitely hoped Marlene didn't turn them out.

"Hush," Marlene said. "I'm only serving it because I want to eat it, too, and it would be rude to eat in front of my guests and not offer it."

Fiona laughed, and the sound lit Jock's blood. The cake was drenched in honey, moist and delicious. He could have eaten three more slices.

"Do you have family here?" Jock heard himself say to Marlene, wanting to thank the woman for the meal, for the peace for a couple of hours.

Marlene glanced up, seemingly surprised at the question. "No. My husband died a couple of years ago, and our son lives in Virginia with his wife. They visit as often as they can."

"Have you thought about moving there?" he asked.

"They offered. I said no. This is my home. My city. I like having neighbors. I like the sounds and voices and smells. My son says I'm strange. He thinks I want quiet in a retirement community with bingo. I do not. I want this life. I'm too old to live how I don't want to live."

He respected that. Even though he felt the opposite—that he was too old to change his life to live the way he wanted. He lived the life now that he'd been dealt. It was only when he looked at Fiona that he wished that wasn't the case.

Fiona stood slowly and a bit unsteadily. "Let me help you clean up."

"My dear girl, no," Marlene said. "I don't mind, and it's only a few dishes. Go on over to your place and spend time with this hunk of a man." Marlene speared him with a glance. "You take care of her. She's feeling that wine."

"I'm fine," Fiona snapped without much heat.

Marlene grinned. "Sure you are."

Jock stood and stepped to Fiona's side, wrapping an arm around her waist and whistling for Sundance, who was dozing near the couch. "Thanks again for dinner, Mrs...."

"Klein," she said. "But call me Marlene."

"Right," he said softly as Fiona's body melted against his. "Have a good night. You ever need anything, just let Fiona know, and I can come over. Run an errand for you. Whatever you need."

"You're sweet. All I want you to do right now is take care of our Fiona."

"I'm not a child," Fiona mumbled in his arms.

He smiled. "'Night, Marlene."

"Good night, Jamison. Nice to meet you."

With Sundance at their heels, Jock walked Fiona to her apartment. She yawned so widely that her jaw cracked, and her hand clenched his shirt over his stomach. "That was so good," she said as Jock shut her apartment door behind them. "How did she snag you in the hallway?"

"I was checking your locks from the outside," he said. "She saw me and the interrogation began."

"Interrogation?" Fiona laughed. "Wow, Jock can be dramatic, I see."

He grumbled, and she continued to grin. Her eyes were a little blurry and unfocused. She'd only had two glasses of wine, but they'd been large glasses, and he noticed she didn't keep alcohol in her apartment.

"I'm going to change. I need to get comfy. Be right back," she announced.

He went to call after her, to let her know he'd see himself out, but she was already in her bedroom, clothes rustling, and he kept his mouth shut. Which proved to be a bad fucking idea.

When she walked out she wore what he recognized as her pjs, aka a torture device for Jock's dick: a tiny pair of cotton shorts and a tank top outlined every goddamn curve, and Fiona had a fuck of a lot of curves.

She obviously wasn't in the mood to let him leave peacefully. "I wanna watch TV." She pulled him toward her couch, her slender fingers around his forearm. "Watch with me."

He didn't want to sit on the couch with an intoxicated

Fiona while she wore those fucking clothes. That sounded like a fucking horrible idea. But she nudged him to sit and then threw herself down, head on the armrest, legs in his lap.

In. His. Fucking. Lap.

He didn't move as she turned on the TV with another yawn. He didn't dare touch her legs and kept his arms at his sides. Her feet were perfect, her nails painted a deep purple. Her legs were shapely, and her skin looked soft as hell.

"*Armageddon*!" she screeched, and his gaze shot to the TV. Sure enough, there was Bruce Willis on the screen, talking to his team of drillers.

Fiona sighed. "I love this movie. In college, Wren came home twice to me bawling my eyes out. By the second time, she realized I was just watching *Armageddon* again."

"This movie makes you cry?" he asked.

She stared at him. "This movie makes everyone cry!"

He didn't respond.

"Okay, well not you, Mr. Emotions Are Weak."

"I never said that."

"Do you think it?"

Again he didn't respond.

She smirked. "That's what I thought. Well, then you can sit there and listen to me cry because, when Bruce shoves Ben Affleck into the elevator thingy on that asteroid, I bawl every damn time. And then the song! It's like they made this movie just to watch people cry buckets, and I fall for it every time."

She didn't even make it ten minutes. Bruce, Ben, and their crew hadn't made it into space yet before Fiona was asleep, her hands clasped against her chest, her breaths even and deep.

Even in sleep, she was fucking gorgeous. What he

wouldn't have given in that moment to lay down with her, wrap his arms around her, and kiss her neck, pressing his hardening dick against her back. She'd wake up, and roll over with a sleepy grin, press those lips to his and then…

And then nothing. *Shut up, Jock.*

He had to move. He carefully slid out from under her legs, and she didn't stir as he grabbed Sundance's leash. The dog needed to go out, so Jock led him downstairs to do his business and then back up to the apartment where Jock gave him fresh water. He went to check on Fiona before he left and found her awake yet groggy.

"What time is it?" She stretched her arms over her head and the edge of her tank rode up, showing a strip of pale, soft skin. *Fuck.*

He forced his gaze to her face, which didn't help matters because she had a fucking gorgeous face, and waking up like this, she was also cute. "Late," he answered.

She blinked at the TV, which he'd already turned off, and she rubbed her eyes. "Shit, did I miss *Armageddon*?"

"Sorry, you didn't get to cry tonight."

She grinned and then began to gather her arms under her to get off the couch. "I guess I should go to bed."

He gripped her arm and helped her up, but in doing so, she stumbled into him, grabbing at his shirt to keep herself upright. Her little body was hot against his, and he waited patiently for her to step away, go back to her bedroom, and put him out of his misery.

Instead she said softly, "Thank you."

There was a lot in those two words. A lot that he wanted to explore but that he absolutely could not. *Nope.* Oh no, no, he didn't want this moment or her voice full of tenderness. He didn't do tender.

He tried to step back but she didn't let go. "Jock."

He swallowed and tried to ignore that he felt her saying his name right in his dick. "Fiona."

The wine was still in her system. He could see it in her eyes and feel it in the unsteady sway of her body. Her fingers uncurled where she clutched his shirt, but he got no reprieve because then she took those hands and slid them right up his chest. "My God, you're so hard," she said, almost to herself.

She had no idea how hard he was right now.

"Do you have a girlfriend, Jock? A wife? Someone you care about?" So much hope in those questions, so much damn hope that he could barely stand it.

There was someone he cared about, and she was right in front of him. "No girlfriend, no wife."

Her fingers dug into his shoulders. "Are you...are you attracted to me?"

Jesus, fuck, she was killing him. He was going to die. "Fiona..."

"Can you please just answer me?"

He reached up and gripped one of her wrists, squeezing. "Have to be blind not to be attracted to you."

She sucked in a breath and her eyes shone, the wet at her bottom lid trembling and not in a good way. "Right. I guess...right."

The pain in her eyes sliced through him. What had he said? He was missing something vital that was going on. "Talk to me."

"My laugh," she said sharply, whipping her hair back so it brushed his arms. "At dinner, I thought...I guess I thought maybe you were attracted to more than blond hair and tits and ass, okay? I thought for a moment that the man who'd made me feel some attraction for the first time in years saw me as more than a body."

He stared at her, unsure how she'd come to that conclusion. "What the fuck?"

She made a sniffing sound as she refused to meet his eyes. "It's fine. Your body language is practically screaming that you want to run away so—"

He wrapped an arm around her back and then dropped down onto the couch on his ass, Fiona sprawled in his lap with her knees on either side of his hips. She yelped, which was fine, because at least she'd stopped spewing the stupid shit that she'd twisted in her head. Thirty seconds ago, he couldn't wait to leave. But now, no way in fuck was he leaving with her under the wrong impression. "Let's get a few things straight," he said. "Are you listening? Are you going to remember this? Because it's important."

She nodded, her hands still on his shoulders. Her eyes were wide now, and dry. She was eager. She wanted to hear what he had to say.

"Yes, I see blond hair and tits and ass. But I'm attracted to you because of what comes with it. You're strong, and sweet, and your laugh is what I think those twinkle Christmas lights look like."

Her mouth dropped open, but he kept going, because apparently he was Captain Romantic now. Where was he getting this shit? *Twinkle lights?* He powered on and rolled his hips, which pressed his hard dick up against her crotch. "See? I'm attracted to you. You're wearing next to nothing, and your face is flushed from wine, and the last thing on my mind is your cute rant about Bruce Willis and Ben Affleck." He reached up and swiped a strand of hair off her cheek, indulging himself in that one touch of her soft skin. "But babe, I can't...I'm not sure what you see when you look at me. Maybe you think there's some deeper shit inside so, if you spend enough time clawing at the dirt, you'll get the diamond underneath."

Her hands tightened on his shoulders, and a small gasp escaped her mouth. "I'm no diamond. You can dig and dig to the brink of exhaustion, nearly killing yourself, and there'll still be more fucking dirt. Do you understand what I'm saying to you?"

She licked her lips, and he tracked her pink tongue. "I understand what you're saying," she said softly. "I just don't believe it."

Fuck. "Believe it," he barked, and she flinched in his arms. "I get it's been hard for you to make connections with people after what happened to you. I'm protecting you, and so you can easily mistake that for..." Shit, he was going to have to say it and watch the hurt flash in her eyes. "For something more."

Yep, there it was, like a solar flare. Her lips twisted in pain.

"I'm not the answer to anything for you. I'm just a guy who plans on keeping you safe."

Her expression hardened, and with a burst of energy she swatted his hand away. "Don't touch me," she hissed and scrambled off his lap.

Regret sliced through him deep. He stood up. "Fiona."

She was already backing away, eyes bright with unshed tears, body shaking with anger. "Fuck you, Jock."

"Fiona," he said more forcefully, "don't make this a bigger deal—"

"How dare you use my past against me? How. Dare. You." She pointed a shaking finger at him. "You think I'm so weak and starved for attention that I'll fling myself at any hard dick?"

"I didn't say that," he gritted out.

"You implied it, and you know it," she said. "You don't want me to get close to you? You don't want this to be anything more than a job? Fine. Tell me. Don't fucking insult me. You don't have to hurt me to push me away, Jock. I've been hurt fucking *enough*."

Tears leaked from her eyes, and he cursed himself. He'd been stupid, so fucking stupid. He didn't know how to handle this, how to be a decent fucking human being.

Her shoulders shook, and a sob burst from her lips just as she turned around to bolt toward her bedroom. He didn't think. He just grabbed her and tugged her to him, her back to his front. She didn't even struggle as another sob fell from her lips. "I'm sorry, Fiona."

"Fuck you," she whispered.

"I'm so sorry," he said, squeezing his eyes shut and burying his face in her hair. "That was fucked up of me. I wasn't thinking."

She didn't speak, but her body shook with silent sorrow, and his heart cracked. If she asked him to let her go, he would, but he didn't want to. He would stand there all night with her clutched to him if she let him.

Finally, she heaved a deep breath and said, "I need to go to bed."

He squeezed her. "Okay."

"I need you to let me go."

"Fiona—"

"You're sorry, I know," she said bitterly.

"I am sorry. I shouldn't have said what I did. I worded it all wrong. But babe, you gotta understand what I meant. It's that *you* are a diamond. Right here, right now, you shine so brightly that it hurts to look at you. I don't want you to go digging at me, thinking we'll match. We'll never match. We'll get you out of this, and then you're free to find and meet someone that'll shine with you, rather than dull what you got."

She didn't respond, and he shook her gently. "Okay, Fiona?"

She didn't respond for a full thirty seconds. He counted. Finally she whispered, "Okay."

He let her go, making sure she was steady on her feet before he took a step back.

She glanced over her shoulder at him and he registered the hurt in her eyes. He took it, and he accepted it, and added it to the other junk in his soul.

Then she turned and walked to her bedroom without a word. And he had to live with the fact that she had cried tonight. But it hadn't been over the movie like she'd wanted. It'd been because of him.

CHAPTER SIX

JOCK hadn't talked to Fiona for a week. A whole seven days. He didn't go to her apartment, and she didn't invite him. No more texts about omelets or roasted chicken salad. The silent message was clear—he was no longer welcome in her life.

When he'd first arrived in Brooklyn to start the job, this had been how it was, and he'd been happy. Talking to people, getting to know them, was not something he enjoyed. He was good at reading people in objective ways—if they were scared or lying. Reading people in relation to how they interacted with him was a whole other story. He wasn't so good at that, and worse, he didn't know how to respond. If someone was lying, he could force the truth out of them through various methods—his nickname was because of his brute force tactics, after all. If they were scared, he was usually happy with that.

But Fiona's feelings toward him mystified him. Confused him. He'd reacted all wrong, fucked it up, and now she wasn't speaking to him. That wasn't okay. Not now that he knew how hot she looked with bedhead and bare feet in her kitchen, how great her laugh was, and how her warm tits felt pressed against his chest. Yeah, he knew all that now, and so he sat in his bare apartment alone slowly going out of his mind as he watched her life from behind a computer. The only glimpses he got of her were when she took Sundance out to the courtyard and when she went to the dog park. She hadn't left for any other purpose. Everything she needed was delivered to her apartment.

He'd almost broken down and talked to Marlene to ask her to check on Fiona. He was so close, this close, from pounding on Fiona's door and demanding she let him in.

He knew what Fiona had been through. Before he'd shown up in New York he'd researched everything he could, even watched the videos of her. He'd seen plenty of violence in his life so he hadn't thought watching her assaults would be different. It had been. He'd only watched a few, unable to handle her cries, the way she fought every single time despite the drugs they pumped into her.

And now...now those images haunted him. He could see them in the shadows of her eyes, like lurking ghosts. He wanted revenge on every man responsible. He wanted to break them bit by bit, slowly and painfully. That was how he consoled himself. Those men were still out there, threatening her, reminding her of how they victimized her. Jock would make them hurt.

He spun away from his computer and snatched a bottle of water out of a case thrown in the corner. He chugged half of it, the liquid leaking out of the corners of his mouth before he took the bottle and chucked it at the wall with a vicious sidearm. The crack of the plastic and subsequent splatter of water cooled his anger somewhat. Now his bed was wet, though. He should have thrown the bottle against a different wall.

Fuck it. He wasn't going to sit here. He had to talk to Fiona. He had to hear her laugh. He had to...fuck, he just had to hold her, if she let him. His willpower had always been solid. Unshakeable. But Fiona was eroding the foundation from underneath his booted feet.

He looked around his apartment to see if there was anything he could take to her, an excuse to knock on her door. With an annoyed huff at himself, he turned away. That was stupid. He didn't need an excuse. She'd either talk to him or she wouldn't.

He took the stairs down to her apartment. It was getting close to dark so she'd be done working for the day, maybe watching TV. He reached her door and listened for a moment. Hearing nothing, he raised his hand and rapped his knuckles on the door sharply. "Fi, it's me."

Nothing. No sound.

"Fiona!" he yelled louder.

He waited a minute—a full minute, he counted—and still nothing. He raised his fist to pound on the door, a growl rising in his throat, when the door across the hall opened. Marlene peeked out, staring up at him. She flinched, and he worked on schooling his face to look less scary.

"She's not answering her door," he said, stating facts.

Marlene narrowed her eyes. "I haven't seen you in a while."

"Been busy," he answered. "You want to try to get her to come to the door? It's important."

"What did you do?"

"Why do you think I did something?"

Marlene opened her door a little wider and leaned against the frame. "Because your eyebrows are fixed in a permanent scowl, that's why. And you're banging on her door with a kind of urgency, like you need to say sorry. Am I right?"

He turned away and knocked again. "Fiona! I'll pick the lock!"

Marlene blew out a breath. "Save your energy. She's at the dog park."

Jock whirled around. "Excuse me?"

"The dog park."

"She doesn't go to the dog park this late in the day."

Marlene shrugged. "She did today. I saw her."

Jock didn't say a word, just turned on a heel and walked swiftly down the hall. *Fuck. Fuck fuck fuck.* He hadn't been watching the camera he'd installed in the hallway outside her door. She'd kept the same schedule for seven damn days. Hell, for a solid year. He'd been complacent, and she'd slipped out. But why?

He'd parked his truck several streets away when he first arrived and hadn't moved it since. His only consolation was that Sundance was with her. Still, Jock picked up the pace until he was all-out sprinting to his truck. He needed to get to her, lay his eyes on her. His skin was itchy, his instincts blaring a warning. He was going to find her, he was going to lay into her for changing her schedule, and then he was going to kiss the fuck out of her.

* * *

Fiona wasn't sure why she'd come tonight. Dinner had been good—she'd made burgers and had some cookies for dessert that she'd found on sale. She'd been all settled to sit down and watch TV but she'd been restless. She couldn't sit still, and Sundance noticed because he'd whined at her.

So she'd gathered his lead and decided to take him to the dog park. Along the way, she grabbed an iced coffee. Sundance walked next to her, his furry body pressed against her leg, and as the sun painted the sky in pinks and yellows, she felt content. It'd been a week of mind fuckery, where she'd worked herself up into a lather of anger over Jock, then self-pity over her life, and then depression about her non-existent future. Rinse and repeat. She knew he hadn't left. He'd promised he would tell her when he did, and sometimes when she was out in the courtyard, she could feel his gaze on her.

That was it, though. She hadn't thought it was possible but she missed him. She missed his hulking presence, his huge hands with thick fingers that were surprisingly dexterous, his rumbling deep voice. She still felt protected, but she didn't have *him*. And she wanted him.

She'd typed so many text messages to him, so many dinner invitations that she then deleted. It was better this way. He didn't want to be anything to her, and so she wouldn't ask him to be. Still, it hurt. In a way, it felt good to hurt. She'd made a human connection for the first time in a long time. That had to mean something.

The dog park was crowded. The weather was pleasant so other people must have had the same idea as her. Sundance's golden retriever girlfriend wasn't there. Because this wasn't Fiona and Sundance's normal schedule she didn't recognize a lot of the owners and dogs. She wasn't in the mood for small talk so she kept her mouth busy drinking her iced coffee and retreated away from the main crowd of barking, playing dogs.

Sundance, again, seemed to sense her mood, happily trotting off to sniff at a corner of the fence. Fiona found an empty bench under the shade of a maple tree and sat down. She wished she'd brought her book. Maybe she should come here more often, especially at night like this. The air was cooler, the smells of the city less prominent. She leaned her head back, feeling the cool air on her face. A breeze blew through, rustling the leaves above her head.

She opened her eyes to see Sundance, nose to the ground, sniffing the fence line.

A black lab walked up to him, and they did the butt sniff dog ritual before the lab bounded off, looking over its shoulder at Sundance. Sundance glanced at Fiona, and she waved him on. "Go play!"

He ran off after his new playmate, and she sagged a bit on the bench, watching as the two dogs nipped at each other in the tall grass. She closed her eyes again as her bones melted a bit, the tension in her neck easing.

She was making a grocery list in her head when something cool and hard touched the back of her neck. "Don't scream," said a raspy male voice, "or I'll shoot that fucking dog of yours."

Her eyes flew open. *Sundance.*

He was on the other side of the dog park, still playing with the lab, paying no attention to her. That coolness against her neck pressed in harder, and she sucked in a breath. "Please."

"I need you to stand up and walk with me, Fiona. Don't do anything stupid. I just want to talk."

"Talk," she said, only able to form one word.

"Yep, just talk. Now stand up casual-like, and let's take a little walk."

She swallowed, panic flooding her senses so that her brain wasn't able to relay to her limbs that they needed to move. "I—"

"Up, Fiona."

Right, *up.* She stood slowly and turned. The cool metal of the gun left her neck, but the threat was still there. A man stood behind her, dressed normally in jeans, a T-shirt, and a leather jacket. He wore no face covering—only a plain ball cap. He wasn't trying to hide his face. She knew in her heart that he didn't want to talk. He was going to kill her. Or at least take her to a place where someone else would.

"Look—"

"Walk, Fiona," he said.

Her feet moved. She didn't know what else to do. Where was Sundance? Jock? A sob burst out of her lips when she thought of her big blond Viking protector. She knew how much his duty meant to him. His identity was heavily tied into his job. If something happened to her...

They made it to the tree line surrounding the park, and that was when the man wrapped his fingers around her bicep in a punishing grip and forced her to walk faster. She stumbled along beside him, and when panic hit her again and she tried to yank her arm out of his grip, he turned and brought the butt of his pistol across her face with a crack.

Oh God, the pain—white hot, like a firecracker across her face. Momentarily stunned, she cried out and stumbled again. This time he dragged her. "Fucking bitch," he muttered.

She could barely think; her ears rang and her cheek was on fire. When she drew her hand away from her face she saw blood, the crimson liquid spreading into the grooves of her fingerprints.

"Don't know why I can't just kill you. No, they want to see you. Maybe another fuck for old times' sake, huh?" He was talking to himself, but his words pierced her like flaming arrows until she was lit up from the inside.

The basement, the drugs, the hands. *No. No way.* She wouldn't go back.

So that's when she fought. She fought like a wildcat, twisting in his grip, flailing her legs, screaming.

The man shoved her to the ground with ease and he pulled up his knee, face snarled with fury, and she knew where that boot was going to go—right into her stomach. She waited for the pain in her ribs, the crack of the bones.

It never came. A large mass flew into the man above her, and then two figures hit the ground with a thud, dust swirling around tangled limbs.

She rolled away as Jock's large body grappled with the man who'd threatened her. Sundance was there suddenly, braced in front of her protectively, lips pulled back in a snarl. Fiona kept her eyes on the men as flesh hit flesh. The stranger grunted as Jock gained the upper hand. He was on his knees behind the man who'd hit her, and Jock's thick forearm was wrapped around the man's throat in a head-lock. The gun lay five feet away in the dirt like a sleeping viper.

The veins in Jock's arm throbbed, and his eyes were a blaze of blue ice. He looked at Fiona, taking stock of her body, before his gaze settled with a deadly intensity on her face. "He do that?"

She nodded.

The man struggled but Jock barely moved, his gaze drilling into her. Jock ignored him and jerked his chin to the gun, five feet away on a patch of grass. "He gonna use that on you?"

"I don't know," she said, her voice barely above a whisper. "He said he was taking me...taking me to th-them."

Jock's nostrils flared just as something shiny caught the light of the setting sun. She didn't even get a chance to shout as the man in Jock's grip pulled a small knife out of his pocket and thrust back, aiming for Jock's side.

Jock twisted at the waist to avoid the slash of the blade, which caused his grip on the man to loosen. Fiona knew ex-actly what the man would do next, and she lunged in the direction of the gun just as the man did. She wasn't fast enough, and just as the man closed his fingers around the hilt of the gun Fiona knew she'd made a big mistake.

The man lifted the gun, his lips curled back in a snarl. Fiona heard barking and a shout as she stared at the black hole of the gun's muzzle.

Then two hands wrapped around the man—one at his throat and one at his forehead. The hands yanked, a sickening crack filled the small space, and the man dropped to the ground in a heap. Behind him knelt Jock, chest heaving, eyes cold, looking like a predator out of a movie.

Fiona shrieked and immediately covered her mouth, staring at the man's now-lifeless eyes as he lay in the dirt path. Jock rose to his feet with a deadly grace. He pulled his phone from his pocket and pressed a couple of buttons. But Fiona couldn't take her eyes off the man's body. She didn't mourn him. She didn't know him, and he'd clearly meant to do her harm but Jock had...just killed him. Snapped his neck. Took his life.

She choked back a sob, the adrenaline draining out of her as Jock said curtly into the phone. "Favor. Cleaning crew needed." He rattled off the park address and then pressed another button and slid the phone into his pocket. He checked the man's pockets but came up empty.

Jock stepped past Sundance and held his hand down to Fiona. "We gotta go."

She stared at his hand, the same one that had killed the man in front of her. She hadn't really thought of all of Jock's skills, hadn't let herself go there and imagine all the ways he planned to keep her safe. That would include killing someone before they killed her.

His hand didn't have any blood on it, because what he'd done had been cleaner than that. But he still had *blood* on it. Blood in her name. Oh fuck, she was shaking so badly her teeth rattled. She still hadn't grabbed his hand, and something passed over his face—Regret? Frustration?—before he shut it down and, with a curse, hauled her to her feet.

With Sundance on their heels, he led her out of the park toward a large truck. He opened the passenger side door, helped her inside, and even buckled her seatbelt as she curled into herself. Sundance jumped into her lap and she gripped his fur, burying her face into his side.

The driver's side door opened, Jock got in, and then they were speeding away. It took her five minutes to raise her head and look out the window. "Where are we going?"

"Away."

"What?"

"There'll be more. We need to move. Not safe here. Need my crew."

"But my apartment, my things—"

"Gotta leave 'em."

"No!" she shouted, the sound surprising her, Sundance, and Jock. The latter darted his eyes her way, his brows lowering. "Fiona—"

"No! I want to go back and pack a bag. Goddamn it, Jock, I don't have a lot, but I have some things, and I want them. I want them because they are all I have, all I've had for ten fucking years, and I will take them with me!"

Jock didn't stop driving, and his face looked set, determined.

"The necklace," she said softly, and at that, he jerked and then stilled as she kept talking. "The necklace you bought me. I want it. It was a gift from you, and I fucking want it. And you will take me back there, Jock, and you will let me pack a bag, and make sure I have my necklace or I'll jump out of this moving truck, so help me God."

He swallowed, and then with a slice of his hand onto the lever of the turning signal, he turned around to go back to her apartment.

She leaned back in the seat, staring out the window, clutching Sundance to her chest.

CHAPTER SEVEN

JOCK didn't regret snapping the man's neck. It wasn't the first life he'd taken, and probably wouldn't be the last. He hadn't stopped working as a hitman for moral bullshit, seeing as he'd killed men who were as dirty as those who tormented Fiona. He'd quit because he was tired of the life and liked hacking better. With his skills, he found he could do more damage from behind a keyboard than with a gun.

Still, he hadn't intended to kill the man. Even though Jock didn't think he'd have gotten much information out of the guy, he would have liked to question him. Even if the bruises on Fiona's face had made him reconsider keeping the man alive. But the man wasn't giving up, and when Jock had seen that gun swing in Fiona's direction his instincts took over. *End him.*

When Jock had arrived at the dog park, Sundance had been frantic, his nose to the ground looking for Fiona. But he wasn't a bloodhound and the dog park was a crazy mix of smells.

Jock had heard something deep in the park, a crack. Like a twig snapping or...a slap. Sundance had heard it, too, and they'd both taken off in the same direction at a dead sprint. When he'd seen that man about to place a boot in Fiona's stomach while he gripped a gun in his hand...Jock hadn't taken too kindly to that. The man had probably been a foot soldier, some low-rank piece of shit sent on an errand to retrieve Fiona.

But it'd been a kick in his own gut to see Fiona's shock that he'd snapped the man's neck. So while he didn't regret it, he still wished the whole situation had gone a different way.

Going back to her apartment was a bad idea, but he couldn't deny her. She was hurt, pissed off, scared as shit, and she wanted her belongings. He didn't quite understand because he didn't have anything of value, but he got where she was coming from. Since they were going back, he'd grab his clothes and his equipment. Then they'd hit the road for DC, where he could team up with Roarke and Wren on their home turf. He didn't know this area well enough and had no hideouts.

He found a shaded parking spot near the apartment complex. "Sundance stays," he said. Fiona opened her mouth and he cut her off. "Sundance. Stays. We get in, get what you need, and get the fuck out. Do you understand?"

She pursed her lips and nodded.

With a soft command to Sundance to stay, Fiona slipped out of the truck. Jock maintained a grip on her arm as they entered the back door and took the stairs. Jock cased her apartment before he let her walk in, and once he deemed it safe, she retreated to the bedroom wordlessly. He grabbed an ice pack from her freezer, and by the time he found her she was filling a suitcase.

She'd done this before, as her movements were practiced. Clothes, some shoes, a shoebox she pulled from her closet, and then a few toiletries. She pulled the necklace he'd bought her over her neck, taking a moment to finger the stones. His throat closed as he stood holding the ice pack with numb fingers.

Finally she zipped up her suitcase and turned to him with wet eyes. "Just let me grab Sundance's things." Her voice trembled.

He nodded.

After she was finished, she took one look at her apartment and followed him out the door. She slipped a piece of paper under Marlene's door and then allowed him to take her suitcase. After a quick glance out the window at the end of the hallway, Jock confirmed his truck was fine. He took her upstairs to his apartment where she waited in the doorway, glancing around as he quickly packed his clothes and laptop. The majority of his weapons were in his truck, but he slipped his Ruger into his boot. When he straightened, Fiona's eyes were on the location of his gun. She darted her gaze up to him and then looked away.

Five minutes later they were in the truck, Fiona's belongings in the cab, and they were on their way out of New York as night descended upon the city.

* * *

He drove with a single-minded focus. Fiona held the ice pack to her face as he'd instructed, but eventually she slumped against the door in sleep. Sundance had settled in the back of the cab, but when Jock glanced at him, the dog's eyes were open, watching him.

"Sleep, buddy," Jock rumbled. Sundance yawned and closed his eyes.

Jock knew the adrenaline running through his system would take a long time to burn out. He would drive until he couldn't anymore, until his body was too worn out and he didn't trust his eyes to stay on the road and keep Fiona safe.

Her cheek had swelled because it'd taken too long to get the ice pack on her face. The sight of it made his hands clench the steering wheel so hard that the leather beneath his hands protested with a squeak. The necklace lay on her chest, and his eyes lingered on the way passing headlights caught the stones. He hadn't thought much of it when he'd bought it. He knew she didn't have a lot, and he knew that he did. He could afford it, and he wanted to give her something. It'd meant something to her. More than he'd realized. He rubbed his chest over his heart, where the sharp pain he'd felt as soon as he'd seen her bruised face had now dulled to an ache. She'd lived with this fear her whole adult life. He'd witnessed it for a couple of weeks, and that was fucking enough for him.

They were in southeast Pennsylvania by the time Jock's hands became unsteady on the wheel, and the road blurred before him. He didn't want to stay anywhere close to the highway so he took an hour-long detour on back roads until he found a small motel tucked behind a gas station. The O'Shaw was a one-story building, about twenty rooms all on ground level. They had vacancy, accepted pets, and boasted color TVs with cable. Good to know.

He jostled Fiona awake. She blinked at him groggily.

"Need to sleep for a bit before I can drive more. Gonna get a room, some shut-eye, then we're on our way again." Fiona nodded, and he grabbed their bags from the trunk. The motel was shaped like an L, and the office sat in the corner. Inside, Jock slammed his hand down on the bell repeatedly until a portly woman lumbered from a back room, glowering at him. He glowered back as Fiona stood at his side, unsteady on her feet, Sundance sitting nearby obediently.

The woman took one look at Fiona's face and stopped abruptly. "No."

Jock ignored her. "Need a room."

"No." The woman said again, never taking her eyes off Fiona. "No vacancy."

"The sign says you have a vacancy, and there are only three cars in the parking lot, ma'am."

Finally she looked at him. "We don't want trouble here. I'm asking you to leave or I'm calling the police."

Fiona seemed to snap out of her sleepy state. "Excuse me?"

"I can call the police now." The woman picked up her phone. "If you're not safe—"

"I'm safe," Fiona said, her voice firming up. Her back was straight, and she gripped Jock's hand as she stared at the woman with clear eyes. "I don't know what I look like. I'm sure I look awful. But I'm telling you, from one woman to another, that however I look is not because of the man standing next to me. He is the reason I'm safe. He is the reason this," she pointed at her face, "is all I got and there isn't more damage. All we want is a place to sleep, and then we're moving on. Please."

The woman's eyes darted between them until finally she placed her phone back in its cradle and sighed. "Okay, but I want no trouble."

"We'll be no trouble," Fiona said, her voice softer.

The woman accepted cash but wanted a valid driver's ID. Jock gave her one of his aliases, and she jotted down the name on the card—Joshua Davis.

"Here are your keys. Room 12. Have a nice stay, Mr. Davis."

Fiona didn't even flinch at the name change.

Jock grabbed the keys, muttered a thanks, and then

steered his small party of three out of the office and to their hotel room.

When he opened the door, he expected worse, but the room was clean if not updated. The TV was ancient, the carpet beneath his feet was threadbare, and a worn Bible sat on the nightstand between the two beds.

The locks were new on the door, though, and the chain lock was sturdy. He checked them before turning to find Fiona standing in the middle of the room, looking around with a dazed expression.

"You want to use the bathroom first? Then sleep."

Fiona blinked at him a couple of times before she registered what he'd said. "Right, bathroom. Sleep."

She walked into the bathroom and shut the door. While the water inside ran, Jock pulled out Sundance's food and water dish. He poured water from the bottle he'd brought, and the dog lapped it up. Jock opened Fiona's suitcase and took out a pair of sweatpants and a T-shirt. When she walked out of the bathroom, he pointed to the clothes on the bed. "Change. I'll be in the bathroom."

She looked at him for a long moment and then grabbed the hem of her shirt. He looked away just as she pulled it over her head. In the bathroom, he splashed water on his face and refused to look at himself in the mirror. He didn't want to think about what had happened or what was to come. He'd worry about it all when he woke.

* * *

Fiona stared at the heavy curtains over the window, listening to Jock moving about in the bathroom. For a large man he didn't make much noise, but these walls were paper thin. Sundance lay on the bed at her feet, his muzzle on his paws, big body at rest. She knew he was worried about her, and if dogs could feel guilt she was sure he did. Not that what had happened to her was his fault, but he hadn't been there and Sundance seemed to pride himself on being there for her.

Jock walked out of the bathroom with his shirt clutched in his fist. Despite her exhaustion, she couldn't take her eyes off his chest. He was massive. She knew that because she'd seen his muscles beneath his shirts, and she'd felt the hardness of his abs. But good Lord, he was a vision. Defined muscles, tanned skin that seemed at odds with his fair hair and blue eyes. He wore a thick black watch and a silver chain with some sort of pendant. And on the back of his upper right shoulder, an eagle soared with an American flag in its grip. Kinda cliché for a military tattoo, and maybe if they'd been other people in another life, she'd tease him about it.

He ignored her, maybe thinking she was asleep. He kicked off his boots, tore off his socks, and dropped his pants.

It'd been so long since she'd seen a man this naked. He only wore a pair of gray briefs that hugged his ass and generous package. After everything that had happened to her, this was a welcome distraction, and she didn't even bother to hide the fact that she was ogling him. Not only was he pretty to look at, she also knew what that big body was capable of.

He turned to look at her and stilled when he saw her eyes open. He didn't move to cover himself, but his abs contracted as he inhaled sharply. Sundance raised his head, and Jock ruffled his ears with a big hand, still watching Fiona.

He padded over to her on silent bare feet, and she didn't move, only waited as he sat on the edge of the bed and gently probed her face. His jaw clenched, and his eyes darkened as she winced from the touch. "Least he didn't break anything. Bruise'll fade."

"How'd you know where I was?" she asked.

"Marlene."

Did she call him? "How—"

"I went to your door. I wanted to talk to you. I banged on your door for a while until Marlene told me you'd gone to the dog park."

He'd come to her door. He'd wanted to talk, after everything that had happened that night when she'd been buzzed on wine. "And you came."

"Had a bad feeling."

"Your instinct was right."

"Yup."

His fingers moved from her cheek to sift through her hair. He didn't seem to realize he was doing it until she leaned into the touch and hummed contentedly. She'd also loved having her hair played with, once. He froze at her movement and withdrew his hand. "You okay?"

"I'm not sure what okay is. I'm here, I'm alive. My mind hasn't fractured into tiny pieces."

"We'll talk more after we get some sleep."

"Can you just tell me where we're going?"

"To DC. To Roarke and Wren. Got some work to do here before we leave to look into what that man planned to do with you. Might stay a day or two."

"Okay."

"We're in Amish country," he said. "Ever been?"

She shook her head and he nodded. "Get you some food after you sleep. They eat well here."

"Okay," she said again, lulled by the softness in his voice. Her body felt heavy, sinking into the mattress.

He stood up and her gaze lingered on his body as he

lifted the covers of the other bed and slid inside. He turned out the light, and she watched his large form roll to face her.

"Jock," she called after a minute.

"Yeah," he said, his voice raspy.

Shit, she knew she should let him sleep instead of bugging him. Why was she being needy? "Never mind."

"What?" He turned on the lamp between them, sending a soft yellow light across his harsh features.

"It can wait. I'll let you sleep."

"Fiona," he growled, "just—"

She huffed. "Why did you come to my door?"

He stared at her, his brows slightly turned in as if he hadn't expected that question. His fingers were curled around the edge of the mattress, and they slowly clenched before relaxing. "I wanted to see you."

"To make sure I was all right?"

His gaze searched her face. "That wasn't the primary reason, no."

She shifted to the edge of her mattress. They were as close as they could get while still remaining in their own beds. "Then why?"

His nostrils flared, and he seemed to be weighing his next words. His tongue crept out to push at the corner of his lips. Finally he spoke. "I wanted to be near you."

That was it, six words. Six words that flayed her open. "Jock."

He rolled onto his back, breaking eye contact. "Go to sleep, Fiona."

"Jock."

"Sleep."

"Jock."

He dug the heels of his palms into his eyes. "Go. To. Sleep."

"Jamison," she whispered.

He dropped his arms back to the bed on two soft thumps then turned his head to face her.

She smiled at him, even though the stretch of muscles hurt her bruised face. "I wanted to be near you, too."

He held her gaze for a long time, and his Adam's apple bobbed as he swallowed. Finally he spoke, his voice a deep rumble that soothed her. "Sleep, Fi."

"Okay, Jock."

He turned off the light, rolled over, and she stared at the bare skin of his back, at the large eagle inked on his right shoulder, until sleep took her under.

CHAPTER EIGHT

WHEN Fiona woke, the clock in the room said noon. She still felt bone tired, like she could have slept another twelve hours. She rolled onto her back and heard the rattling of Sundance's collar. His wet nose nudged her elbow, and she dropped a hand to the side of the bed to scratch his ears.

The tapping of keys drew her attention, and she lifted onto her elbows to see that Jock had turned the corner of their small room into a damn control center.

She'd known he had computer skills—he'd said as much, based on all he'd done to secure her life—but it was still a shock to see his large body hunched over his laptop. His legs were braced far apart, and he only wore a pair of jeans. His hair was damp and the air smelled like soap. His feet were bare, and the sight of him sitting there with all that skin exposed sent a bolt of heat down her spine. She was going to have to talk to him about wearing more clothing.

The bed frame made a cracking noise as she sat up and swung her legs over the side of the mattress. Jock swiveled his head to her, his gaze raking her body, lingering on her bare legs before lifting back to her face. She hadn't bothered with the sweatpants he'd laid out for her, choosing to strip down to her underwear and an oversized T-shirt. Maybe she should have worn the sweatpants.

She cleared her throat. "Morning. Or afternoon."

His eyes went a little soft. "Coffee and sandwich by the TV for you."

She looked to where he pointed to see a massive coffee in black Styrofoam and a small wax-paper bundle. "You left to get food?" How had she not heard him?

"Had it delivered to the front desk, tipped the receptionist to bring it to us."

"Oh." That was nice. Her stomach growled as she stepped onto the carpet. "Thank you. Sundance fed?"

"Yep."

He was back to his computer. She sat on the edge of the bed, sipping the coffee and munching on her sandwich. It was good—bacon, egg, and cheese on a croissant. She didn't recognize the name on the wrapper so the food must have come from some local place. She fed some of the leftover bacon to Sundance and then walked to her suitcase. "I'm going to shower."

"Hot water knob is sketchy. Give it time before you step in to make sure it doesn't burn you."

He said all this without looking at her. She held her clothes to her chest, staring at the back of his blond head. Did he realize how much he went beyond the call of a normal protector? He was worried about her burning herself in the shower. Maybe another person would find him overbearing or controlling. But to Fiona...well, she'd spent so much time on her own without anyone watching out for her. So the way he treated her was like having the sun shining on her face.

She remembered what he'd said, that she was latching on to him because he was someone she could trust, that she could depend on, but she knew in her heart it wasn't only because of that. It was the whole package.

"Jock."

He grunted.

"Jock," she said again. Finally he turned, and when their eyes locked his large body stilled. She smiled at him. "Thank you."

He held her gaze for a long time before he gave her a nod and turned away. Satisfied that she'd conveyed what she wanted to, she went to shower.

The hot water was in fact a little touchy. It took a long time to warm up and surged a couple times with a temperature spike. So once she got the temperature where she wanted it, she didn't touch the damn thing.

It felt good to get clean. She lathered her hair twice just because it felt so nice, and shaved and coated her body in her favorite honey-scented shower gel.

After her shower, she dried off, pulled on a pair of jeans and a top, and wrapped her hair in one of the motel towels. After moisturizing her face, she walked out to find Jock hadn't moved.

He did that head-to-toe scan thing he always did and patted the chair next to him. She sank down into it and pulled her knees to her chest, wrapping her arms around them. He turned away from his computer and leaned into her space. She froze as his hand came up to brush her bruised cheek. His eyes went dark, and a muscle in his jaw ticked. "Getting darker."

She swallowed. "I can put makeup on it. That'll do the job of covering it up."

"When we leave, yeah. Don't want to draw attention."

"Okay."

He squeezed her knee and turned away.

"So what's the plan?" she asked.

"Thought about driving straight through to DC, but I wanted to give Roarke a heads-up first. Did that this morning, and now I'm checking on your apartment security, seeing if anyone has been by."

Fiona bit her lip. "I hope Marlene stays in her apartment and doesn't try to be a hero if anyone comes around."

Jock shook his head. "Called her son. He's on his way up to visit her. Might take her home with him for a bit. She'll be fine."

Oh God, Fiona's heart was going to burst. "That's...that's perfect. Thank you for thinking of her."

Jock looked down and away, the praise clearly making him uncomfortable. "Woman makes good brisket."

Fiona smiled.

"So, we stay here another night. Roarke's gonna find us a place to stay in DC that'll be easy to hide away." His eyes cut to her sharply. "Game's changed, babe. We go from defense to offense now. All you gotta do is hang tight until we win."

"Oh," she said softly.

"Let me get some more things done here. Drink your coffee, do your face up, then we'll get you out of here. Take a walk, get some more food. Okay?"

She felt a bit like she was floating. She'd steered her own boat for so long, and she was so damn weary. Amazing how someone else making the decisions made her feel *more* free. How was that possible? She wasn't sure, but it was. "Okay, Jock."

"You all right?"

"I'm good."

He reached out and pulled on the towel until it slipped from her head. Her hair tumbled around her shoulders, and he ran his fingers through the damp ends. "Good girl," he said, so quietly she barely heard the words. She closed her eyes, enjoying the gentle tug on her scalp. Was this what Sundance felt like when she rubbed his ears? She needed to do it more often. Eventually the hand in her hair withdrew and the typing resumed. She opened her eyes to watch him as he worked intently, fingers flying across the keyboard. The screen changed fast as he switched from window to window to window.

Maybe she should have been more scared or worried, but she knew that she was better off right now, in this motel in nowhere Pennsylvania, than she'd been in ten years on her own. Jock was wrong. He wasn't made of dirt. He was something else, like rock hard steel. Glistening metal. She saw it all. And she'd work herself to the bone to make sure he saw it, too.

* * *

When Fiona emerged from the bathroom, the bruise was hidden beneath makeup. Jock tilted her face this way and that, but he couldn't see it. "Got skills," he said.

She smiled. "I'm a little rusty on makeup application. I used to wear it a lot but not so much anymore. Glad I still got it."

Jock had thrown on a shirt while she was in the bathroom, and now he sat down on the end of the bed to tie his boots. Sundance danced near the door, eager to go outside. "So where are we going?" Fiona asked.

"There's a park nearby where we can take Sundance. Also a couple of shops. Soft pretzels, smoothies, coffee. Not sure what things are going to be like once we get to DC so..." He let his voice trail off.

"So enjoy some things now?" she finished for him.

"Yeah, that's about it."

Fiona clipped on the leash, and after Jock stuck a gun in his boot—when Fiona wasn't looking—they left. The park behind the motel was an annex of an industrial complex, and the grounds were well taken care of. It was a weekday afternoon so not many strolled the pathways or lounged in the gazebos, but they saw a few people.

Sundance was happy to be outside and enjoyed exploring his new surroundings. After grabbing some soft pretzels and smoothies, they retreated to a shaded gazebo. Fiona poured some water for Sundance into a portable dog water dish, and then they sat in silence, enjoying the slight breeze and relatively cool shade.

Fiona looked more relaxed than he'd seen her since they'd met. She sipped her drink and poked at a praying mantis, then gave Sundance some of her soft pretzel. She caught Jock watching her and said, "I know, I know. People food is bad, but he's such a good boy and so I give him treats. I swear I don't do it a lot. Don't judge me."

He hadn't said one word about what she fed Sundance. The dog was hers. "I don't care what you feed him."

"Oh," she said, and her cheeks colored.

"Had a dog when I was a kid, fed that thing under the table every day even though my mom told me not to. He lived to be fifteen years old and died when he got hit by a car, so whatever. Feed the dog bacon if he wants it. Who gives a fuck."

Fiona's lips twitched. "That's what vets say, by the way."

"What do they say?"

"'Feed the dog bacon if he wants it.'" She lowered her voice and puffed out her chest, imitating him. "'Who gives a fuck?'"

She was funny, but he refused to laugh. "That what I sound like?"

"What do you think, Sundance?" she asked the dog. "Was that a good Jock impression?"

Sundance blinked his eyes at her.

"Sundance says yes," she announced.

"That so?"

"Yep, we have a system."

He hummed under his breath and gulped some of his smoothie.

"So...what was your dog's name?" She asked the question tentatively, like she knew probing into his life might not be welcome.

It usually wasn't, but this was Fiona. She probably didn't realize it, but he'd let her in more than he had anyone. "His name was Rex. He was a mutt. Lab and something mixed. We were never sure."

She inched closer and closed her lips around her smoothie straw, hollowing her cheeks as she sucked up the drink. He tried in vain not to look. "Where'd you grow up?" she asked.

They were doing this, the whole backstory thing. Whatever. "Trailer park in Indiana. Lived there with my mom, older brother, and Rex. Yes, my mom's still alive. No, we aren't super close although I send her money every month. She refuses to leave her trailer park because she's screwing the maintenance guy. I haven't seen her in years." And he didn't say a goddamn word about his brother.

Fiona didn't say anything for a long time, and he didn't look at her. He hated talking about himself, and most especially his past, but he had to admit it felt kinda good to purge it all. He popped the cap off his smoothie, poured the rest in his mouth, and tossed it into the nearby trash can.

He avoided Fiona's eyes. He didn't want pity or understanding or...anything, really. He didn't want to deal with
the naked emotion he'd see in her expression because she
wasn't good at hiding anything. So instead he leaned his
head back, closed his eyes, crossed his arms over his chest,
and waited.

Silence followed, and normally he would have been per-
fectly happy with that, but something about this silence was
thick, cloying, suffocating. He finally lowered his head and
opened his eyes to see Fiona staring off into the park, biting
her lip. She turned to face him and it was obvious she was
struggling to find the right words. "Sorry about your mom."

Yeah, he was sorry, too. Every goddamn day. "Thanks."

She took the hint, nodded, and didn't ask questions about
his brother. A breeze blew through the gazebo, lifting her
hair so the ends tickled his arms. He could smell her
shampoo—a sweet, fresh scent. Fuck, he'd never paid
attention to the way a woman's hair smelled before. This
was all kinds of fucked up, yet he couldn't bring himself
to care anymore. If she hadn't gone to the dog park, if they
hadn't had to leave town, if they were two people without messed up lives...What would have happened when he
knocked on her door last night?

With a sigh, Fiona scooted over until their thighs
touched, and then she leaned her head onto his shoulder, relaxing her body against his. He tensed for a brief moment
before forcing himself to loosen up.

When he'd observed her, he'd noticed how she avoided
physical contact with anyone. But she voluntarily touched
him. She'd done it when they went to the street fair, and she
did it now. He didn't have a whole lot of experience with
sexual assault survivors. He'd done research while prepar-
ing to protect Fiona, but every person was different. And

reading articles from therapists—where everything was black and white—was nothing compared to dealing with an actual, real-life person. Fiona wasn't a statistic or a case study. She was a person with a past, present, and future.

He slowly uncrossed his arms and settled one around her shoulders. Fiona's lashes fluttered, and she pressed into him deeper. His heart rate sped up, right there in public, and he willed himself to be cool, to calm down. But Fiona smelled so good, and she was so damn warm, and soft.

An elderly couple walked by and the woman turned toward them in the gazebo. She smiled and then said to her husband loud enough to hear, "What a sweet couple."

They kept walking, and while something settled in Jock at those words, some sort of puzzle piece slotting into place, Fiona quickly jerked out of his arms.

He frowned at her but she wouldn't look at him, busying herself with throwing away her half-empty smoothie cup and fixing Sundance's tangled leash. Finally she looked at him, and he didn't miss the wetness pooling in her eyes. "I think...I'd like to go back now. I'm not feeling well."

He rose to his feet quickly. "Are you okay?"

"Just tired," she said, but she wouldn't look at him. "Headache. I just need to lay down."

He didn't believe her and wondered what had made her jumpy. He didn't pry, though. Fiona deserved her privacy, and if there was something she wanted him to know, she'd tell him. They walked back to the motel in silence, and when they were safely secured inside the room Fiona washed off her makeup, revealing the livid bruise that made his teeth clench. She stripped out of her jeans and slipped under the covers, pulling them up to her chin. Her breaths evened out almost immediately, and he was embarrassed at how long he watched her sleeping form, the way her hair lay around her in a blond waterfall.

Then he turned away and lifted the lid on his laptop. He and Roarke needed to get back on the forums where women like Fiona were bought and sold to see if there was chatter. That man at the dog park hadn't killed Fiona—he'd wanted to take her somewhere, to someone. This time, Jock and the crew weren't just after the ringleader—they were after the whole damn operation.

CHAPTER NINE

WHEN Fiona awoke, she heard the sound of muffled voices, and she tensed for a moment until she realized the talking was coming from the TV. Jock was in the other bed, legs stretched out in front of him, crossed at the ankles, feet bare.

He was shirtless again. Bastard.

She stared at him for a long time, admiring the curve of his biceps, the shape of his short beard, even the perfect curl of his long golden eyelashes. When had she ever noticed a man's eyelashes?

Jock turned his head slowly to face her, as if he sensed he was being watched. He didn't speak and neither did she. Her heart hurt because, for a moment in that gazebo, she'd believed in them. She'd been able to have the fantasy that they were a couple, that Jock wasn't only with her to watch over her but because he wanted to be. *I wanted to be near you.* Those words echoed in her head, made her want things that he'd told her not to want. When that woman had walked by and made that comment, she'd shattered the illusion, made Fiona remember they weren't any of that.

Her life was in danger, her cheek hurt, she was scared out of her mind, and yet all she could think about was

Jock. Her mind was consumed with his presence, his small smiles, his rare laughs. The way he looked at her, his gaze now altered from one of protection to one of grudging attraction. It might have been a long time, but she knew the difference.

"Jock." Her voice was raspy with sleep, and her brain wasn't firing on all cylinders. All she knew was that she was tired of this tension between them.

He didn't say anything. His steady gaze on her was his only response to his name.

"Jamison," she said, softer this time, enjoying the way his name fell from her tongue.

His eyes went liquid, less blue ice and more gentle waves. "Yeah."

Her hand crept out from beneath the sheet and curled around the edge of the mattress. She wasn't sure she was this brave anymore. Freshman year of college Fiona? Oh yeah, she'd been brave. She'd flirted and kissed and made out. She'd done all of that because she liked the attention and knew she could get it easily with a smile. But now . . . it'd been so long. She was curling her toes around the edge of the cliff and debating whether she was going to jump. All she needed was a strong breeze to convince her. "If I . . . If I came over there and got into bed with you, what would happen?"

He didn't say anything, but his chest hitched—she saw it just as he swallowed. His one hand she could see was fisted on his thigh.

"Fiona." Her name was a warning. A yellow light. She planned to speed right on through.

"What would happen, Jock?"

"Why are you doing this?"

"Why aren't we doing this?"

His nostrils flared. "I don't know how to—" He stopped abruptly.

Her heart was pounding in her ears and heat was pooling in her belly. She shifted her legs restlessly beneath the sheets, and he watched the movement. "You don't know how to do what?"

"Handle you." He said the words rapid-fire. "I don't understand what you see in me. Why you think I know how to do this... with you... after all you've been through."

Oh God, that was it. He was worried about fucking this up. She'd avoided touch for so long that she thought she was used to going without, but a couple of careful skin-to-skin contacts with Jock and she realized how damn touch-starved she'd been. She knew in her heart, though, that it was him. No other person could have reminded her how good it felt to be held. She didn't want to be touched by anyone else, just him, and the fact that he was worried about fucking it up only proved her point. So she jumped off the cliff.

She slowly slipped out from under the sheet and dropped her feet to the carpet. She sat on the end of the bed, needing to gather some emotional strength before she stood and crossed the foot to Jock's bed. Only a foot. *One. Foot.* But she knew that one foot would change a lot. Everything. Jock wasn't pushing her away, not yet, and the flush on his chest, slowly rising up his neck, told her he didn't want to.

He cared. He cared about touching her wrong, dredging up bad memories, making her feel unsafe. Didn't he know that she'd never felt more safe in her life?

She stood, and his eyes immediately dipped to take in her body. Her T-shirt brushed the top of her underwear as she shifted her weight. When his gaze once again met hers, the swirling blue was no longer gentle waves—it was white water rapids. She brushed her hands on the outside of her thighs and took one step. One step was all she needed to bring her to the side of Jock's bed.

He breathed rapidly, his chest expanding and contracting as he kept his hands pinned to the bed with a grip on the sheets. "Fiona."

Another warning, so close to red that she thought for a moment he'd say *stop* or *no*, or worse, he'd get up and walk away. But all he said was her name. So she blew out a breath and placed a knee on the edge of the bed, swinging her other leg over him until she settled into his lap, straddling him.

He was hard. She hadn't looked before, hadn't dared, but she could feel it, a steel rod nudging up, seeking her heat. She'd thought when she felt this again that she'd bolt in terror, but right now, it was...okay. Non-threatening. Because of Jock.

"You do know how to handle me," she said. "You've been doing it for weeks. And you're doing it now, letting me have control."

His eyes narrowed. "I don't know."

"Don't do this. Don't make me feel like I'm throwing myself at you," she pleaded. "If you don't want me, then tell me, but don't hurt me just to be noble. If you have one care about me, don't do that."

He shuddered beneath her, and his eyes closed briefly. The veins in his neck stood out, and she longed to run her finger down them, to feel his pulse beat beneath her touch, sure and strong. Finally he lifted his hands from the sheets and laid them on top of her thighs. He squeezed her flesh once, and she could see when he stopped fighting, when the clench of his jaw eased, and he let his big body give in to what he wanted. "You know I care. And you know I want you."

"Do I?"

"You do," he said, his fingers once again tightening on her thighs. Other than that, he didn't make any other moves to touch her. And God, it'd been so long that she wasn't sure how to do this anymore. She'd been sexually active before that awful night she'd been taken, but that had all been teenage fumbling. She'd lost out on those formative years where she learned what turned her on, how to study a partner.

She began to panic a bit. "I want to do this, but I'm not sure...It's been..."

He slowly raised his hands from her thighs, closed his fingers around her wrists, and brought them to his chest. She placed her palms flat on his pectorals, covering the tattoo that said *Loyalty* in script over his heart.

"It's been long for me, too," he said, in a voice that was more gentle than she'd thought he was capable of. "We don't have to do anything. Up to you. I won't touch so you can just...explore. Take your time. That what you want?"

That sounded great. Access to Jock's body without worrying about her own reaction to being touched? Heaven. He was so damn warm and hard, silky skin stretched over muscle. He had a spattering of light hair across his chest and a small trail leading from his belly button down into his waistband.

She nodded eagerly. "I'd like that a lot."

He smiled then and folded his hands behind his head, where he reclined on a pillow. "Whatever you want, babe."

She started by brushing her hand over the coarse hair on his chest, feeling it rasp along the backs of her fingers. His nipples were tight beads, and she thumbed one, halting when he sucked in a breath. He let it out slowly and didn't take his eyes off her. She continued her exploration, tapping on his ribs like they were piano keys and tracing the grooves in his abs. He was so beautiful, his body a work of art.

She was getting used to the hard feel of him between her legs. He didn't move at all, didn't buck his hips, although there was some tension in his thighs where her butt rested on them. He was holding himself in check, for her.

He'd said his nickname meant brute force. Was that how he fucked? With unbridled power? Or did he maintain control the whole time like he did the rest of his life? Could she get him to let go?

She leaned forward, wanting her lips on his skin, needing to taste his salty flavor. She ran her mouth along his collarbone and then slipped up his neck. She darted out her tongue to taste that vein, the one that pulsed with his lifeblood. At the feel of her wet tongue, he jolted beneath her. When she opened up her lips to suckle on the skin, he made a small sound, a brief moan he choked off.

He was worried about scaring her. That she knew. But God, she craved his noises, she wanted to know how she made him feel—it was a power trip to have access to him, to know she could break through that stoic façade.

She ran her lips along his jaw line, nipping at his short beard. Then she planted her hands on the bed and leaned down, so close that all she could see was the swirling blue of his eyes. She licked her lips. "I like touching you."

"I like you touching me." He was looking at her lips.

"Should I kiss you?"

"Do you want to?"

She nodded and chewed the inside of her cheek.

The corner of his mouth tilted up. "Then yeah, babe. You should kiss me."

What if she was a shit kisser? What if she knocked his tooth out? Bit his lip? Sucked on his tongue too hard—

"Thinking too much. I can practically hear it." He placed a hand on the back of her neck and drew her forward until their lips touched. That was it. Then he stopped, only to mumble against her, "Don't think. Just kiss."

She closed her eyes and pressed her lips against his. For a moment, there was no movement, just this chaste kiss. Jock moaned and opened his mouth and then swept his tongue across the seam of her lips. She felt like a virgin as she gasped, and he surged inside.

He plundered her mouth, conquering it, taking everything she had and making it his, and she loved every single minute of it. She curled her hands into his shoulders, pressing closer, losing herself in the kiss, in their duel of tongues, in this wonderful man who made her feel so fucking precious.

Her head spun, her clenched stomach unfurled, and those butterflies that had been locked inside flew away. She felt... open. Gutted. Uncaged.

He broke the kiss first, breathing hard, and pressed his forehead against hers. She lifted her fingers and placed them on his damp, swollen lips, wanting to confirm that that had happened. They'd kissed. He'd owned her.

He pressed kisses to the tips of her fingers, blue eyes boring into hers. "That was some kiss."

It was, but that had probably been beginner's luck. She had no idea how to do any of this, and her inexperience shamed her. She tried to cover it up with a joke. "I'm sure that's what you say to all the—"

"Don't," he barked out firmly. "Do not bring anyone else into this. Do you understand? There is no one else here. It's just you and me. And Sundance in the bathroom."

She swallowed. "Okay."

"Okay." He folded his arms behind his head again. "You want to keep on exploring, you go ahead."

Oh goody, yes, she wanted to do this. She wanted ... She shifted so she sat on his thighs, and his eyes darkened a bit as she ran her fingers down his stomach, his bellybutton, to that trail of hair leading into his pants. "Can I—?"

"Whatever you want." His voice was strained, veins in his arms bulging.

This was hard for him, she realized, to lay back and let her do what she wanted. He probably liked control in bed, but for her, he was allowing her to lead as best as he could. "Are you sure this is okay?"

"Babe, I'm good. I'm lying in bed with your hot body straddling me. I just had the best kiss of my life. And if I'm reading you right, you're about to free my dick that's threatening to tear through my fly. I'm fucking good. Trust me."

Okay, well that said it all. She pursed her lips together and tried not to laugh, but the giggle burst out anyway. He rolled his eyes, but she could see he was amused, too, his face flushed, his lips curved upward. "Great, now you're laughing."

"You're funny."

"No one has ever called me funny."

"Well, maybe they never saw you like this."

And just like that, his smile froze and then his face softened. "Ain't that the truth," he said under his breath, so low she barely heard him. Then he nodded. "Go on then. Explore."

She scratched his lower stomach with her nails, just to get him back for rolling his eyes at her. He grunted softly but, other than that, remained still. He wore a pair of jeans with a zip fly. She unbuttoned them and then slid down the zipper. He wasn't wearing underwear. She raised her eyebrows at him.

"Didn't have anything clean," he said, but there was a wicked glint in his eyes.

All she saw were tufts of coarse hair, blond like on his chest. His dick had lengthened down his leg, and she tried to figure out how to reach down and pull him out without hurting him.

He must have figured out her dilemma because he said softly, "Slide back a bit, babe."

She did, and he shimmied his jeans down past his hips until the root of his cock was visible. She got distracted by his V-cuts and missed that he had reached inside of his jeans. She shoved him away and slipped her hand inside, wrapping her fingers around the hot, hard length of Jamison Bosh.

How had she gone so long without this? Memories flew at her, but they were good ones. That first fumbling at a high school party with a member of the soccer team. He'd been tall and lithe, so handsome with brown eyes and long, dark lashes. They'd found a closet, and she'd touched him, felt a hard dick in her hand for the first time.

This was better. Jock was thick and so damn hot, like if she held him too long he'd burn her hand. She pulled him out and kept her grip on him. She'd always vowed cocks could be pretty, and Jock's was, long and flushed red from blood, the tip leaking a bit with pre-come.

She stroked him a couple of times, and his hips jerked until he settled. When she glanced up at him, his teeth were clenched shut, eyes like a foamy waterfall.

The only time she'd had a dick in her mouth, she'd been forced to. She shoved that thought away just as Jock's hand closed around hers. He stroked with her a couple of times, showing her the pressure he liked, the speed. Except...she wanted to bend down and lick the liquid at the tip, to feel her lips wrap around the spongey head. To suck and lap at him on her own terms. Because she wanted to.

She scooted back farther and planted a hand on the bed, leaning down.

"Fiona," he said, another yellow warning that she ignored.

She stuck her tongue out and licked the head. His hand smacked the bed, a loud thump that made her flinch.

"Sorry," he guttered out. "That...shit, it surprised me."

She relaxed and grinned at him. "You said I can do what I want, right?"

"Yup," was all he said.

"Tell me what you like and don't like."

"Not much I don't like about this. Just don't bite my dick off, and it'll be fine."

Right, watch the teeth. She took just the head in her mouth, laying her tongue along the underside, and reveled in the groan Jock made, followed by the swift inhale of his breath. That was it; she'd done that. She'd made him feel this good.

She lowered her head as far as she could go, which wasn't much, just until her lips met her fist, and then she pulled back, sucking as she went.

"Fucking—just like that," he said between gasps. "Just like that."

She began to blow him in earnest, wanting to make him come apart under her, to spill into her mouth, to give it all to her. She wanted to own him the way he owned her with his kiss. She chose this. It was what she wanted.

He began to churn his hips, not a lot, just enough that she knew he was close, that he was trying to rein it in but was failing. She loved that. She sucked harder, jacking him with her hand on the same rhythm until he placed a hand on her neck and pushed her away slightly. "Gonna come."

She didn't stop. She didn't want to. She wanted him in her mouth, down her throat, and although he warned her again with another shove on her shoulder, she ignored him. On a jerk and a pained grunt, he came. His dick pulsed, and semen filled her mouth, the taste bitter but oh-so-satisfying.

He twitched a couple more times, until his body re-laxed back onto the bed. She let him slip from her mouth, and then she crawled up his body, knowing her mouth was curved into a triumphant grin. He met her with bright eyes and a smile of his own before he cupped her jaw and kissed her.

CHAPTER TEN

FUCK, she was beautiful. And not just because she'd made his brain leak out his dick, but because she was Fiona. She was smart and strong, and so damn brave. He was the weak one, the selfish one, because he couldn't push her away, even though he didn't deserve her.

She tasted like him, and he nibbled her lips as her hot body lay on top of him. When she pulled back from his kiss, her face was flushed, eyes a little glassy, and she shifted restlessly, her legs tangling with his. What she'd just done...had turned her on. Fuck, she was perfect.

"Can I touch you?" he asked, trying to soften his voice as much as he could. He didn't know what she was comfortable with, if his touch was welcome.

She bit her lip and uncertainty crossed over her features for a moment. That was enough to cool his sense of urgency, to once again make sure she had the control, that he let her set the pace. "I...yeah, I think I want that. I just..." She winced, like whatever she'd meant to say had hurt her.

He gripped her biceps. "I'm gonna roll you to your back, okay? Then I'm gonna touch you, and if there's something you don't like, you gotta tell me."

She blinked at him and then nodded. He rolled her, careful not to settle his weight on top of her in a way that made her feel trapped or caged. It was his turn to explore now, but this wasn't for fun; this was a fact-finding mission. He planned to study her, listening for every gasp, every inhale, because he wanted to know what made her feel good, what turned her on, what would make her forget all the ways she'd been touched opposite of that.

She lay on her back, staring up at him a little fearfully as he stretched out beside her on his side. He wasn't quite sure how to do this...He'd never been slow, or gentle. He paid enough attention to his partners in bed to get them off because it was better for him when they did. That was it. Self-serving. This, with Fiona...this had to be selfless.

She was shaking slightly, staring up at him with a wary expression he didn't like. "Are you—"

"Please, Jock," she whispered, and her eyes moistened. "Just...please."

Her hands were straight at her sides, and so he picked up the one closest to him, sliding his lips from her wrist to her fingers and pressing kisses on each fingernail. She relaxed beneath him before he even got to her ring finger, and a small smile curved her lips. Her legs shifted again, and he could see the damp spot on the fabric between her legs. Fuck, he wanted that. Then he chastised himself. He would only take it if she offered. This wasn't about him.

He lifted her T-shirt to below her breasts, careful not to touch them yet. Her stomach was soft and slightly rounded. For a small woman, she had curves and full hips. Her hands fluttered at her sides, but she didn't stop him as he lowered his head. He pressed a kiss above her belly button and squeezed her hip, running the backs of his fingers down her ribs. She sucked in a breath and the skin shuddered beneath his mouth. He smiled and kissed her more, adding his tongue.

Her legs were moving constantly now, and he lifted his head to find her mouth open, breaths coming fast. Her hands gripped her shirt where it rested below her breasts, and with a sharp inhale, she lifted slightly and pulled it over her head.

When she settled back onto the bed, wearing nothing but her underwear, she froze, her wide eyes on him, arms once again stiff and straight at her sides.

He'd known she had full breasts, but fuck, seeing them in front of him was like nothing else. "Fiona," he said as he touched the bottom swell of her breast. "Fuck, you're gorgeous, sweetheart."

She shivered beneath his touch, and the tension left her body. The trust she was placing in him…he was not worthy. He leaned down, nuzzling between her breasts just as her hand came up and slipped into the hair on the back of his head. She was okay with him at her chest, touching her breasts. Great, because he hoped to spend a lot of time there.

On her back, her large breasts had fallen a bit to the side, and he lifted one, rubbing his thumb over the stiff peak.

"Oh," she said softly. "Jock."

He closed his lips around the nipple and sucked. She jerked beneath him, her hand tightening in his hair. He closed his teeth around her, not biting, but letting her feel their edge, and she moaned a high-pitched whine. He pulled off and moved to the next breast, laving attention on that one until she was a trembling mess beneath him, her breasts wet from his mouth, her body a beautiful all-over flush.

She rubbed her thighs together. "Please, I need—"

"I know," he rumbled. Except this part…he was nervous. He knew how to touch a woman, but not Fiona. And he wanted this to be good for her, not so she'd ask him to do it again, but just so that it was *good for her*. She deserved for this to be good. He always worked well under pressure, but he'd never felt pressure like this.

He ran his finger along the waistband of her underwear. "Can I take these off?"

She blinked at him, and her gaze shifted to where he still wore his jeans, although they were hanging off his hips. "Can you—can you be naked too?"

He grinned. "'Course." He shucked off his jeans and returned to his place at her side. "Now?"

She nodded.

He drew the underwear down her legs and laid them beside her on the bed. He couldn't take his eyes off the apex of her thighs. A patch of curly blond hair stood out on her pale skin, right above her clit. But the rest of her...she was bare. Bare and glistening with her arousal. Jesus fucking Christ, he could smell how turned on she was, he could see how it had begun to coat the crease of her thighs.

He hooked a hand around the back of her knee and slowly drew her legs apart, watching her face. She was okay. In fact, she appeared very turned on. There was no wariness there.

"Gonna touch you, okay? Not inside, just outside, where you're wet."

She blinked rapidly, and it was as if his words released the last of her nervousness because she smiled. "Okay, Jock."

He massaged her thighs first and ran his fingers up their inner sides so she could feel when he touched her, when his fingers finally slid over her most sensitive flesh. She jolted but stilled quickly. When he brushed her clit, a beautiful moan left her lips and her hand came up to grip his arm.

He froze, wondering if she was going to push him away,

but she only arched her back and dug her blunt nails into his skin.

He did it again, dipping between her lips before dragging two fingers to swirl around her clit. "Oh God," she said this time, her eyes falling closed.

He continued to touch her, stroke her, careful not to enter her, because he'd told her he wouldn't—but fuck, it was killing him. She was so wet, wetter than he could remember a woman getting, and hot as fuck. His fingers weren't enough.

"Babe," he said, and her eyes, which had narrowed to mere slits, widened slightly to take him in. He stopped roaming with his fingers and cupped her possessively. "Would you let me put my mouth on you?"

Her eyes popped open, big and round. Her mouth dropped down but she didn't speak.

He smiled at her. "Babe, my mouth. My tongue. Between your thighs. I'm dying to taste you."

Her eyes fell closed briefly, and her hand flexed where she still held his wrist. "I—yeah," she said breathlessly.

He moved slowly, and for once, he didn't have to will himself to go slow. He wanted to draw this out. This was for her, but he was enjoying the fuck out of it.

He pressed a kiss to her bellybutton, to her hip, into the hair above her pussy. Then finally, finally, he managed to wedge himself between her legs on his stomach, her thighs over the backs of his shoulders.

She gripped the bed tightly, and she looked on the verge of flight. "I feel very exposed, vulnerable," she said, and her honesty flayed him alive.

"I get that, babe. But this is still your show. You're in control. I'll stop, I'll go slow, I'll go fast, anything you want. You might feel vulnerable and exposed, but you got all the power."

She shivered, and her legs convulsed on his shoulders. Then she smiled and brushed her hand along his temple. "I don't know what I want right now. I just know I like how it feels when you touch me. And I want this."

He blew on her wet lips, and she jerked and then laughed. "Oh my God, that feels weird."

"Weird, huh?"

"Yeah, weird."

"Tell me if this feels weird, too." He cupped her ass, pulled her to his mouth, and licked.

She cried out and her thighs squeezed his head, hard, smashing his ears, but he didn't care, not at all. If she wanted to crush his skull in the vice of her thighs while he lost himself in the taste of her, then he didn't give one single fuck. Her hand tightened in the hair on top of his head, and she gave him one single command. "More."

He lapped at her. He sucked her clit and swirled his tongue around it. He moaned into her, knowing the vibrations would drive her insane, and they did. She went wild. She ground into his face, not holding back now as moans and cries and other sounds erupted from her throat. She bucked so hard when he sucked her clit that he nearly rolled off the bed, but she'd given him his orders—more—and he wasn't going to let her down. He was going to stay down there, his mouth on her, until she came, until she forgot everything, until she knew what it was like to be cherished.

Her moans turned into words, chants—"More" and "Oh God" and "Jock" and even a whispered "Jamison" that went right to his dick. He was hard again, thrusting into the sheets like an animal, wishing he was fucking into her tight heat. But he didn't want his mouth off her either. He focused on her clit and massaged her ass, and he could feel the moment the orgasm hit her because her thighs tightened around him to the point of pain, and then she screamed—an actual scream followed by whimpers as her hips churned against him. He lapped at her through it, holding her trembling body until finally her thighs collapsed onto the bed, her body went limp, and she fell silent.

Her hand hadn't loosened from his hair, though, and she gave it a sharp tug. Fuck, he loved that.

He reluctantly let go of his now-favorite place in the whole world—her pussy— and moved up her body. He hoped she didn't notice his hard dick grazing her thigh as he lay down next to her. Her hair covered her face because of all her thrashing, and he felt a swell of pride at her disheveled bed head. He brushed her hair off her face, eager to see the happiness in her eyes that he'd put there. But then she curled into a ball, tucked herself into his chest, and burst into tears.

* * *

He'd broken her. Oh God, he'd broken her. He didn't know what to do. She was tucked against him, her tears wetting his bare skin, but he had no idea if he was supposed to hug her or . . .

He settled his hands at his sides, and then she heaved another sob and he barely repressed a growl. Fuck it. He gathered her into his arms and held her against him. She didn't push him away so he guessed he'd made the right choice. He was sick to his stomach, and his cock was having no part of this, thankfully. Wouldn't want to hold a sobbing woman against his chest with a hard-on.

"I'm sorry, Fiona," he said into her hair, not sure what he was sorry for, but it had to be something he'd done, right?

She flung back her head, nearly clocking him as she narrowed a teary glare at him. "You should be!" she spat.

He jerked back at the force of words, and ice rattled down his spine. Alarm spiked through him. "Did I hurt you? Did—"

"No!" she hollered on a wail and then clunked her forehead back into his chest. He had no idea what to do now. Completely out of his element. He didn't do tears, emotions. What had he been thinking? Why had he thought he could handle her on his own? That he could be . . . some kind of healing force? Like what, if he gave her great head, she'd suddenly forget about what had been done to her?

He hated himself in that moment, hated what he'd done, that she was still naked and vulnerable on the bed. Had he pushed her into this? He was going to throw up.

He made to get off the bed, to leave her alone, but as soon as he put several inches between them, she lashed out her hands, fingers digging into his shoulders as she peered up at him with a tear-streaked face. "Where are you going?" she asked on a shriek.

He froze and then lay on his back. "Thought you wanted to be left alone—"

"No!" she yelled and then threw an arm and leg over him and clung to him like an octopus. At least her sobbing had stopped. Now she was reduced to small sniffles into his shoulder.

So he didn't move. He lay there with his hands pinned to his sides, staring at the ceiling. If this was what made her happy, he'd stay like this for hours. Fuck the fact that he had to piss or that he was hungry or that his calf was cramping. He'd stay.

Finally she lifted her head, hair in a mess around her blotchy face. "I'm sorry I yelled at you," she said on a sniff.

She could yell at him all she wanted. "I'm sorry if I hurt you. Or if I did anything you didn't want."

She shook her head. "No, that wasn't it." She nibbled her lip and looked away. Was she...embarrassed?

"Fiona?" he called.

"I'm mad at you," she said, but there was no heat in her words. In fact, there was tenderness. He stayed silent because she needed to get something off her chest, and he was more than happy to take some of her burden. "I'm mad because that was single-handedly the best intimate experience of my life." He still didn't talk because the words were penetrating his self-loathing, piercing holes in the regret.

"I'm mad," she went on, "because all these years, I could have been working on knowing how I like to be touched, and how I like to touch, and I could have made that better for you."

He drew her into his arms, pulling her onto his chest so she straddled his stomach. "There was nothing wrong with any of that. It was amazing for me. I wanted it to be amazing for you."

"It was." Her voice trembled, and he saw the tears gathering again. "They denied this to me for so long—"

He knifed up so he could sit with his back against the headboard, Fiona sitting in his lap. He had important shit to say, and he wanted to be on her level when he said it. He gripped her face, forcing her to look at him. She did, with her hand on the outside of his. "Don't give them that power, Fiona. Do. Not. They are not here. What happened in this bed was between you and me, and they don't get to come into this. Do you understand?"

She shook her head. "But you're wrong. They are always here. Always. They find me, and they taunt me, and they remind me they can get to me anytime. They do have that power."

He wanted to throw something. Like this entire bed.

Just take it and toss it against the wall and revel in the destruction of splintered wood. When all he really wanted to do was pummel the faces of the men who'd hurt her. "That's no more, Fiona," he said with finality. "No. More. They are not here now. You'll get that power back. It'll be yours. And until then, you can have all mine."

Her face crumpled like a folded napkin, and she fell forward, tucking her head under his chin, her body once again shaking, but this time with silent tears. He rubbed her back until her breathing evened out. He thought she was asleep until she spoke softly against his neck. "I—think I'm hungry."

"Oh thank fuck, because I'm starving," he said.

And with that, her body shook again, this time with laughter.

CHAPTER ELEVEN

IF someone had told Fiona a month ago that she'd one day be sitting in a hotel room with a man who didn't speak in full sentences, eating pizza after he'd just gone down on her, and then she'd cried on him, well...she'd have thought they were crazy.

But yet here she was, sitting cross-legged on the motel bed, a pizza box in front of them, watching TV while Jock sat at the nearby table tapping away at his laptop. That was where he'd been since he'd called for the pizza. He'd also eaten three-quarters of the pizza himself, which was great because her appetite hadn't been as big as she'd thought it was.

She didn't know what to do now. Should she feel awkward? Should she act awkward? The thing was, all she wanted to do right now was walk over and crawl into Jock's lap, curl up like a cat, and let him hold her and protect her and take care of her.

And that felt dangerous. Very dangerous. She didn't know much about Jock's life at all. He'd warned her not to push him, but she had, and now that he had reciprocated her feelings...she wasn't sure what to do. Yes, he knew about her past and treated her with kid gloves, but she didn't delude herself into thinking this was anything but acted-upon attraction. He thought she was beautiful and had a nice body, he'd told her. That didn't mean he wanted to keep her forever.

They'd let Sundance out of the bathroom, and now he lay on the bed with her, his head on his paws, eyes on her. She ruffled his ears. Sundance wouldn't be around forever either. The only person she could count on was herself. And this attachment to Jock... She couldn't do this, couldn't rely on him, especially when she knew she could fall for him further so easily.

Jock wouldn't be by her side for the rest of her life. If she had any self-preservation or respect, she'd thank him for showing her real pleasure and go back to how they'd been. She didn't want to ice him out—she was grateful after all, and he didn't deserve that—but she couldn't turn into a stage-five clinger on the guy. His rejection the first time? Stung. His rejection a second time? Permanent damage.

Her stomach protested the grease, and she dropped her uneaten crust into the box. Like a dog, Jock's head went up and his gaze zeroed in on the crust. "You gonna finish that?"

She bit back a smile. "No. You want it?"

Yes, he did. He was looking at it like it was candy.

She placed it back on her plate and took it over to him. He snatched it up and ate half of it in one bite. That had been a large slice. Goddamn it, why was his eating like Cookie Monster endearing? *Knock it off, Fiona.*

"So what's the plan?" she asked.

"Tomorrow morning," was his answer.

She dropped the plate in the trash. "I'm sorry? What's tomorrow morning?"

He typed something into his phone. "We leave. Got a

place outside DC we can stay. Wren and Roarke are there now getting it kitted out for us."

"'Kitted out'?"

His eyes sliced to her before returning to his phone. "Security."

This all felt…this all felt like too much. So many people were involved and for what? For her? That man in the park, no matter what he'd been planning, had died because of her. How many more until this was all over?

Doubt and insecurity swamped her like a rising tide. Maybe she should just go, get on a plane to the Caribbean and hide away in a small village. A place with bad Wi-Fi. *But with what money, Fiona?* She sank down onto the edge of the bed, feeling helpless. She didn't even have money to buy a plane ticket.

What if she just…let herself get caught? Maybe she could take the place of another young girl, someone who could stay innocent…

"Stop!" came a barked voice, and Fiona jerked, the sound breaking her out of her thoughts. She stared at Jock, who had twisted in his chair and was sending her a wicked glare.

She glanced around the room. "Are you talking to me?"

"You think I'm talking to Sundance?"

"Well, I didn't do anything that would require you to yell at me."

"No?" His voice was low, threatening. "Tell me what you were just thinking." She hesitated a beat too long in answering. He turned to face her, the old chair squeaking under his weight. "Fiona—"

"No," she snapped right back as anger welled in her blood. "You don't get to demand what I'm thinking. My thoughts are mine, and I'll tell them to you if I want to!"

She ended on a shout, expecting Jock to fire back. Instead his expression lightened, and if she wasn't mistaken, a smile began to form on his face. "Why are you smiling?" she huffed.

"I like it when you let out some of that fire in you," he said.

That…ugh, why did that turn her on a bit? She turned away from him and crossed her arms across her chest.

He didn't speak for a while, but he didn't move either. "Will you tell me what you're thinking, Fiona?" He paused. "Please."

He hadn't kept secrets from her, had he? He wasn't forth-coming with information, but he answered when she asked. He'd done nothing deceptive. Despite her claim that her thoughts were her own—they were!—she also found herself confessing to him. Because he was Jock, and he knew how to care for her no matter what baggage she laid at his feet.

She called to Sundance, and he jumped off the bed before dropping to his haunches at her side. She ran her fingers through his thick fur.

"I don't feel worthy of all this," she said, not looking at Jock but instead into Sundance's kind eyes. "You. The money you are spending that I *will* repay some day. Wren and Roarke's time. I'm just one person. I'm not going to cure cancer. My last job was to make a quiz on BuzzFeed for readers to find out which *Game of Thrones* character they were. And you…you probably do amazing things, worthy things, you probably put bad people behind bars and protect good people…"

Fuck, the tears were dripping down her face. She didn't even notice until Sundance flinched as one landed on his nose. "And instead you're spending time with me." She ran out of steam then and fell silent.

There was no movement out of the corner of her eye. No squeak of the chair, no hand motion, no sharp, deep voice. Nothing. He was watching her, though. She felt the searing heat of his gaze on her like the needles of a tattoo gun. Branding her.

Finally she lifted her head. That's when he spoke, his voice so deceptively quiet that she wondered if she'd finally pushed him over the edge. "Do you not think you are good people?" he asked.

He didn't wait for an answer. "I realize I haven't been forthcoming about my past, but you shouldn't be under the delusion that I'm some saint, that I'm out here doing God's work or some shit. I'm not King Arthur, babe. I do bad shit, and I do good shit, and in the end, hope the scales are balanced toward the good. Not so sure that'll ever be the case, though."

She swallowed and forced herself to meet him squarely in the eye.

"When we met, my goal was to protect you. That was it. Then it switched to revenge. But now? Fiona, I've been digging. You're not the only woman they torment. And they're still in operation. So don't give me this 'I'm one person' bullshit because you're not. You're one of many. So these are bad guys that I want to do something worse to than put behind bars."

She sucked in a breath. Of course, how could she have been so fucking selfish? "I didn't... okay. I just worried this was all for me, and—"

"Stop you right there, sweetheart. If I tried to take down every sex trafficking ring in the world, I'd never get through a small fraction even if I lived until ninety and worked every day. So this one is personal, and that's because it's you, so I better not hear another fucking word about whether you are worthy."

That was it, Jock had spoken, and she had no comeback, no retort. All she could do was fall into those blue depths and pray she didn't drown. "Okay."

With a nod, he whipped around and went back to work.

* * *

Fiona was keeping her distance. He let her. She had wounds to lick and things to sort in her head. He wanted to pull her close, though—kiss those full lips and cup her round ass, feel the press of her tits on his chest. But he didn't. That meant she'd slept in a separate bed from him the night before. He'd never had problems falling asleep, but last night he'd stared at her still back for a good hour before his eyes finally closed.

This morning she was quiet, pensive. She wasn't cold to him, but she didn't act like they'd been naked together the day before. He'd never craved physical touch before. Sure, he liked it, but he'd never felt like he'd die if he didn't get a woman's hands on him. As they prepared to leave the hotel room, he couldn't take it anymore. "I do something wrong?"

She jerked up from where she'd been stuffing her bag. "Sorry?"

"This..." He gestured at the distance between the two of them. "That my fault?"

"What's your fault?"

Why was he doing this? Why couldn't he let it go? "The fact that you haven't really looked at me at all and keep giving me those polite, vacant smiles."

That exact smile faded from her face right now. She straightened and blew a strand of hair out of her eyes. Her hands twisted in the hem of her shirt, a long thing that she

144   MEGAN ERICKSON

wore over tight leggings. "Jock, I—" She looked down at Sundance, who sat obediently at her feet. "No, you didn't do anything. I just need some distance."

He knew people played games, but Fiona wasn't like that. She wasn't trying to manipulate him, make him chase her or some dumb shit. She genuinely wanted space; he could see it in her eyes. He couldn't blame her. She'd been alone for a long time, and now he was in her face 24/7. It would take some adjusting. It was taking *him* some adjusting. "No problem."

She looked sorry. "I—"

"Fiona, it's fine. Matters to me if you're uncomfortable. Take all the distance you need."

She gulped and finally dropped the hem of her shirt she'd been twisting. "Thank you."

Those two words. She said them a lot, and every time it squeezed his heart. And now his dick. With a nod, he hauled his bag over his shoulder. "Ready?"

"Yes." She picked up her bag, grabbed Sundance's leash, and then they were out the door while the sun was still rising over the horizon.

* * *

As he drove, Fiona closed her eyes and fell asleep. They'd had to wake up early and her hair was still damp from her shower. She smelled so fucking good, and he had to sit in this damn car surrounded by her scent. It was kinda torture.

He had to stop being so distracted by her, so instead of thinking of baseball stats to get his mind off Fiona and her body, he went through everything he'd been working on in the hotel. First, Tarr had taken care of the body in the park. Second, Roarke was kitting out the townhouse they'd be staying in. They'd debated between a remote location, like a cabin, or somewhere like a quiet neighborhood in a Virginia suburb. They'd settled on the latter, believing they'd be less likely to be caught unaware with nosey neighbors around. Jock didn't like the idea of somewhere remote, where he could be ambushed by too many enemies. At the townhouse, only a few men could attack them without attracting too much attention. Jock could handle that all on his own even without a state-of-the-art security system.

When Fiona woke up, he needed to tell her that they would play the part of engaged couple. One of their stops today? To get her a ring.

It was late morning by the time she straightened and rubbed her eyes. She stretched on a yawn and then turned to him with sleep lines on her face. "Sorry, didn't realize how tired I was."

"Gotta stop to make," was all he said in answer as he got off the highway.

"Oh? I hope it involves food."

It did.

He parked at a mall, and Fiona frowned at it. "A mall?"

"They got food there, and jewelry stores."

"Jewelry stores?"

"Need to get you a ring."

She stared at him. "Jock, explain with full sentences."

He twisted in his seat and draped his arm over the steering wheel. "We're going to be living in a townhouse together. If anyone asks questions, like neighbors, we're engaged."

"Why do we have to be engaged? Why can't we just live together as boyfriend and girlfriend? It's 2018, not 1953."

"I don't want anyone fucking with us. You having a ring

on your finger with me in public tells everyone else to just back the fuck off."

"I think you overestimate the kind of male attention I get."

"I don't," he retorted. "Now let's go."

Sundance couldn't come with them, but it was a cool day so they kept the windows down, told him to stay, and left food and water. Jock didn't plan to be long. They went right to a jewelry store, and even though Jock wanted to just point at one and buy it, he gestured to the case. "Pick one," he said quietly so the sales associate didn't hear.

Fiona whipped her head to face him. "What?"

"Pick a ring."

She was still staring at him when the woman from behind the counter—her name tag said Bethany—flashed them a smile. "How can I help you?"

"We're traveling, and my fiancée here left her engagement ring at home. We'd like something temporary." He smiled, trying to pull out charm he didn't have. "Don't like seeing my woman's finger naked."

Bethany beamed, like that was the most romantic thing she'd ever heard. "Of course! Well, I'd be happy to help. Is there a budget?"

He ignored her and looked back at Fiona, who was still gaping at him. "Pick a ring, sweetheart. Whatever you want."

She snapped her jaw shut and blinked, and he could see when she forced herself to click into character. Her lips curved into a small smile as she stepped closer to the glass, where Bethany was eager to pull out expensive shit, he was sure.

Fiona pointed to a simple gold band with a small round diamond. "That one."

Jock squinted at it and pointed to the one next to it, with a larger diamond. "That one."

She whirled to face him. "Jamison," she hissed.

Oh yeah, those fiery eyes and his name—right to his dick. "Fiona," was all he said back on a smile.

She rolled her eyes and crossed her arms over her chest. "The one he pointed out, please," she said to Bethany.

The woman pulled out the ring with manicured hands, and when she went to slide it onto Fiona's finger, something in Jock made him pull Fiona's hand away and hold out his, palm up.

Bethany froze, and he told himself to be a little less forceful. *Talk, Jock.* "I'd like to put it on her, if that's all right."

There was a feminine sigh, and he turned to see another sales associate looking at them with hearts in her eyes. *Christ.* Bethany dropped the ring in his palm. "Of course."

He slipped it onto Fiona's finger, and it fit surprisingly well. He twisted her hand back and forth. "Feel good?"

Fiona was staring at the ring, and she didn't say a word. "Like it?" Jock prompted.

Her gaze shot to his, and then she nodded. "Yes, it's very pretty. Thank you."

She needed to stop saying thank you, especially when they were in public. And because she was looking up at him with round eyes, her expression soft, he leaned down and kissed her. He kept it chaste, not because he wanted to but because he wasn't sure if Fiona wanted his tongue in her mouth in the mall. When he pulled away, he saw Bethany and the other sales associate watching them as if they'd just kissed after being pronounced husband and wife.

He paid for the ring with cash and pulled Fiona out of the store with a firm grip on her hand. They made a beeline to the food court where he got a cheeseburger sub and she ordered a massive salad. They ate in the car with Sundance, who was thrilled to see them when they returned.

Fiona didn't eat as much as he would have liked, and she spent a lot of the time rotating her hand to catch the sparkle of the diamond in the sunlight. When she took it off and slipped it into her purse, he frowned. "Why'd you take it off?"

"Well, I don't need it on right now in the car, do I? And I don't want to scratch it up any more than possible so you can resell it for close to its value."

"Resell it?"

Her brows drew in. "Yeah, resell it when this is all done."

He crinkled up the empty wrapper from his sub and tossed it into his small trash bin in the truck. "I'm not gonna resell it."

"Wha—"

"It's yours. You can resell it if you want, but I'm not taking it back."

Her mouth dropped open. "Jock, what the hell? Why not?"

"Do I need a reason? I don't want to."

"You can't just buy me a ring."

He tilted up his chin. "Who says?"

She sputtered and blinked at him. "My God, you're serious."

After checking to make sure she had her seatbelt on, he put the car in gear. "Yup."

She fell silent after that, and it took her five minutes—he counted down—before she reached into her purse and slid the ring back on wordlessly. He smiled at the windshield in front of him.

* * *

They reached the townhouse late in the day. By then the sun was setting, Jock's shoulders were killing him from driving for too long, and he was fucking starving. He pulled into the driveway, and the garage door went up. He couldn't even muster a smile for that, but he was pretty damn pleased Roarke had been watching for them.

He pulled inside and threw the truck in park just as the garage door started closing again. Fiona turned around to watch it. "Is that on a sensor or something?"

"Roarke," he said in answer.

"Huh?"

"Roarke's inside waiting for us."

"Roar—" Her eyes widened. "Wait, does that mean—?"

The door to the house flung open, light spilling into the darkened garage. "Fionaaaa!" a voice shrieked and then a small figure with jet black hair leaped down the few steps and slid across the fucking hood, to land on the other side where she clasped a surprised Fiona in her arms.

Jock got out and raised an eyebrow at Roarke. He shrugged with a small grin on his face. "She's been working on that move."

Jock whistled to Sundance and grabbed their bags as the women were still embracing. Wren was stroking Fiona's hair, and something about the loving way they looked at each other made Jock's heart clench. Then they began to admire the ring, and he was done witnessing the reunion. They were safe in a place packed to the gills with security. The offense started now.

He brushed past Roarke and made his way into the house, Sundance at his heels. The women followed them and then split off so Wren could give Fiona a tour of the small townhouse.

Jock dropped their bags on the kitchen counter, immediately searched for the nearest pizza place, and ordered two large extra cheese pies with some wings. He nearly wept when he opened the fridge and found beer inside. He grabbed one and turned around to see Roarke perched on a stool in front of the small breakfast bar. "I see you got my housewarming gift."

Jock twisted off the top and took a long pull. "Needed this."

"Talk to me."

"'Bout what?"

"Well, you were pretty adamant in your texts. Make this place like Fort Knox then prepare to work. So what're we doing? And why can't all this be done remotely?"

"Because I'm gutting the operation, and that means I gotta stay in the area."

Roarke stilled and then leaned forward. "I'm sorry, what?"

"This isn't about protecting anymore. I'm taking down every bastard involved with what happened to Fiona. Darren's down. Now's time to take out his minions."

When Darren Saltner was arrested, they'd suspected someone else would rise up to fill his shoes. If Maximus was carrying through on his threat against Fiona, then he had to be protecting something else—like his investments.

"I'm sure they're running scared or fighting each other for top dog," Jock continued. "I don't give a fuck about them because they're all going to pay."

Roarke inhaled sharply. Jock could see the gears turning. If there was one thing about Roarke, it was that he didn't like to be told what to do. Jock knew it rankled him that

Maximus had told them to stay away from this operation, to let it thrive. But none of them really wanted that. They knew what kind of damage this did to women like Fiona.

"And Maximus?" Roarke said softly. "He's watching us. Even if he can't trace any of this back to us, he's not going to care. He'll hold us responsible. It'll start a war."

"Then I guess we start a war." Jock drained the beer and tossed the bottle into the sink with a clatter.

"Who you doing this for?" Roarke said sharply. He pointed up the stairs where the women had gone. "Her? You? Jonathan?"

Jock clenched his jaw at his brother's name but didn't answer.

Roarke sighed heavily and ran his hands through his hair. "Let me talk to the crew. You understand we gotta ask them to sign off on this, right? Bringing this shit storm on their heads without a heads-up or a chance to get away is shitty."

He was right. Marisol, Erick, even Dade—they'd be drawn into this by association. Jock nodded.

"I'll ask if they want in, or if they want out."

"Explain—" Jock cut himself off, gritting his teeth. "This is for me. You do this for me and Fiona, I'll owe."

Roarke nodded and rapped his knuckles on the table. "I will."

CHAPTER TWELVE

FIONA hadn't seen her friend since Fiona had dropped out of school. Once she discovered her tormentors were watching her, she'd cut ties and run as far away from Wren as possible to protect her. What if the men tried to hurt Wren again?

It'd broken Fiona's heart to distance herself from Wren. Even though Wren reminded Fiona of what had happened, she was also the only one who understood even a fraction of the terror from that night. It had bonded them.

Wren had tried to keep in touch for years, but Fiona had moved so much that she assumed her friend had given up. She hadn't known that all these years Wren had been learning how to avenge Fiona, and that it'd all come to a head earlier this year. While Roarke had been getting revenge for the death of his brother, Wren had been working to take down the men who'd hurt Fiona. The thought of Wren putting herself in harm's way for Fiona took her breath away. She mourned all the years she'd avoided Wren, all the time they had lost.

Now they sat cross-legged on the large king-sized bed in the master bedroom of the townhouse, which incidentally was the cutest thing Fiona had ever seen. The home sat on a quiet block off the main street of a small Virginia town. The neighborhood consisted of six rows of town-houses, four wide. Theirs sat along the side of a cul-de-sac. In another life, this would have been perfect, a home that would be more of a starter for some, but for Fiona it was all she needed. But this wasn't real; this wasn't hers—a home she'd worked hard for and earned—and the ring on her fin-ger was an act.

The master bedroom was done in lavender, and Fiona's gut clenched at the sight of it. It'd been her favorite color back when she'd lived with Wren. So her friend had gone out and decorated the room with Fiona in mind.

Wren held Fiona's hand in her own, her fingers tipped with black polish. "I know you made me promise never to tell anyone—" Wren began.

Fiona shook her head. "No, it's fine."

"But can I explain better? Our last phone call was rushed. And I really want to make sure you understand how seriously I treated that promise. Because I knew how much it meant to you."

It did. It was the one thing Fiona had made Wren promise. That after Fiona returned and got well—sort of—that they'd put it behind them. Now Fiona knew Wren hadn't. Not one bit. She'd dedicated her life to revenge. "Okay."

"I only told Roarke when I felt like I had no other options. He wanted to protect me, too, and I had gotten in over my head. Then when Maximus mentioned you, we couldn't let you hang in the breeze. We've taken down one boss but we haven't been able to dismantle his operation. His men are the ones looking to save their skins by cutting off loose ends."

Fiona swallowed. "Me." Back in New York, Wren had explained the complicated web to Fiona. And while she was still sketchy on this mysterious hacker, she knew the threat was real.

"I'm sorry," Wren said. "This is so much deeper and even more fucked up than I thought."

"Me too," Fiona said. "I didn't think it went high, but Jock explained it does. And if it wasn't for him, they'd have me again."

Wren's hand squeezed hers. "I heard. I'm sorry."

Fiona shrugged. "If you hadn't started the attack on the sex ring, someone else would have. I was a loose end that was always going to be cut one day. You might have sped it up, but at least you know someone named Jock who's pretty good at protecting me."

Wren tucked a piece of Fiona's hair behind her ear, and God, Fiona had forgotten how good it was to sit with a friend and just relax.

"Is Jock treating you okay? I know he's a little rough, but he's a good guy."

Fiona jutted out her chin, her immediate instinct to defend and compliment Jock. "He's a *great* guy. He's kind and smart and gentle." She snapped her mouth shut as Wren's eyes widened. Her cheeks burned, and she had to look away.

"Fiona." Wren's voice was barely above a whisper. "Did something happen between you two?"

Yes, their mouths had been on private parts. Fiona cleared her throat as she remembered the sight of Jock's head between her legs, those blue eyes—

"Oh my God." Wren tugged on Fiona's hands. "Tell me! Jock is so...so...cyborg."

Fiona burst out laughing.

"He is!" Wren said, laughing along with her. "I love the guy, but he's half computer."

"He's not with me," Fiona said, twisting the ring on her finger. "He's not at all." She lifted her head to focus on Wren and spoke seriously. "I haven't dated. I have avoided anyone touching me. I tried and couldn't do it. And I know Jock isn't some magical person that's going to heal me, but he's showing me I can be healed. I can move on from what happened. I can be whole again."

"Fiona," Wren whispered. "Sweetheart, I'm so glad."

"I like him. I feel safe with him. And so if all this had to happen for me to meet him and to see you again, then it was fate. Or something." She looked up quickly. "I'm not saying I'm going to marry him or he's my Prince Charming, but he's who I needed right now. And I didn't realize it." Even as she said the words, though, imagining moving on to someone other than Jock didn't sound as appealing. She liked *him*. She wanted *him*. For now, what they had would have to do.

She gave herself a little shake. "Enough about me. Tell me about Roarke! I remember you mentioning your brother's best friend in school. And now you're together?"

Wren's face flushed. "Yeah. And he fought it, then I fought it, and who knows what the future holds, with the kind of lives we live. But we decided to stop fighting against each other and fight together. I love him, so much. And every day, he lets me know how much he values me."

"I'm happy for you," Fiona said. "So happy."

"I'm still mad at him for spying on my life for ten years."

"What?"

"Oh yeah, the sneaky hacker. Remember when I won gas for a year from that radio show?"

"No!" Fiona gasped.

"Yes! He made sure I won. How freaking creepy is that?"

"Creepy and kinda romantic." Fiona said.

Wren snorted. "Whatever." But she was smiling as she picked at the hem of her jeans. "We should probably get back to the guys. I want you to know, though: you're not alone, not at all. We're going to talk to our crew, and if I know them, they'll join us to do what we need to do. This is just beginning, and we're not going to sit back and let them fuck with you. Okay?"

"This is weird," Fiona confessed. "I've been alone, watching my own back for so long…"

"I know," Wren said, scooting closer and drawing Fiona into her arms. "It kills me that you went through that. But it's over."

Fiona closed her eyes, clinging to her friend, worried about how fast she was falling, how quickly she was relying on Wren and the rest of her crew. She didn't have a choice now, but when this was all over she'd have a tough one to make.

* * *

By the time the pizza came, Fiona wasn't sure if she was more hungry or more tired. Wren and Roarke had left, and so it was just her and Jock in this strange, furnished townhouse, eating pizza off nice ceramic plates that Wren had picked out.

Since they'd walked in the door, Jock's entire body language had changed. He held himself straight, blue eyes hard like flint. This was Jock in work mode, she realized. Jock hadn't liked running. At all. Now, while he was mounting an offense, he was more in his element.

"What did you and Wren talk about?" he asked.

She jerked, for a moment worried he could read her mind

and would recall all the things she'd said to Wren about him. "Girl talk."

He leveled a look at her.

She shrugged. "Just...about all this. I think she feels guilty for everything. But she's not responsible for what happened. Only *they* are."

Jock finished the last of the pizza and closed the box lid. "You get what we're doing here, right? And you accept it?"

"We're going after them."

"So they can't hurt you anymore, or others."

"Yes."

"I hate that this has to involve you. If I could, I would have done this all without you even knowing, without you having to think about it all again. Because we're going to have to ask you some questions, maybe identify some pictures."

He didn't get it. "I'm reminded every day. Every single time I get my mail, I worry about what's going to be in it."

A muscle in his jaw jumped.

"Every time I close my eyes, I remember. Their faces, their touch, the needle in my veins that kept me compliant. I remember it all. You can't wipe that away."

"We will," he rasped out with a slam of his fist on the counter.

She shook her head. "You can't. You don't have that power."

He looked away, his fists clenched at his sides. She needed him to understand. She wasn't sure why, but he had to get it. He had to see how damaged she was. "Stay right there," she said. She ran upstairs, pulled down the orange shoebox from where she'd stored it in the closet of her bedroom, like always, and walked downstairs, holding it with both hands even though it was like carrying fire.

Jock stood exactly where she'd left him, eyes like a hurricane. She threw the box on the counter in front of him so the lid fell off and the flash drives and pictures spilled out.

He glanced down, and when he saw what was in the box pure pain slashed his face and he grimaced as if he'd been struck.

"There," she said, pointing to the pictures, the top one showing her tear-streaked face. "That's what I've been through. That's what's in my head. Right there, Jock. I can't tell you how grateful I am for what you're doing, but I need you to understand that I'm not going to come out the other side of this as if nothing happened. I'm still fucked up, and I always will be, no matter if those monsters are still breathing air or not."

She hated seeing him like this. He was still staring at the photos with his nostrils flaring and shoulders heaving, as if he'd just run a marathon. He slowly raised a hand and flicked away the top photograph to see what was underneath. That one was...He shuddered, and with a roar he picked up the box and hurled it at the wall. Photos scattered, flash drives went flying, and she ducked to avoid a CD that went whistling by her head.

"What can I do?" he shouted. "Tell me, just tell me, and I'll fucking do it!"

She dropped her arms from where she'd hid behind them to avoid the debris. She was shaking, but none of this was new to her—these photos, the fear, the memories clawing up her throat.

Jock was a solid mass of fury. His face was red, hair mussed, eyes a blue-hot blaze. For her. And for some reason, his anger sucked something ugly out of her, calmed a bit of her brain where all the fear lived.

She stepped toward him, her bare feet treading over the

photos that had been sent to terrify her. She'd let them hold a lot of power resting in that shoebox. And now she was walking over them, on her way to a man who made her want more—something better, a future.

She swallowed and placed a hand on his chest. God, he was vibrating. "You've done more in the last few weeks than I ever thought possible." He didn't relax at all, but his gaze bored into her as she stepped into his space, trapping her hand between their bodies. "You made me believe there's more out there for me, a different kind of life than I've been living. There's always going to be that shadow over me, and I can't pretend it won't be, but at least I know the sun is still there, and it'll shine again. You showed me that. Do you understand?"

He didn't speak for a long time. Finally the muscles beneath her palm stilled, the tension leaving them. "Jock?"

"I want the sun for you," he said quietly. "I want that more than anything."

God, *God*, what had she done to deserve his words? Karma for something. She wasn't so sure she'd earned it.

She was scared, terrified, worried what would happen when this was all over. Would they both still be standing? She wasn't naive enough to pretend this wasn't dangerous. But right here, right now, she wanted this for herself. "Do you know how to give me the sun?"

His hands rested lightly on her hips. "How?"

"Kiss me," she whispered. "That's how."

He didn't waste any time. He pulled her to him tightly and crashed his lips onto hers. He tasted spicy, like the pepperoni from the pizza, and a little bitter from the beer he'd drunk. She reached up and wrapped her arms around him, feeling like she'd die if she didn't climb his big body right now.

He groaned her name into her mouth, and she wrapped
a thigh around him. God, he was so tall, and with his arms
around her he blotted out everything until there was only
him and her and this moment.

"Please," she said, gasping as she tore her mouth from his.

With a rumble in his chest, he picked her up, and she
wrapped her legs around his waist as he strode out of
the kitchen and up the stairs. To bed. He laid her on
the sheets and she thought he'd cover her with his body
immediately but instead he straightened and closed his
eyes, heaving a great breath, as if he was seeking control. She didn't need it, not now. She wanted him as out
of control as she felt.

"J," she called, shortening his name because she couldn't
get any more sounds out.

His eyes snapped open. Something crossed his face,
something devastating and beautiful at the same time, while
the moon caught on the flash in his eyes. He gripped his
shirt with one fist at his upper back and pulled it over his
head in one, swift, sexy-as-hell motion. Did he have any
idea what he looked like?

She sat up and spread her legs on either side of his where
he stood at the foot of the bed. She clasped his hips, a silent
plead to stay put. He did. His chest contracted and expanded
as he breathed, and she leaned in, just enough to press a kiss
below his belly button, right where that trail of hair started.
His skin was so damn smooth, silk over steel.

She lowered his zipper and reveled in his soft groan as
she wrapped her hands around his hard cock inside. She
stroked it a couple of times before she scooted back on
the bed. He watched her with hungry eyes as she tried to
look sexy. She sure felt sexy under his gaze. "I want..."
How did she say this? She wasn't a prude, but *fucking*

didn't seem like the right word, and *make love* sure as hell didn't.

He bent over her with a knee on the bed between her legs. His hand skimmed up her side under her shirt to rest with his thumb along the side of her breast. "What do you want?"

She licked her lips. "I want you inside of me."

Jock's hand spasmed where it held her. Then his head dropped forward, like he couldn't hold it up anymore, and he groaned. "Baby..."

"Please."

"Last time—"

"Was last time. I want to try this." Shit, what if he got that monster touching the entrance of her body and she freaked out?

It was like he could read her mind. "You can say stop at any time. I'll stop."

She bit her lip. "Okay."

"I'm serious. Won't do it unless you promise you'll say stop if you want to."

Her heart melted. "I promise."

He smiled at that. "Gotta get you naked."

"You first."

He watched her for a moment longer before rising. He dropped his pants to his ankles, kicked them off, and then stood in front of her, gloriously naked, a freaking perfect statue. They could put him in a textbook on the study of musculature because it was all there shifting under his skin. She'd never seen a man like him. His dick was hard, hanging hot and heavy between his legs. He gave it one rough stroke when she spent too long looking at it. She blushed and met his eyes. He was smiling a sexy, self-confident grin that she rarely saw.

"I love to look at you," she said softly. "Your body, your strong face, but most of all your eyes. They're more expressive than you think they are."

He leaned over her and began to unbutton her jeans. "Don't know about that. Just think most people don't bother looking."

"They're missing out." She lifted her hips to scoot her jeans down over her butt. They got tangled in her ankles for a minute before she kicked them off.

"If you say so," he said as he took her shirt off, along with her bra. Then she was below him, naked, and he was looming over her like her own Viking conqueror. She ran her hands over his beard. "What was high school Jamison like? I bet you got all the girls, the head cheerleader and the prom queen."

His lips twitched. "I didn't."

"Impossible."

"Late bloomer. I was scrawny as fuck, awkward and shy. Grew four inches after I graduated high school and put on forty pounds in basic."

"What's the equivalent of puck bunnies for the military then? Stars-and-stripes bunnies?"

He laughed out loud this time. "Wasn't much of that, either."

"How is that possible?"

"'Case you haven't noticed, I'm not a charmer. Didn't go to bars, dance, none o' that shit." He leaned down and brushed her nose with his. "Why you asking me about this? You want me to tell you again that you're special?"

"No, I guess I want to believe that you were happy once."

He froze over her, his muscles hardening to stone. Oh shit. She'd fucked up, gone too far. She didn't know what he'd been through, but she knew him well enough to have seen the scars and wounds he carried inside. Goose bumps raced over her skin. "Jock, I'm sorry I—"

"I was. Okay? I was, then I wasn't. Now I'm feeling pretty happy unless you're gonna make me rehash shit I don't want to rehash while I'm naked in bed with you."

She pursed her lips together, hiding a smile. "No, Jock."

"I'm gonna kiss you now, then."

"That's a good idea."

CHAPTER THIRTEEN

HIS tongue licked into her mouth, more demanding than he'd been before, and she reveled in it. Jock was safe; he would protect her. She didn't have to worry. He'd stop if she wanted to stop, and he'd fuck her hard if she wanted that instead. Which she did. Oh yes, she did.

She hadn't been a virgin when they'd taken her, but she'd been inexperienced. She was still a little nervous when Jock's hand slid down her thigh with a smooth confidence and then yanked her leg up over his hip. He thrust against her, a beautiful roll of his body, and she gripped his ass, loving the power in his body that he was using all on her, for her pleasure.

The hard ridge of his cock rubbed against her clit, the feel of skin on skin deliciously erotic. Her skin heated, and she could feel the flush of arousal spread through her body. She clung to him and sucked on his neck, knowing she was leaving a mark and *wanting* to do it.

"Wanna go down on you again, baby," he rasped into her hair. "Been thinking about it nonstop since last time."

She pulled off his neck and admired the red mark. "I've been thinking about it since you did it."

He moaned and slid down her body, pausing to press a

few kisses to her breasts, her stomach, her hips, and the top of her mound. He knelt on the floor at the end of the bed and tugged her to him. After settling her thighs over his shoulders, he blew on her wet, heated folds. She squirmed, clutching at the hair on the sides of his head. She must have yanked a little hard because he grunted. "Oh shit, I'm sorry," she said.

He grinned. "Nah, I like it. Love how aggressive you get. You know you do that, right? You pull and scratch." This was embarrassing, and she tried to wriggle out of his grasp. But he wasn't having it and clamped his hands around her thighs. "No, don't. I love it. I love how hard you dig those nails into me. Do it all, baby. Bite, smack, draw blood, I don't give a fuck."

"You're perfect," she breathed, before she had a moment to consider her words.

The corner of his mouth lifted. "Nah, just lucky." Then he lowered his head, nuzzled his nose into her clit, and gave her skin one long, slow, hot-as-hell lick.

She arched her back and clenched his hair in her fists. Oh God, he was so fucking good at this. Once he started, he didn't let up. Growls and nips and swirls, like he was feasting on her, and she wanted it, wanted to be his five-course meal.

When his tongue dipped into her entrance, her body seized. She hadn't been expecting that, and he slowly lifted his head to peer at her. His face was wet from her, his lips plump and red, and it turned her on to see him covered in her. "That all right?"

She had trouble speaking. "I—yeah, it just surprised me, I guess."

"Gonna add my fingers, baby. Can you handle that?"

Fingers. Thick and dry and it hurt...

"Fiona." His firm voice brought her back. "We don't—"

"I want you to." She hated how her voice trembled.

She could see the gears working in his head before he said, "I'll talk you through it, tell you what I'm doing. No surprises."

She swallowed. That sounded okay. "All right."

He smiled at her. "Gonna rub your clit here. It's so swollen and a little hard because you want it bad, don't you?"

She nodded and bit her lip, her eyes fluttering closed as he pressed on it with his thumb.

"You're soaked, Fiona. So it's gonna feel good when I put my fingers inside you, all right? Just one. I'm fucking dying to feel how hot you are inside. Bet you're soft as fuck too."

His finger circled her entrance, and she opened her eyes to find him watching what he was doing, his hungry gaze on her most intimate place. She was spread for him, her legs braced wantonly over his shoulders. She reached down and brushed the hair on top of his blond head. He met her gaze and she smiled.

"You okay?"

"Yeah."

"Ready for me to go inside you? It's just me and you here, and I'm gonna make you feel good. You know I can, right?"

"Yes, J," she whispered.

A shudder wracked his body as he slowly pressed a finger into her. "Tell me how it feels."

Full, she felt full. Jock's thumb was on her clit, his other hand cupping her butt, and a thick finger was stretching her, filling her, reaching deep inside where she wanted to be claimed by someone who cared about her. Jock. Jamison. J. It would be him.

He crooked his finger, and at first she jolted, and then a warmth spread through her core, like he'd turned her insides to molten lava with one touch. "Oh God," she gasped, pushing into him, her body automatically knowing what to do as her hips rocked.

"Yes," he murmured and tongued her clit for a moment. "You look so damn beautiful right now."

His finger felt so good, and when he added another, she thought she saw stars. He was working on a place inside her that was twisting her inside out, baring everything she had. Her hips rocked harder, and she gripped the bed, seeking purchase to get those fingers deeper, harder.

Jock's head lowered again, and when he sucked on her clit, the fireworks went off. All the colors exploded behind her eyes and she screamed, clenching tightly around his fingers. She wasn't sure what her body was doing. She didn't have control. All she knew was that Jock owned her now with his calming voice, smooth hands, and wicked tongue.

Lips nibbled hers, and she opened up her eyes to see Jock looming over her. He was cupping her, and she felt soaked, wetter than she'd ever been in her life. He rubbed her gently as he pressed a kiss to the side of her mouth. "How was that?"

She would not cry again. But goddamn she'd needed that, like a cleansing. "That was incredible."

He grinned, all cocky man, and she didn't even care. He deserved it. She reached down and wrapped her fingers around his thick shaft. She loved his dick, loved the feel of it in her hands, the way the veins stood out underneath the skin, and the softness of the spongy head. She stroked him, and he rocked into her. "Fuck."

She spread her legs on either side of his hips, even

though her limbs were like jelly, and ran the tip of his cock over her wet folds. "I want this inside me, too."

His eyes popped open and he pulled back a bit. "You sure?"

"Positive."

He nuzzled her nose, kissed her jaw, then her lips, all while she stroked him, mixing his pre-come with her own juices.

He broke the kiss. "Let me get a condom."

"You have some?"

"Don't usually keep some on hand, but picked up some after the hotel."

She didn't comment on his optimism, just glad he'd thought to get some.

He broke away from her for a moment to roll on the condom and then he was back on top of her. He let some of his weight fall, bracing himself on his forearms, hands nestled in her hair. "Hope I can make this good for you."

"It's already good for me," she whispered.

He swallowed. "Guide me in then, baby."

He was giving her this, the control. She placed her feet flat on the bed, angled her hips, and pressed the head of his cock right at her entrance. Then she let go and grasped his firm, muscled ass. She squeezed and pulled him against her.

He didn't push harder, didn't thrust. She knew how much control this was taking him as his entire body was a trembling mass of tension. The veins in his neck stood out as he held himself back. And she loved him for it. She really did.

The head of his cock breached her, and she was so sensitive from her orgasm that she gasped. He stilled. "Okay?"

Her answer was to squeeze his ass harder and continue to pull him inside of her. He kissed her as his shaft slid inside, filling her more fully than his fingers had, impossibly full. It seemed to go on forever, that delicious drag of his length inside of her, until finally, his balls rested against her skin, and they were locked together. Jock twitched above her, and his hips jerked as his eyes fell closed, and his head dropped down. "Fuck, you feel like a goddamn dream. Pinch me, baby."

She pinched his ass and his head righted as he grinned at her. "Nah, guess I'm awake."

"Take over," she said.

He tilted his head in question.

"Go on," she said. "Give it to me. Let go. I want to feel you. I want you to take me. Make me yours."

He settled his weight on one arm, and with the other cupped her cheek as his hips rocked gently. His thumb brushed the corner of her mouth, over her bottom lip. "Make you mine? You have been since the moment you shot me."

She felt the tears coming, and no fucking way would she cry right now. "Do it, J."

Fire sparked in his eyes, so damn hot that it seared her. She braced, but he only tilted back his hips, pulling his cock out to the tip and then slowly coasting back inside. Her eyes eased closed at the stretch of him filling her.

"Keep your eyes open," he said on another soft thrust of his hips. "Want you to see it's me."

She listened, staring up into his blue eyes as he took his time, easing in and out of her body, one hand sifting through her hair as he dropped soft kisses on her jaw, her neck, and her lips. He didn't speak, and he didn't have to because everywhere he touched her was a promise, a gift.

She began to rock her hips with his, slow at first as she focused on his rhythm. His breath sped up, and he bit back a curse, so she knew he liked it, that he was affected. It spurred her on. She dug her fingers into his shoulders and moved with him, eyes locked on his. He surrounded her, his touch, his smell, his body, and it blocked out everything but that moment, them in the bed together.

She was going to come again. She could feel it gathering, and it felt so big, so much. Jock had her clutched to him, her face pressed into his neck, her body cocooned into his, cradling her.

"Beautiful," Jock was muttering into her ear, his voice a deep, gravelly rasp. "So fucking perfect, my Fiona. Jesus fucking Christ."

She sucked on his skin, the spot where his shoulder met his neck. There was a muscle—she couldn't remember the name right now—but it was gorgeous on Jock, soft skin over hardened power.

He let out a groan as his hips stuttered, the rhythm falling apart, and he clenched his fingers in the sheet by her bed. His muscles strained, body vibrating, and the sight of him like that rocked her. Fiona's orgasm roared down her spine, shattering her, and she clenched around his cock, her hips working as she clung to him. He arched his back as he pulsed inside of her.

He fell onto the bed on his forearm, still inside of her. Her hands fell from his shoulders to rest on the bed. She wasn't going to move for about a hundred years. Already, she could feel her thighs begin to ache. Jock's heavy pants filled her ear and though she longed to run her fingers through his hair, her muscles weren't working. She could only lay there, eyes half-open, as Jock smoothed the hair off her forehead with a shaky hand. "Baby?"

"Mmmph," she mumbled.

"Huh?"

"Can't move," she managed.

"Am I too heavy?"

She rolled her head back and forth. "No, too fucking good at fucking."

He laughed, the gorgeous sound filling the room, and that got her to smile, too. He looked five years younger when he laughed. He stopped to press a kiss to her lips. "I'm gonna pull out, help you get cleaned up, then we'll sleep. I'm not sure I can think anymore; my brain is boiled."

"Mmm, same," she said on a yawn. Her eyes closed, and the heat of Jock's body left hers.

A minute later, something pressed between her legs, something warm and damp. She shifted restlessly. A blanket covered her, and she snuggled into it. Sometime later, a warm body pulled her into an embrace, and she nuzzled into it, loving the feeling of being surrounded by big arms and a masculine scent. She fell asleep to the steady beat of a heartbeat she knew would never fail her.

* * *

"You're a stupid idiot."

Jock hadn't realized he'd missed Marisol until he heard her voice again.

"You'll owe me? Fucking *owe* me?" She stood in his kitchen, a petite, green-haired spitfire wearing black and hot pink. Large hoops dangled from her ears as she gestured wildly. "Erick and I aren't going to do this just so we can claim you owe us, dumbass. We're all stuck together now. I knew that the minute we banded together for Flynn. None of us thought that was going to be the end. Hacking's always a goddamn, never-ending web."

Yeah, he'd missed her. She stomped over to the fridge and opened it up. "I need a candy bar or some shit."

Fiona was watching Marisol with wide eyes, and yeah, Jock knew the feeling. She'd shown up with Erick and hadn't stopped ranting since they'd told her the plan and asked if she wanted in. Erick stood along the far wall, a huge grin on his face. Jock was happy to see Erick in a good mood. During the last mission, Erick had revealed that he and Flynn had secretly been lovers. Jock hadn't known Erick before, but Roarke had expressed many times that Erick wasn't his usual joker self since Flynn's death.

Marisol grabbed a leftover muffin and bit into it as she turned around. She stopped when she saw Fiona. Her body went tight for a moment before her face softened—something Jock hadn't thought she was capable of doing. Then she gave Fiona a tender smile. "Hey there, kitten."

Fiona returned the smile. "Hi."

"Marisol, Fiona. Fiona, Marisol," Jock said as introductions.

Marisol shoved the rest of the muffin in her mouth and swiped her hands on her black jeans. "Nice to meet you." She cocked her head. "Jock treating you okay?"

Fiona nodded. "Yeah, of course. He's been wonderful."

Jock felt his chest puff up just as Marisol raised her eyebrows. "Wonderful? Huh. Jock can be human. Who knew?"

"Shut it, Marisol," Jock rumbled, but she just grinned at him. When they'd first met, he wasn't so sure about her. She was sarcastic and flirty and dug under his skin. But eventually they'd fallen into a brother-sister relationship full of banter and insults. He'd found he missed it after the last mission was over. But now Marisol was back, full of that same fire.

"What you been up to since I saw you last?" he asked her.

"I thought I was supposed to shut it?" She punched him in the arm.

"Answer."

"I don't know, Grumpy. Here and there. Out and about. Honestly, I was getting a little bored and was about to start some shit just to keep life interesting."

"Well, we got you covered."

"I have such great friends." Marisol beamed at him. She wore a deep purple lipstick, which made her teeth look even whiter. She turned to Fiona. "So, Wren's my girl, and you're Wren's girl, so therefore you're my girl. It's, like, math or something. And I'm super excited to take down some assholes who've made my girl's life miserable. Do I have that right?"

Fiona's lip trembled, and Jock went into protective mode. In one step he was at her side, and she curled into his chest. She didn't make a sound, but her shoulders shook with silent tears. He glared at Marisol over Fiona's dark head. "What the fuck?"

Marisol held up her hands, actual alarm on her pretty features. "I'm sorry! What did I say? I'll take it back."

Fiona pushed on Jock's chest, but he didn't move. She pushed again and mumbled, "Let me go."

He did, and she left his arms, reaching for Marisol. "No, you didn't say anything wrong. I just..." She inhaled sharply and her voice dropped. "Having people at my back is going to take some getting used to."

Marisol's face fell, and now she looked like she was going to cry. "Oh kitten, we aren't at your back. We're the front line."

Fiona threw back her head and, in a teary shout, hollered,

"You people need to stop saying nice things or I'll never stop crying!"

Marisol headed right for the wine rack. "That's it. We're drinking."

"It's not even noon," Jock snapped.

"I don't give a fuck," Marisol said. "This girl needs a drink. I need a drink. Erick, you want a drink?"

"Sure," he said.

"Wren! Roarke!" She called to where they sat in the living room, hunched over their laptops. "I'm breaking out the pinot. Who wants a glass?"

"No thanks!" Wren called.

"I'm good," Roarke said.

Marisol poured three glasses of wine and doled them out.

"I don't get one?" Jock said.

She cut her narrowed eyes to him. "No, I'm annoyed at you."

He laughed. "What did I do?"

"I don't know. You probably did something, and you'll do something else soon." She clinked glasses with Fiona, who seemed enamored by Marisol. "Quit pouting, Jock. If you really want a glass, pour it yourself."

Instead, he snatched Marisol's, drained half of it, and then handed it back to her with a smack of his lips.

Her eyes widened. "See! I knew you were going to do something that annoyed me!"

"Self-fulfilling prophecy," he said as he walked into the living room to join Roarke and Wren.

They were sitting close, dark heads bent over their laptops. At Jock's entrance, Roarke leaned back and stretched his arms over his head. Jock took a seat on the edge of a large recliner as Erick joined them, taking a seat beside

Roarke and leaning back with his ankles crossed. Marisol's voice filtered through to the living room in conversation with Fiona. For the first time in days, maybe weeks, Jock felt his nerves calm.

"So," Wren said. "Update on Darren is he's awaiting trial, but word is he might take a plea. He's not really safe anywhere, but he might be safer in jail. Plus he doesn't want them to look further into him and add charges."

"And his crew?" Jock asked. "Was the one I took out in the park working for him? Or hired separately to take out Fiona?"

"One of his," Roarke said. "That taken care of, by the way?"

Roarke didn't know all of Jock's past. Or his connections. "Yeah, got a friend. It's done."

Roarke eyed him but didn't dig. That was one of the things Jock liked most about Roarke. He was a good judge of character, but he didn't pry. He let people tell him their stories when they were good and ready. The only time Jock had opened up about himself to Roarke was when he had a 2:1 vodka ratio in his blood.

"Are these guys still active?" Jock asked.

They'd learned that Darren and his crew had put up a shopping list of sorts on the Dark Web. Buyers placed an order, and Fiona had been one of those orders.

"Not now, but I think they are just laying low. There are a lot of people making money off this, including Maximus," Roarke said. "They won't be down for long."

"I'm looking into whether they moved operations. They have to know we found their shopping list. So they might have set up on another site. I'm digging into the coding to see if they left a trail for their buyers," Erick added.

"I'm still going through Darren's phone contacts," Jock

said. On their last mission, Wren had copied Darren's phone, and Jock was still verifying all the names. "We know they want her so my priority is to keep her safe."

"Of course," Wren said. "And that's what I want you to focus on. You're the best at that, and we'll pick up the slack on finding these guys. I don't know how far Darren's network extends, and I'm sure Maximus has cells all over the country."

"One at a time," Jock growled. "We'll figure out how they communicate, because they are probably all linked, and we can take them all down."

The room was quiet, then Fiona's laugh sounded from the kitchen. Jock let it settle over him, filling him full to bursting. When he met Roarke's gaze, the man nodded.

Jock nodded back. *Game. On.*

CHAPTER FOURTEEN

JOCK shifted in the passenger seat of Roarke's car and cringed when his foot collided with about half a dozen Diet Coke cans. He glared at Roarke, who sat in the driver's seat peering out the window of the parked car. "Trash can too bougie for you?"

Roarke didn't even look at him. "Don't give me shit. I get it enough from Wren. She's trying to get me to quit. I explained I could be doing heroin so maybe she should be glad it's only diet soda."

Jock made an annoyed grunt, and Roarke turned his head. "What, isn't there something you're addicted to?" He looked Jock up and down. "Camo? Thick-soled boots? Silence?"

Jock would have smiled normally because that shit was funny, but instead all he could think about was how he had never been addicted to anything. It wasn't in his personality. He was good at leaving shit behind when it didn't suit him. He'd never collected things as a kid. He liked to read and play sports. He got good grades. He dated but was never really into any girl. They were just...company.

Except now? He was addicted to Fiona. The realization hit him hard and fast. He'd been sitting in this car for only five hours, and he was jonesing for her. Sweating, antsy, irritable. What was she doing? Was she okay? Did she miss him? Most of all, he wanted to hold her, feel those firm tits pressed to his chest, listen to the catch in her voice when she settled over his lap and felt how hard he was for her.

Jock took his eyes off the door of the building in front of them for a minute to stare out the passenger window. Based on the information Roarke had pulled from the forum where buyers could find Darren's "shopping list" of women, a lot of profiles led back to local IP addresses. On the forum, the dialogue between the men seemed to be familiar, enough so that Jock and the crew believed the men were friends of Darren's. It would make sense—friends would be less likely to rat each other out.

So they were working on a file of Darren's associates, friends, acquaintances. Darren wasn't the only one bankrolling this operation. He had to have his high-class friends helping. And when they found the money, they would find how to shut it all down. It was only Tuesday, and they'd been at it since Sunday. It'd been too many hours observing pieces of shit who had mistresses, hit on their secretaries, and made a lot of racist jokes to their buddies. Once they had profiles of enough of these guys, they'd sit down with Wren and Fiona and see if either of them recognized the men or their voices.

Jock was over it. He burned for Fiona. This was unsettling as fuck. He didn't know how to handle this...desire. Was this what Roarke felt like about Wren? And if so, how did he let her out of his sight?

"You usually think a whole lot quieter." Roarke's deep voice filled the car, and Jock glanced over at him and quickly focused back on the office building. They were waiting for a fucker named Henry Chamberlain II, a friend of Darren's who they believed liked to shop for women on-line with his cronies.

"Guess I got a lot on my mind," Jock answered.

Roarke was still watching him. "Probably stupid to ask if you want to talk, huh?" Jock didn't say anything, and Roarke popped open another can of diet soda, taking a sip immediately. "Uh, okay. So, you want to talk?"

Not really, but he had things he was curious about. "How did you do it with Wren?"

"Do it?"

"Watched while she worked on the undercover mission, while she went out with Darren." He curled his hands into fists on his thighs as he felt anger swell inside of him. "How the hell did you function when Wren was kidnapped by him?"

Roarke stared at him for a minute with wide eyes, maybe remembering when he'd been shot and Wren had been taken. They'd found her in a warehouse where Darren's father and some of his men had held her. Wren and Roarke narrowly escaped with their lives after the warehouse was lit on fire. "I . . . I'll answer, but can I ask you where this is coming from? This about Fiona?"

Jock swallowed and looked away. He tried to loosen his fist, but his fingers wouldn't uncurl. "Just want her safe," he heard himself say softly. "Thinking about Wren, and now I think I know how you feel. Don't know how you did it."

"You falling for Fiona that hard?" Roarke's voice was cautious, like tossing a softball and hoping Jock caught it and didn't whip it back at his head.

Jock nodded, his gaze glued to the door because he didn't know what he'd say or do if he looked at Roarke. The man was one of the few that Jock would consider a friend. He was a good guy, loyal and smart. Blood ties mattered to him so he could understand how Jock felt about losing his own brother.

Roarke looked at the windshield and braced his tattooed hand on the steering wheel. "If you want to know, I'm not sure. At the time, I just...did it. I got through it because I had to, because I couldn't come apart. I focused on the mission and getting revenge for my brother. That helped, but I was still sick over Wren being involved the entire time. I also drank a lot." He gave a husky laugh.

Jock processed the words. "So I need to focus on the mission."

Roarke hesitated before answering. "I mean...yeah. The mission is for her. So you're taking care of her by doing it, you know?"

"Yeah." Roarke was smart.

"But it's okay to not be okay. It's okay for you to want to hit something, to yell, to lock her in a room and throw away the key so no one can hurt her. It's not okay to actually do that, because she's not a Disney princess, but it's okay to lose your mind a bit over worrying."

"I worry so much," Jock said. "Thinking of anyone harming her..." He shook his head. "Makes me fucking rage."

"I get it," Roarke said. "Do I ever. But one thing that got me through the last mission was not to get too emotional, to focus. I was no good to Wren if I was a fucking basket case. She needed my skills."

"Never had to worry about being emotional. Even with—" He didn't say his brother's name. Roarke knew. "I was cold about it."

"That's because you weren't protecting him," Roarke said, his voice so damn kind that Jock nearly broke. "You were getting revenge. With Fiona, it's different."

It was, and Jock didn't have experience with this shit so it was going to take some getting used to. "Thanks."

"Sure, I mean, you know you can always talk to me, right? Never thought to say that before because you don't really...talk."

Jock snorted, and smiled a genuine smile, the first one in hours. "Yeah. Yeah, I know."

"Good," Roarke said. He blew out a breath and tapped out a beat on the steering wheel. "So is this guy ever gonna show or what? I'm hungry and want some damn tacos."

Henry Chamberlain II was a friend of Darren's back from their days in the same fraternity while they were business majors at Cornell. Jock immediately disliked him because he couldn't be anything other than a pretentious fuck with that name. He was currently the COO of Halloran Pharmaceuticals. Again, probably a pretentious piece of shit.

They knew he'd been at work today because Marisol had called pretending to be a vendor and Chamberlain's secretary had confirmed he was in the office but couldn't take her call.

"Maybe he snuck out or something," Roarke said, glancing at his watch. "Doesn't he have minions to work late for him? It's eight o'clock."

Jock didn't say anything. He wanted to be home, too. But he was focused now on protecting Fiona. And the way to do it was to look into these assholes.

The door opened just then, and a tall man stepped out wearing a tailored suit and polished oxfords. He carried a leather briefcase and adjusted his tie as the doors closed behind him. Jock picked up the DSLR camera on his lap and began to snap photos. Luckily, the sun was still up so he didn't have to worry about needing artificial light. They'd found a few photos of Henry online, but most looked dated. Plus, they wanted to record his voice. Fiona was blind-folded a lot and said she'd need to hear voices as identification. That had Jock wanting to punch a wall.

As he continued to snap photos, Roarke dialed Chamberlain's cell phone number, which had been easy to obtain.

They watched as Chamberlain stopped abruptly, furrowed his brow on his pinched face, and slapped at his pockets. The phone rang three times before he pulled his cell from his pocket. His lips moved, and his voice filled their car. "Chamberlain."

"Hey buddy, it's Paul! Paul Wilcox. How are you?" Roarke's voice was completely different, and Jock smiled.

Henry was still standing on the sidewalk. "Paul?"

"Yeah, how's it going?"

"You sound a little different. Everything okay?"

"Yeah, sorry, got a weird cold thing. Fucking kids in daycare have got me sick year round."

"Yeah, I heard you and Yvonne had two. How are they?"

Roarke grinned at Jock. Chamberlain believed the ruse. Paul Wilcox had a small family blog on YouTube—each video only got a couple hundred views, but Roarke studied the videos and knew enough about the guy's life and how he talked to be convincing. That wasn't in Jock's skill set so he was impressed at Roarke's acting ability.

Roarke, posing as Paul, rambled on about the kids before asking Chamberlain about himself. He made up some party invite as the reason for the phone call out of the blue, after confirming Chamberlain couldn't attend because of a work commitment. The whole time, they were recording Chamberlain's voice.

"So you good? How are things?" Roarke asked just as

Jock gave him the thumbs-up. Chamberlain was buying it and talking enough to give Fiona plenty to listen to.

"Yeah, things are good. You should come up sometime. The guys and I have some parties...you know the kind." Henry smiled, and it was a smile that made Jock's back go straight.

"Yeah? Even with Darren away?" Roarke went out on a limb and asked.

"Yep, the parties are still going on," Chamberlain said. "Got one coming up."

Roarke met Jock's gaze and swallowed. "Well, sounds good. I gotta go. Family calls, but I'll give you a buzz if I want to come up."

"You do that. Nice catching up with you, Paul."

"You too," Roarke said. He ended the call and leaned back in his seat. They watched Chamberlain walk to his car, a silver Lexus, and get inside. With a slight roar from his engine, he pulled out of the parking lot and drove away.

"So it doesn't matter if Darren is away," Roarke said. "I know he was the boss. Wren showed me her research. So I'm thinking a new boss is in place, or some big players banded together."

"Something like that. A venture that makes that much money, they got some plans in place. Always. A way to keep that money rolling in," Jock said.

Roarke nodded. "Yeah. Fuck." He started the engine. "Well, tomorrow is another day."

"Another profile. Another piece of shit," Jock muttered.

Roarke sighed, and Jock closed his eyes, glad as hell that he was on his way back to Fiona.

* * *

Fiona knew what Jock had been doing all week. He didn't talk about it to her, but she knew. He'd leave early in the morning—she'd get up with him and make him coffee. He'd drink it silently while she babbled on about random shit. Then he'd kiss her forehead, ruffle Sundance's ears, and leave. Sometimes he came back early afternoon, sometimes around dinner, and other times, he'd be in the kitchen in the morning when she went down to make coffee.

So she kept herself busy. Wren came over a lot, but she couldn't be there all the time because she had her own life and was busy on a freelance job with Erick for money. Marisol also swung by a lot with food and alcohol, which was appreciated.

So Fiona made a home. She didn't know what else to do, and she'd always wanted a house to fill with love and pretty things. She had a ring on her finger, a fiancée with massive biceps, and a dog in a townhouse. So she ordered wall decor. She went to the flower shop nearby and made planters. The first day they were on the porch, she watched out the window for when Jock came home. He walked down their sidewalk, checking out his surroundings like he always did, jiggling his keys. When he saw the planters, he stopped, walked around one and then the other. He stepped back to eye them both, cocked his head, and then, so quick she almost missed it, he smiled. She lived on that smile for a solid twenty-four hours.

She also baked. A lot. She dug up her late grandmother's recipes and made cookies, brownies, pies, and a peach cobbler.

Tonight, she was making blueberry buckle for no other reason than that she liked blueberries, and it could be re-heated for breakfast or dessert. Blueberry buckle was a dense coffee cake with a blueberry layer and a sweet,

crunchy streusel layer on top. Fiona thought it was delicious, and she knew Jock would, too. He was a sucker for
fruit desserts.

She'd eaten dinner with Sundance and made the buckle.
The timer on the oven beeped, and she hopped up from the
couch where she'd been reading, grabbed a mitt, and pulled
the dish from the oven.

Her eyes rolled into the back of her head—it smelled
that good. She placed the plate on the stovetop and
grabbed a toothpick to stick in the cake to test if it was
done. The toothpick came out clean, and she grinned. Of
course, she'd prefer to eat it with someone, but she was
alone. Again.

She needed to quit whining about this. Jock wasn't
actually her fiancée. He wasn't really even her boyfriend.
She had no idea what they were. She knew she trusted him
and he wouldn't hurt her. But she didn't know anything
about him—how did he have money? Where was his family? Did he even like dogs? He could have a lovely life in
Wisconsin with a Midwest accent and two kids. Fiona had
no *freaking* idea who Jock really was. She knew he was
great at knowing her body and said a lot of nice things. But
that didn't make a boyfriend or a lasting relationship. On
the other hand, she couldn't imagine not being with him.
Her heart was twisted up inside, and she hadn't talked to
Wren about it because Fiona was a little scared about what
Wren would say.

So Fiona just needed to eat her blueberry buckle, finish
her book, and go to bed. She opened a cabinet and drew a
plate out just as she heard the car keys jingle in the front
door. Jock must be home—he'd left in Roarke's car. She
placed a square of the dessert on a plate just as Jock walked
into the kitchen. He tossed the keys on the table and made

a beeline for her so quickly that she backed up against the counter.

"How—" She didn't get a word in because his big hands were gripping her head and his lips were on hers—firm, pressing—and she gave a soft sigh and opened her mouth. He slipped his tongue inside, probing, licking, owning. She clutched his shirt at his waist and melted into him. He pulled back and licked his lips, face inches from hers. "Sweet."

"Thanks," she whispered.

He shook his head. "Taste like sugar."

"Oh," she blushed. "I made a dessert."

He turned his head and spotted the plate sitting on the counter. "Again?"

She shrugged as he let her go and snatched up the plate. "I like to bake. Gives me something to do."

He didn't use the fork she'd placed near the plate for herself. With his fingers, he picked up the cake—which had to still be hot—and shoved half of it into his mouth.

He began to chew and immediately opened his mouth to suck in air. "Hot," he said around a mouthful.

"I would have warned you but you didn't give me the chance." She poured him a glass of cold milk and watched as he downed it. He apparently didn't learn his lesson, though, because he swallowed and then immediately shoved the other half in his mouth. "Fucking good," he mumbled around the mouthful. He swallowed that too and drank more milk. "Not even gonna complain about how much weight I'll put on eating this shit. Fuck it. Too delicious to care."

She liked Jock's body, but she also liked that it looked lived in. Used. Not a model posed on one of her book covers. Not that those weren't fun to look at.

She ran her fingers over his stomach and cut her own square. "I'm glad you like my baking."

His arms wrapped around her waist from behind, then his lips were at her ear. "Like it a lot. Like you more, though."

See? Why did he have to say sweet shit? It was on the tip of her tongue to ask him questions, probe into his life, but why do that if this relationship was strictly about this mission? Why ruin this moment where his breath smelled like blueberries and sugar and his arms were warm and safe around her?

"How was, uh, tonight?" she asked instead.

His arms tightened briefly. "All right. We're making progress. We'll have profiles for you and Wren to look at next week."

"Great," she said softly.

He pressed a kiss under her ear. "Eat your thing. Finish your book. Then come to bed. I'm gonna shower, then wait for you."

Right, he'd wait for her, then he'd touch her, then he'd make her come, then she'd make him come, and they'd fall asleep. Because this was her dream life. Not her real one. And fuck it, but she'd earned herself some dreams. "Okay, J."

He blew out a breath and a shudder ran through his body, something that happened every time she called him J. She didn't know why. Another question she didn't ask.

Another kiss and he was gone. She did indeed eat her cake, finished her chapter, then went upstairs to the bedroom and a very clean and very naked Jamison Bosh.

CHAPTER FIFTEEN

"I don't like this." Jock's face was thunder, and Fiona appreciated the anger on her behalf.

"I don't either," Roarke glared. "You think I didn't try to talk Wren out of this?"

Fiona squeezed Wren's hand. "We talked about it, and we're okay. We can do this."

Jock's jaw ticked and Fiona smiled at him. She knew the smile didn't reach her eyes. This wasn't anything to smile about. This was going to be painful and humiliating, but it was necessary.

It'd been a week since they'd arrived at the townhouse, a week where Fiona could pretend she had a normal life. That she wasn't being hunted or that all of this would go away once the threat did. That she'd be on her own again before too long.

At least she had Sundance. He sat at her legs now, his body leaning against hers. She threaded her fingers in his fur and he turned to her, blinking those big eyes. She blew him a kiss, and he tossed his head.

During the past week, the team had spent every minute working on profiling Darren's crew and associates. And now Wren and Fiona had about twenty profiles to go through to see if they recognized anyone from the time they'd been taken in college.

Fiona knew he hated to see her anxious or upset. He was her protector, a big bulldog who wanted to stand between her and anything that dared to hurt her. She was falling for him, but it was a painful fall. There was nothing glorious about falling in love with Jock when she knew there was nowhere to land. Nothing to cushion her because, after this was over, he'd be gone on his next mission. She didn't doubt that he cared for her, but it was the kind of care bred of protectiveness. It wasn't a lasting love, built on humor, common interests, and goals.

Hell, she didn't even have goals. Her main focus had always been just to stay alive.

Wren's hand squeezed her knee. "Hey, you okay?"

Oh right, they had profiles to look through. *Focus, Fiona.* "Yeah, I'm ready to do this. Let's get it over with and then I can drink an entire bottle of wine."

It was just the four of them. Erick and Marisol were working elsewhere, and that was great, because this wasn't something Fiona wanted an audience for. She sat on the couch with Wren, a coffee table in front of them, Roarke and Jock looking on. She took a deep breath as Roarke slid an envelope across the table, and Wren opened up the first file. Jock began to pace. Fiona got distracted by the shift of his ass in his pants and the way his thighs stretched the seams. God, he was a beautiful hunk of man.

"Fiona," Wren said.

She smiled at her friend. "Yes, sorry, looking now."

The first file made her breath catch. The eyes in the picture stared back at her. She knew the guys and Marisol had spent a lot of time working on these profiles, staking out the men to get as much information on them as they could, including pictures. Whoever had taken this picture got this man's photo head-on. And it was the eyes that Fiona remembered. The hard, cold, beady eyes. He'd wrenched her hands behind her back, and he'd hissed in her ear not to scream or he'd slit her throat. He'd been the muscle.

"Harvey," she said softly. That was what the others had called him, although the file listed him as Clive Baskins. He'd always be Harvey to her. "Him. He was the enforcer."

Jock's body went still. "Enforcer?"

Fiona swallowed and glanced at Wren. She was deep in thought, staring at the picture. "He was the one I saw taking you away that first day, wasn't he?" Wren asked.

Fiona nodded.

"What do you mean by 'enforcer'?" Roarke asked in a gentle voice while Jock's face got redder by the minute.

"I mean he was the one they brought in if I tried to fight. He was strong, and he knew where to, um, hit—where bruises weren't too visible on camera."

The energy in the room snapped like lightning, and then Jock was moving, right out of the living room. She heard the sound of his footsteps up the stairs, then the slam of a door, and then a loud crash followed by a roar. Fiona flinched, her stomach souring. She hated this, hated this so much, even though it had to be done. "He can't…" Her voice dropped to a whisper. "Please tell him not to get upset. I don't like it."

Roarke nodded once and then went off after Jock. Wren watched him go before turning to Fiona with wet eyes. "I'm so sorry. I wonder every single day, what if I stayed, what if—"

"They would have done the same to you," Fiona said. "And it's done. Please Wren, I can't deal with what-ifs, I can't. Because there's no going back. It is done. What-ifs make it hurt more."

Wren nodded tightly. "Sure."

"Okay." Fiona closed Harvey's file and placed it to the side. "That's the keep pile." She went for a smile, and Wren returned it.

They'd gone through two more files, not recognizing either of them, when they heard the sounds of footsteps down the stairs. Jock went right to her and sat down, drawing her into his arms. "Sorry," he said into her hair. "Shouldn'ta...shouldn'ta done that. Didn't mean to scare you."

She leaned into his touch and squeezed his forearm. "It's okay."

"Hate seeing you upset, hate hearing about it all..." Fiona didn't say anything as a tremor ran through Jock's body. "I'll be here for you, though. Right here. Getting through this with you. I'll keep my cool." He pulled back and pressed a kiss to her forehead. "Won't happen again."

"I like that you're angry for me," Fiona said. "I do. But today...I need steady, J. I need you to be strong for me because, when you're strong, it props me up."

And like that, his back went up, his eyes went hard and determined. "Steady," he murmured.

"Yeah." She patted his thigh before focusing back on the files. "Okay, I'm ready to start again."

They went through another ten profiles with Fiona recognizing a couple of names and voices. The last profile was of a man named Henry Chamberlain II. Fiona didn't recognize the name or the face.

"Got his voice, too, and we think he's a part of this. He mentioned something about holding more parties."

Fiona's anxiety spiked through her like a lightning bolt.

They often used the word *parties*, as if this was all con-
sensual fun and games. Roarke tapped at his phone before
holding it out to her to listen.

*"Yeah, things are good. You should come up sometime.
The guys and I have some parties...you know the kind."*
The tinny voice filled the room, and Fiona's blood went
cold. She knew that voice, she knew the way he said *parties*, with a hard *r* like a pirate. She knew the way he
smelled, the way his hands felt on her skin. She knew it all.
He was the one who'd ordered her. There'd been several
men, but this one was the reason she'd been bought.

"Yeah? Even with Darren away?" Roarke's voice said
on the phone in answer, with a slight accent.

"Yep, the parties are still going on," the man said.
White, they'd called him. There'd been a Blue and a Black
too, like some fucked-up version of *Reservoir Dogs*. She
felt like her body had been yanked back in time. There she
was again. On a bed, the red light of the camera penetrating
through her grimy blindfold, damp with her tears.

White's voice, laughing as he used her. Telling all his
friends what a great *party* this had been. A sharp needle had
pierced her vein, and she was no longer crying because she
was floating, floating from the pain and the smell, and the
feel of those hands.

"Fiona!" a voice shouted and she jolted, her mind snapping back to present day, to Jock and Wren and Roarke,
who were all staring at her with concern and sympathy, and
fuck, this was all too much. Too damn painful...

"Him," she whispered, eyes on her wringing hands in her
lap. "He bought me. It was him."

"Knew he looked like a smarmy fuck." Jock's voice was
tight, and she wondered if he'd ever get to the point when
he'd be disgusted with her. When she'd have to say more,

when he'd face these men who saw her as nothing but flesh and holes. Would Jock look at her through different eyes?

"I need to shower," she said abruptly. She clenched her fingers in Sundance's fur, which grounded her, but all this talk…she needed to get clean. She needed soap, scalding hot water, a robe, and her bed. Alone.

"Fiona," Wren whispered.

Fiona finally met her friend's eyes. There wasn't the pity there she expected. There was love, nothing but love shining out of Wren's deep brown eyes. Fiona brushed Wren's hair behind her ear. "I'm okay. Well, I'm not okay, but I'm not bad. I need a shower, and I need my bed." She lifted her gaze to Roarke's. "I can answer more questions later. I need a break."

Roarke waved her on. "Of course. You don't need to explain to me."

She nodded and looked to Jock. But he stood with his back to her, looking out the living room window into their backyard. He didn't turn around, and she didn't call to him. Instead she turned around and walked upstairs, Sundance at her heels.

She stripped quickly and scrubbed her skin until it was pink and painful. Then she pulled on a big pair of sweatpants and a large sweatshirt—even though it was eighty degrees outside—and crawled under the covers. She stayed like that for a long time, Sundance lying beside her, his big body warm and soft.

Voices filtered up from downstairs. Eventually she heard the front door open and close. Then there was silence. She closed her eyes and opened them a little while later to a darkened room. Jock was beside her in bed, his eyes open and alert. He lay on top of the covers, wearing a pair of pants and nothing other than his big black watch.

He was watching her. She stared back. He didn't reach out to touch her, didn't say a word, just watched.

"Hi," she said softly, feeling the sleep leave her body as if it was a receding tide.

"Hey," he said back.

"I didn't mean to fall asleep."

"You're allowed."

"Where's Sundance?"

"Fed him and let him out. He's downstairs now with a bone."

"Thank you."

He didn't reply.

She didn't feel like herself. Her skin felt itchy and tight, the bed beneath her body like quicksand, uneven and waiting for her to move so it could give way.

"I don't know how to be," she confessed. Wren had always been able to get Fiona to talk when it was dark—sometimes she even drew her into a closet. So here, in this darkened room, Fiona felt like she could open up. "Maybe I don't know how to be because I don't know myself. During the years I was supposed to be figuring out who I was, I was recovering from what they did to me—to my body and my mind. And now...I don't want to be defined by what happened to me. Even with you..." She swallowed. "I know you because of what happened to me. Why couldn't we have met like regular people? At a dog park, or a grocery store where we both reached for the same bunch of bananas and our fingers touched. So we would have laughed awkwardly and started talking, then you'd ask me out." He stared at her, and that made her smile. "Okay, I realize you don't laugh awkwardly, but you know."

She rolled onto her back and stared at the ceiling. "I want

to be something else, something not connected to my past. But that's not possible, is it?"

He didn't speak for a long time, and when he did, his voice was low and gravelly. "Can be."

She rolled her head to the side. "So how do I do it? How do I move on?"

"Cauterize it. Take care of it, walk away."

"Jock, I'm not like you. I don't think that'll work for me."

"That's the point of this mission, isn't it? To shut down everything so you can move on."

She turned onto her side. "Well, sure, but my past is still my past. I'm still haunted."

He made a *tsk* sound, like one of disgust, and it irritated her.

"What? You have a past, don't you? You walk around pissed off and determined to raze the earth. You're telling me you were born like that? Or something happened that made you that way? Even if you cauterized it, as you say, it sure as hell changed you."

His body went tight, so tight that she could feel the vibrations of tension through the mattress. "You don't know a thing about my past."

Each word was an arrow, shot straight and true with fire. He meant for that to hurt. And it did. "You're right. I don't."

"Past is over," he spat, and the fire in his blue eyes sparked. "Done with. Taken care of. That's the way it's going to be for you."

He didn't get it, not at all. "Humans don't work like that—"

He knifed up in the bed and swung his legs to the side. "Humans *can* work like that," he snapped as he stood up and turned around to face her. "They can, but some of them are just too weak to put in the work."

Wow, that cut was deep. She flinched. "Excuse me?"

For a moment, indecision crossed his face, but then he hardened again. "You'll be fine. Once this is over, you'll be fine, and you'll move on."

There was something to this conversation she was missing. She wasn't sure they were even talking about her anymore. "J, you can't just demand it—"

"You'll be fine!" he roared and then stomped out of the room. She heard his feet jog down the stairs and then Sundance's tags rattle.

She wore heavy layers of clothing and lay underneath a comforter, but she felt cold, so damn cold. She was sleeping with a man she didn't know, a man who she struggled to read, who she feared couldn't interact on a basic emotional level. She was putting so much of her effort into him, and what would she get in return? He'd taken such care with her this far but it was clear that, as this went on, he was only capable of so much. Or he was reaching his limit.

She closed her eyes, let the tears fall, and then went back to sleep, still unsure who or what she was, but knowing she sure as shit wasn't going to get over her past because a man demanded it.

* * *

Jock sat on the couch in the dark, staring out the patio doors to their backyard. Sundance sat at his feet panting, as he'd just run around outside for fifteen minutes.

He didn't like how he felt unbalanced and anxious. Anger, he was used to. He lived with anger so deep in his marrow that it was a part of him. It fueled him just like the blood in his veins. The anger had dulled over time to manageable levels so that he wore it like second skin. Everything else he was feeling, though? It was itchy and uncomfortable.

He knew he'd been out of line with Fiona, but he wanted... Well, he didn't know what he wanted. For her to be better, happy, fulfilled. That was the point of this mission, at least for him. He could act like a savior and say it was for the good of other women. That would be what a good guy would say, but he wasn't really a good guy. He never pretended to be. His actions were often fueled by selfish rather than altruistic reasons. Preventing the abuse of other women was a great side effect of taking down these men so Fiona could breathe free.

When Jock had taken down the men who killed his brother, he'd been able to breathe again, right? He'd been free, easy. But now that breath was stalling in his lungs, and the anger that had dulled was again surging to the front, demanding attention. He'd taken care of this, hadn't he? He'd destroyed the terrorist cell over there in that fucking desert and taken revenge for his brother. He'd done that so he could move on.

His hands curled into fists on his thighs. Had he moved on? Or had all his anger and pain still living in his veins been dormant until someone like Fiona made him remember? Had he been telling her she'd be fine or was he trying to convince himself that he was?

He flicked his fingers at the dog. "Go to Fi," he said.

Sundance nudged his leg with his wet nose and trotted off, nails clicking on the hardwood floor. Jock didn't want her up there alone, but he didn't think he was welcome. He didn't deserve to sleep up there after the things he'd said to her. Was she angry with him? He'd have to apologize tomorrow, except he wasn't sure what the hell to say.

His phone buzzed, and he pulled it from his pocket. He glanced at the caller ID before answering. "Tarr."

"Hey, man," Tarr said, his voice deep. "I'm in your town on a job. Wondering if you need anything."

He didn't ask how Tarr knew where he was. Tarr knew everything. He thought for a split second about asking him to find Henry Chamberlain II, chain him up in a basement somewhere, and wait for Jock to show up and pummel him with his fists. But he had to discuss it with the team. They were looking to take down each guy and didn't want to spook anyone into splitting or covering their tracks better. "Nah."

"Saw her buying flowers," Tarr said quietly.

Jock's body went tight. Tarr had been watching Fiona. Jock thought about the flowers sitting on his front porch right now. "Come again?"

"She's pretty, man."

"You cannot be fucking serious."

"Just saying."

"You draw any attention to her—"

"You know me," Tarr cut him off, voice low and vibrating through the line. "I'm clean, I'm careful. And your business will always be my business."

"We're good," Jock announced. "Took care of the mess in the park. We're good. No debt."

Tarr was quiet for a moment. "Don't insult me."

"I'm not."

"You fucking are." A moment of hesitation, then he clipped out. "I saw her recently."

Jock closed his eyes. *Her* was Tarr's sister. Jock was the reason Tarr's sister was breathing, and they both knew it. Jock asked, "She good?"

"Yeah, man, she's fucking great. Happy. Pregnant again, third kid, gonna be an uncle a-fucking-gain and who do I owe that to?"

Jock didn't say a word.

"Who do I owe, Jock?"

Again, he stayed silent.

"I owe you. I'll owe you forever. So don't insult me and tell me the debt is paid."

Jock didn't say a word again.

Tarr sighed.

"This personal for you? The blonde. Not like you to take things personal."

Nope, he'd only taken one job that was personal, for his brother, and even then, he was ice cold about it. "Maybe it is this time."

"You need me, you know where to find me. I won't be in town long, but I can get here quick again. Got it?"

"Told you that you don't owe me. No marker. Did what I did for selfish reasons."

Tarr laughed, and it was a light sound, surprising from the large ginger with the gravelly voice. "You took a bullet to the arm to save my sister for selfish reasons? Not sure we're using the same dictionary."

"Fuck off," Jock said with a small smile.

"Sure, I'm gone. Take care of that woman. I'll keep an eye on the hit. There's been some talk but I'm keeping an ear on it."

"Talk about what?"

"Some guy buying hits. Not sure how they're connected, but I'm looking into it."

"Sounds good."

"Till next time." Tarr ended the call.

Jock leaned back in the chair and scratched at his stomach. Buying hits wasn't good, but his was old and no one gave a shit about him anymore. At least he hoped so. Tarr was right. He needed to focus on his woman. Even if he woke up tomorrow and she didn't want to speak to him. He'd apologize, some way, somehow, and he'd work as hard as he could to help her get her life back.

CHAPTER SIXTEEN

JOCK never got the chance for a proper apology. He slept on the couch and woke up to the sound of the coffee maker. He stood up, stretching out his back. He was too damn big for that stupid fucking couch.

He walked into the kitchen, running the words *I'm sorry* over and over in his head, but then stopped short as soon as he saw the figure standing at the counter whistling and spinning a mug. Fiona was not in their kitchen. That was…

The man turned around, and Jock stilled. Dade Kelly was standing in his kitchen at six o'clock in the morning, making coffee. Jock hadn't seen him in a month; his hair was longer, sweeping across his forehead in a rich brown, and he was clean shaven.

"Hey there, Jock," he said with a white-toothed smile. He kept on whistling as the coffee maker beeped and then helped himself to a cup. He turned and leaned back against the counter and blew over the top, peering at Jock over the rim. He had an accent, one all his own that didn't really have a place. Jock figured he made it up on purpose, to disguise where he was from or where he'd been. He said Jock's name like *Shoke*, which always got under his skin.

Jock didn't trust Dade. Most of them didn't, but Dade

had pulled through for them last mission. Dade was a man who didn't live by hacker ethics and was loyal only to himself. Case in point, he'd broken into Jock's townhouse and was showing zero remorse.

"Kelly." Jock grabbed his own mug and poured a cup of coffee. He stood across from Dade, waiting.

Dade grinned. "No outrage on how I got in here? No threatening me physical harm? Not that I suspected emotion from you, but yet I'm still disappointed."

"What do you want?" Jock took a sip of coffee.

"I was incommunicado for a bit so I got Roarke's message late. All it said was that I could experience blowback. And since I'm the curious sort, I figured I'd fly my ass to the States to see what you assholes got yourselves into this time." He glanced around the room. "Nice place. Potted plants outside are a nice touch."

"Wasn't my doing," he said.

Dade's smile stretched wide. "Oh, I know that. Fiona likes the nursery down the street. She was there twice last week."

Jock slammed his coffee on the counter and took a step toward Dade, anger surging through him hot and heavy and violent. Dade had been watching her. Jock would have put a fist through the guy's smug face if he hadn't heard a soft. "Jock?"

They both turned to see Fiona standing in the doorway. Her hair was in disarray, some of it falling out of her ponytail, and her face was lined with sleep. She wore a T-shirt and a small pair of sleep shorts. Bare feet with red painted toenails. She looked beautiful, soft, and vulnerable. She also looked scared. Her eyes darted between the two of them, and she gripped the frame of the doorway with white knuckles. "Who's that?"

Jock turned to glare at Dade, who was still smiling, the fucking asshole. "Saved by your fiancée, it seems," he said softly.

Of course Dade knew about everything. He always did. Jock counted to three to calm himself. "Fiona, this is Dade Kelly. Dade, this is Fiona Madden." That was it. That was all he said. Fiona still looked a little confused but not as scared.

Dade rolled his eyes and took a step forward. "Hello, beautiful. I'm part of their crew. No need to be scared of me. Lots of people are, but you don't have to be." He held out his hand. She stared at it and then at Jock. She was waiting for his okay. That hit him somewhere soft. He gave her a nod, and she stuck out her slender hand, placing it in Dade's palm. "Oh, well, nice to meet you."

"Same. Now I know Jock is glaring at me, but that's just because he doesn't like me much. I actually don't mind him and find him mildly entertaining with his big silent thing, but that gives you some context as to why he's not welcoming me with open arms." He held up his coffee mug. "Helped myself. Hope you don't mind."

She shook her head. "No, it's okay."

"Would you like some?" He reached for a mug and looked at her with raised eyebrows.

Irritation made Jock snarl and snatch the mug out of Dade's hand. He was tired of the man's charming act—sweeping in here all nice and *hello beautiful*, and *would you like coffee?*

Fuck that, Jock knew how Fiona took her coffee. One sugar with a splash of milk. He made her coffee, spilling some on the counter in his annoyance before shoving it at her. Some sloshed over the top of her shirt, and she gasped as the hot liquid hit her stomach. "Fuck, sorry,"

Jock mumbled and grabbed a napkin, dabbing at Fiona's shirt.

"Jock, just…it's fine. It's fine!" she snapped. He froze, and she took the napkin from him with pursed lips. "It's fine," she said again. "Go drink your own coffee. Thank you for mine." She took a loud sip as if to make a point.

Jock slinked back to his coffee—embarrassed, irritated, sexually frustrated, and off-kilter. Meanwhile Dade had watched the entire thing with his arms crossed over his chest and that ever-present smirk on his face. "Well, as much as I'm enjoying watching this actual blossoming romance with a clearly experienced and articulate hero, I have some things to go over with you two."

"This needed to be done at six in the morning?" Jock asked. "Couldn't have called a meet with Roarke and Erick?"

"You know I like to make dramatic entrances," Dade said. "It's my thing."

"Like I give a fuck about your thing," Jock growled.

Dade waved off his tone as if it was nothing. "So I did some digging. You all think Maximus is after her, right? Cutting loose ends and all of that?"

Jock gave him a tight nod. Out of the corner of his eye, Fiona took a sip of her coffee with a steady hand.

"That's not it." With that sentence, Dade shrugged. That was it. He just shrugged. "Got any breakfast?"

Jock was going to strangle him, just crush his fucking windpipe. "Don't make me hurt you. What's it about, then? Why did that man come after her in New York?"

Dade opened up the refrigerator, stuck his head inside, and grabbed a piece of cold pizza. After unwrapping the foil, he picked off the black olives and took a bite. Cold. "Oh, that guy? Hired by one of Darren's friends. Fiona isn't the only one they grabbed and let go. They're bringing back their favorites for a little *throwback party*." Dade's only show of disgust was a slight spat on the last word. "Fiona here was a favorite of—"

"White." Fiona cut him off in a dead, emotionless voice. Her hands shook slightly around the coffee mug, and her pale face lifted to meet Jock's eyes. "There are more girls, Jock. Like me."

The room was silent. Jock stared into her eyes, wishing he could take away her pain, just rip it out of her right now and replace it with peace, but if he'd learned anything from last night, it was that he couldn't do that. No more than he could do it for himself.

Finally Dade spoke again. "Yes, it's Chamberlain who's calling in all the big dogs to find Fiona again. These parties—they are just games for bored, rich men. One where they hold all the power.

"Sick fucks," Jock hissed.

Dade shrugged. "Pretty much."

Fiona's eyes were huge in her pale face, and Jock went to her, unsure if she wanted to be touched, but as soon as he got close she took one step and collided with him. Fell into him. Melted into him. He wrapped his arms around her and let her burrow into him so hard that he swore she'd entered his body.

Her hands gripped his shirt and he rested his cheek on her head. He held her and didn't say words, didn't bother, because what was there to say? She had a sick-fuck asshole who'd already assaulted her trying to relive the past and play with her life like she was nothing.

She was far from nothing. She was goddamn everything.

Dade finished his pizza and tossed the ball of foil in the

trash. He sipped his coffee. "I'll leave you two alone for a bit. As far as I know, Maximus's threat to her was just a threat. He surely knows what his underlings are doing and doesn't care. I have digital eyes on Henry. And I'll catch the rest of the crew up to speed."

Fiona let him go long enough to swipe at her nose and look at Dade. "Thanks for looking into this."

"Gonna want proof," Jock said. "All you got."

"'Course," Dade said. "You know I'm thorough. I'll say this, though. You want these guys? All of them? You want to save these women? We get an in to that party. And that *in* is in your arms."

Jock went still, his blood freezing in his veins. "No fucking way."

Fiona made a sound beside him, but he ignored her, shoving her behind him as if Dade had just threatened her. Well, he had threatened her. Letting those men anywhere near her again? Over Jock's dead body.

Dade cocked his head. "Something to think about. Thanks for the coffee. And the pizza. See you later, lovebirds."

Then he walked out the front door. Jock still didn't know how he'd gotten inside. When he turned around, Fiona had her arms wrapped around herself, her body wracked with shivers.

"Hey—"

"I just want to drink my coffee," she said. "I want to eat my blueberry buckle. I want to watch the morning news. And after that...after that I'll deal with all of this. Until then, I want to pretend we are normal. Normal fucking adults with our major issues being that we both forgot our Wi-Fi password and that we left last night's leftovers out overnight so they spoiled. Okay?"

Jock nodded, even though he wanted to reach for her again.

"Okay." She blew out a breath. With that, she grabbed her coffee, her buckle, and left him standing in the kitchen, wondering when the hell he'd given over his heart to a woman who was currently his fake fiancée.

* * *

"This motherfucker, swanning in and out," Jock grumbled, "annoys the shit out of me." Jock looked like he was going to murder someone. After Dade had left, Fiona hadn't bothered to speak to Jock other than to comment on random news stories. He'd sat in a recliner with his laptop, all angry and glaring, and she hadn't wanted to deal with it. She was still mad about the night before, and he hadn't said one word about it. Not that he'd had a chance, what with a strange guy in their kitchen.

She wasn't sure what to make of Dade. He'd introduced himself as part of the crew and Jock hadn't corrected him. He'd smirked a lot and was charming, but she'd sensed it was an act. There seemed to be no depth to his personality and she got the impression he wanted it that way. He covered up whoever and whatever he was with a shallow foreign charmer.

Still, he'd looked into her situation and given them information they hadn't had yet. They'd known Chamberlain and his crew were still hosting parties. What they hadn't known was that one of those parties would be a *throwback*—and Fiona had been cordially invited, along with other women. Fiona's heart ached at the thought of women like her trying to move on without someone like Jock and his crew at their backs.

A knock came at their front door and she unfolded from the couch to answer it.

"Got it." Jock was already up, his laptop on the coffee table, and he was on his way to the door. Whatever.

She heard the voices of Wren, Roarke, and Erick. Her friend rushed in first, followed by her boyfriend and brother. "So I heard you met Dade," Wren said, a smile on her face.

"That asshole and his goddamn entrances," Roarke said. "He can't be a normal person, no. He's got to make everything dramatic."

"I admire his creativity, to be honest," Erick said.

"No one asked for your opinion," Roarke snapped.

Erick made a face at him.

"You two can shut up," Wren said, "because Dade cracked part of this mission for us, okay?"

Jock again looked murderous, and Roarke and Erick looked cowed.

"Um," Fiona spoke up, "he's...interesting."

"That's one way to put it," Wren muttered. "Look, I trust Dade. I worked with him for years, and he's weird as hell but smart."

The men were already pulling out their equipment and setting up shop in the townhouse like this was Central Command. Wren sat down on the couch beside Fiona while Roarke sat on the floor at her feet, laptop on his lap. She idly played with his hair while chatting with her brother.

Fiona watched Wren's fingers slip through the dark strands and admired the way Roarke leaned into her leg. This was love and comfort and familiarity. They knew each other's past and accepted each other. They understood each other's motives and desires and goals. They'd scratched and clawed and dug beneath the murky outer layer of anger and pain to worm their way into each other's hearts. Meanwhile, Fiona could barely speak to Jock right now. The tension and awkwardness between them was nearly suffocating.

He'd warned her, hadn't he? He'd told her she could dig all she wanted, and all she'd find was more dirt. For a brief moment she'd hoped that she saw some light shining through the cracks, but maybe not. Jock's past had calcified his soft parts permanently. There was no room for her. So while he'd shown her how to find pleasure again, he remained stuck in the anger of his past.

He looked up at that moment and met her gaze. Something passed across his blue eyes, something warm, but then it was gone, and his head dipped again to focus on the screen in front of him. Code was reflected in his eyes. Cold, sterile, black and white binary. God, her heart hurt.

"Dade sent all his information, and now I see what we missed," Roarke said. "Fuck. I knew they were talking in some code, but I was so focused on believing Maximus was after Fiona that I didn't dig deeper."

"What do you mean by 'code'?" Fiona asked.

"As you said, each guy was a color, right? Well, these girls they want back are all animals. I noticed them mentioning *Pink Zebra*, but I'd assumed the code was for a product they wanted, not a specific girl for a specific man. So whoever Zebra is, she's been requested by the guy who goes by Pink. Dade's right. They're bringing back their favorites."

Fiona's heart stopped. She remembered now. White had called her … "Lion," she whispered. "My hair … he referred to me as a lion."

Roarke nodded, eyes sweeping her face. "Yes, there are several references to locating the white lion."

"Where is the party?" she asked.

"We can't figure that out," Roarke said. "Dade doesn't know, and he's trying, but what we really need is to get a lead and follow someone there."

"What about the other girls?" She dared to ask the question as the sinking feeling in her gut deepened.

Roarke opened his mouth, but Jock cut him off. "No."

Roarke whipped his head to face him. "What do you mean, no?"

Jock only glared, his jaw tight.

"What?" Fiona asked, not understanding.

"Jock," Wren said, "what is it?"

Roarke and Jock were in a stare down, communicating something silently, a battle of wills over...what? Fiona wasn't sure. Until finally Jock swore, smashing his fist into the arm of his chair. Jock looked away first.

But Roarke didn't look victorious when he craned his neck to peer up at Fiona. "They have all the girls already. They are waiting to find you and then the party starts."

Fiona's heart bottomed out. Oh God, the girls. The other girls were currently in their clutches, probably scared as shit. And what was worse—they knew what was going to happen. They knew the pain and the terror, and they were just waiting. Waiting for her. And she was selfishly hiding.

She pressed her fist to her mouth as tears burned the backs of her eyes. She turned furiously to Jock, needing to yell and scream, and he was the easiest target. "What, you didn't want Roarke to tell me the truth? You wanted to keep that from me?"

"Because I knew you'd get upset," he fired back. "Dade got in your fucking head, and now you want to use yourself as bait to save those women."

"Wait, what?" Wren said. "No way. No."

"Dade suggested that?" Roarke said.

"I'll do it," Fiona said, still glaring at Jock because anger was the glue holding her together. "Help get me out of this townhouse and find a way for Chamberlain and his friends to locate me. I'll lead you to the party, and we'll rescue everyone."

"No problem. Let's just steal the Eiffel Tower while we're at it and fly to the moon," Roarke muttered. Wren smacked him.

"Jesus fucking Christ, what is it about you women wanting to do the most dangerous shit?" Erick said. "Marisol entered the enemy's house posing as a caterer. Wren used herself as bait to catch Darren. You just want to waltz into a goddamn sex ring party. What the fuck, for real? Next mission, no one is valentine or bait."

"You want to know where this is, right?" Fiona asked. "They'll all be in one place. We can rescue the other girls and arrest the men. And do whatever computer voodoo you all want to do. There. Done."

Jock's eyes bulged out of his head. "Are you fucking serious? And what if we somehow lose you? What if they hurt you the minute they grab you? There are so many goddamn variables, and I'm not okay with any fucking one of them!" he roared.

"I don't give a fuck if you don't like it!" she yelled back, her hands trembling where they rested on her thighs in fists. "This is what I want to do. I want control. I want to go in and face them and watch them go down. That's what I want, and you don't get to sit there and take that away from me!" She ended on a screech and the entire room went still and silent. Her heart was racing, and she felt nervous sweat drip down her neck, but still she held her ground. These guys were the best, right? They could perform miracles. They'd taken down Darren. They could get her in and out of this party safely. Or she'd go down trying.

Finally, Sundance broke the silence. He inched forward on his belly and whined, clearly uneasy with the tension in the room. Fiona lowered her hand to him and he eagerly nosed it, his eyes big and round and apprehensive. "Sorry for yelling, buddy," she murmured.

"Fine." Jock's voice rumbled across the room. "You want the control, we'll give you the control."

She waited to see encouragement in his eyes, strength, anything to give her something to go on, but all she saw was anger, swirling there like a tornado. He was cutting her off. She could see it plain as day, and it felt like he'd lopped off her arm.

All she could do was swallow and nod. "Thank you."

"You sure?" That was Wren.

"Positive," Fiona said.

Roarke began to talk, laying out how they'd get her noticed, how they'd protect her, and what they'd do once she was at the party. A lot of the words went over her head, and she knew they'd explain all she needed later. So for now, she got another cup of coffee, more cake, and didn't look at Jock. It hurt too much.

CHAPTER SEVENTEEN

THIS was over. It had to be. He'd told her there was nothing good in his core, and she'd figured it out. He could see it now in her eyes, in the way she looked at him. He could only hope that, after all this was over, she wouldn't regret letting him touch her. He knew he'd carry the memory of her for the rest of his life.

Fiona wanted to act fast. She seemed frantic about the other women, and Jock wished she didn't have such a big heart. Why couldn't she be selfish? Hide away and let this all blow over? Let them find another way? If they had more time, they could look harder at the codes on the message boards, on the shopping lists. They could crack where the party was. They could...protect her.

All Jock wanted to do was protect her.

"So what does Chamberlain and his crew think about the guy who tried to take her in New York?" Erick tossed a couple of salted peanuts in his mouth while they waited for Fiona to get ready upstairs with help from Wren and Marisol.

"Don't know. They'll never find him," Jock said.

"Never find him?" Erick frowned.

Jock shook his head. "Got a guy."

"You got a guy that takes care of bodies?" Erick's voice went shrill at the end.

Jock just stared at him.

Erick blinked a couple of times and sighed. "Never mind. I'm not surprised."

Roarke turned from where he was fiddling with something on the kitchen counter. He held up a half-inch-long metal cylinder. "This is her tracker. Easiest place to implant it will be in her scalp right at the back of her neck. Her hair will cover the cut."

Once she came downstairs, she'd get a tracker embedded beneath her skin, and Jock didn't feel one ounce of regret for the pain she'd feel. He wanted to know where she was at all times. "The plan," he said. "Let's go over it."

Roarke lifted his brows. "Oh? So you're the crew leader now, huh?"

"Last time, you led because it was your woman. This time I lead—" He cut himself off and gritted his teeth. "This time I lead."

Erick opened his mouth as if he wanted to ask a question, but Jock shot him a glare so quick that Erick's jaw shut with an audible clack.

"You're still on their secret forum, right?" Jock asked Roarke. The man nodded. "Good. So you post asking for more information on the White Lion. Once they give it to you, slip that you've seen her around town. When they press for details, you'll tell them she's always at Trikes Coffee over on Sixth every day around three. You know because you work across the street. She's hot and caught your eye. Got it?"

Roarke nodded again.

"I want a list of every animal and every color mentioned

on the forum. Get Dade's help if you have to. I want to try to link every color to one of these men and identify as many women as we can. How many women we looking at?"

"Twelve. Fiona would make a baker's dozen." Erick tapped on his laptop's track pad. "Seems like they're getting antsy about finding her. Chamberlain won't give up."

Jock curled his lip. "That's what we're banking on."

Footsteps sounded on the stairs, and the men turned to look. Wren and Marisol came down first, Fiona after them. She wore a pair of jeans and a soft top—casual sweatshirt material that somehow looked elegant as it hung off her shoulder. She wore Converse shoes. And that rock on her finger. She looked like a happily engaged woman about to grab coffee with friends, except her eyes were troubled.

Jock didn't say a word. He stayed motionless because he was worried that if he moved a muscle, his body would take over for his brain and his only actions would involve locking Fiona in the bedroom and not letting her go. So he stayed put and listened to Roarke talk to her about the plans. She nodded, eyes wide, and he could see she was trying to be brave. While Roarke implanted the tracker in the base of her skull and Marisol gave her a couple of stitches, Fiona kept her eyes on Jock.

He still didn't say anything, but he held her gaze.

"Are you sure about this?" Roarke asked.

Fiona nodded. "It's for the other girls. I mean, it's kind of for me, but I can't sit by and know there are other women like me suffering. So yes, I'm sure, even if I'm scared."

Jock wanted to tell her this was killing him. He wanted to say he was sorry, he wanted to kiss her, he wanted to do a million things but he couldn't bring himself to do a single one. He felt out of control and he hated that feeling—the heavy beat of his heart in his chest, his damp palms.

When Fiona grabbed her purse and gave a round of good-byes, Jock's gaze drifted over her shoulder. She didn't come to him, and he didn't go to her. She walked to the garage door.

"Jock?" Wren whispered.

He still didn't move.

Fiona looked at him one last time and he stared at the wall in front of him. He felt her disappointment, her hurt; it thickened the air around him and his heart, and he was surprised he didn't collapse under the weight of it.

The door opened and shut.

Marisol hissed, "You're a fucking dumbass."

He moved to glare at her, and that one movement unfroze him because he was already moving toward the door to follow Fiona.

* * *

Fiona's heart felt like it was breaking. Jock had looked right through her, as if they hadn't shared everything, as if he hadn't promised he'd care for her. He'd told her he didn't want to talk about his past, and she'd prodded and lost him. So that was that.

Despite all of it, she knew she wouldn't want anyone else at her back. Jock was nothing if not thorough and duty-bound.

She started to pull the garage door shut behind her but something stopped it. She tugged again and then turned around to see what was the matter.

Jock stood in the doorway, his large frame blocking out the light from inside the house and his hand firmly on the doorknob. She tugged again. "I'm trying to shut the door."

"We need to talk."

She stared at him. "Excuse me?"

"Talk," he barked at her.

Oh hell no. "I think we've both said all we've wanted to say."

He pulled the door right out of her hand, shoved his way through, and shut it behind him so they were alone in the garage. He towered above her, and when she stepped back, he moved forward. He never took his eyes off her. "Have we?" he said, his voice deceptively soft, and the tone sent a chill down her spine.

She swallowed. "I thought we had, and now might be too late."

"Maybe but I still got things to say."

"And I'm just supposed to listen now that you finally decided you have something to tell me?"

His brows dipped, and his chin jerked down. "I—Will you please listen to what I have to say?"

He'd asked and said please, in that voice, the one that he used when she called him J.

She nodded. "Okay then."

His shoulders dropped a bit, but he didn't speak right away. He stared down at the floor, and his lips twitched, as if he was mouthing words. It was one of the most endearing things she'd ever seen. He wanted to get it right, her big, silent man who hated full sentences. He was trying for her. If that didn't make her heart start stitching back together, then she didn't know what would.

"I'm sorry," he finally said, and just those two words made her knees weak. "For what I said last night. I—" He winced and then said under his breath, "Fuck, I hate talking."

"Keep going." She didn't want to move for fear that she might spook him.

"I said I was over my past, and I wasn't lying. But I didn't know better. Lived this way for so long that I didn't realize I'd just grown to live with the..." He fisted his hand in his shirt over his heart. Hard. "Anger. It's so deep in my DNA now that it's me, who I am, and I didn't stop to think that my past still lived there. I'd let it fester, and it's like a cancer that'll never kill me, but I'll live with forever."

She could barely breathe. He'd said all that. Just vomited it all out right there on the oil-stained garage floor of the townhouse they'd lived in for a week. She hadn't known he was capable of speaking all those words in succession, let alone baring that much of his soul.

"I want you to get better." His voice was dredged up over broken glass, or maybe that was the ragged edges of his heart. "I want you happy. Maybe I'm not made of dirt the more you dig, but I'm sure as hell made of scar tissue and fucked-up shit. I can't even...can't even talk to you about why I'm so fucked up. Don't want that in your head. Some days, can't believe you touched me, and other days, I think I never should have let you. But I was weak. And I love you, Fiona. In a fucked-up way with whatever real emotions I have left in me. Not much is there, but all of it loves you."

She gripped his shirt, needing to anchor herself, needing to know this was real and not a dream. But no, he was right there. This was Jock's smell, and his skin, and his soft, familiar T-shirt. These were his blue eyes on hers and his full lips mouthing those words in that deep, syrupy voice.

Tears slid down her cheeks and he watched them but stayed silent. He'd dropped everything—all the walls, all the fortifications. This was J, spilling out his heart to her. And she refused to believe there wasn't much of it.

Absolutely refused. It was big and warm and beat solidly beneath her palm as she laid it over his chest.

He loved her. He—big, dependable, loyal, and strong Jock—loved her, a woman with a messed-up past and not much to show for it besides a shoebox full of photos and a dog.

She'd never known how much she wanted to hear those words until she met Jock. She'd never wanted to hear them from anyone else, and she hadn't thought she would as long as she lived. She'd earned that, his love. She'd fucking earned it.

He slid his hand into her hair, his hot palm cupping her cheek. He pressed a kiss to her forehead and her temple. "It's going to kill me to watch you do this. But I will because it's important to you. Sorry I can't be what you want, but I'll spend the rest of my life making sure you're happy, even if I'm not by your side."

She was tired of him speaking, something she never thought she'd feel. She reached up, gripped his face, and pressed his lips to hers. The kiss was full of salty tears as Jock slid his tongue inside. She moaned into his mouth and pressed closer to him. He held her tightly, his kiss pouring desperation and love down her throat. When he finally broke the kiss, he pressed his forehead to hers, panting slightly.

He stepped back, shoving his hands in his pockets, and she could see the walls coming up, the ice freezing over in his eyes. "You need to get going."

She did, but she wasn't ready. Not now that he'd dropped all this on her.

"Jock," she said, the tears coming faster now. "J."

He flinched at the name, like he always did, and she wanted one last thing before she left. "Tell me who called you J," she asked. "Someone in your past did, right?"

The ice was moving fast, and he was nearly frozen over until he blurted out one word. "Brother."

"Your brother?"

He nodded and took another step back, toward the door. Even as she asked, she knew the answer. "Where is he now?"

Jock opened the door. "He's dead."

Two words. Two words that gave her a glimpse inside. How much more would he give her if they had the time? How much pain could she take away if only he let her?

"Good luck, Fiona. Remember you got us at your back," he said.

"Thank you," she whispered.

He gave her a nod, ice cold, and shut the door.

CHAPTER EIGHTEEN

THE coffee had been a bad idea. Maybe Fiona would be happy about it later, when she needed to keep her wits about her and not crash. But right now, the caffeine was surging through her system, making her hands shake. She'd already spilled it on her hands three times as she walked quickly away from Trikes Coffee Shop. She truly did like it there. The one barista was a nice college kid who flirted with her, and they had really great cranberry orange scones. Maybe she should have bought one. Would she have the chance to get another?

The back of her neck itched where the tracker was embedded, but she didn't dare touch it. Its irritation comforted her. That was her link to the crew, and even if she wasn't sure she'd get out of this party in one piece, then at least the tracker would lead them to the other women.

The memories were coming back now. A few names, a few voices. Women she'd long forgotten about—blocked out, because it was bad enough she had to relive her own memories—she didn't want to relive others', too. But they had been there. Young, like her, scared out of their minds, drugged and bruised. As far as she'd been aware during her time in captivity, they'd let all the women go. It sounded crazy, but it just went to show how fucking untouchable their captors all thought they were. They'd been right, at least so far. But not anymore.

She'd left her hair down, and the weight of her thick hair was heavy, but it was also her most recognizable feature. She couldn't believe that these men wanted them back. Over the intervening years some of the women had probably married, had children, and wouldn't have twenty-year-old bodies anymore. Which made her think...maybe this was it. Maybe they weren't getting out of it this time. One last hurrah and then they'd silence all of them. A baker's dozen of women removed for no other reason than that rich men had wanted to play with toys and then got bored.

She really hoped she got a chance to kick Henry Chamberlain in the balls. Hard. Maybe gouge out his eyes.

The plan was for her to leave Trikes on foot and walk a few blocks outside of the neighborhood, where she expected they'd take the opportunity to nab her. Screams there would draw no Good Samaritans. Even now as she walked out of Columbia Heights, she heard about five arguments coming from apartments all around her.

When they came, she would have to put up a good fight. They'd already expressed surprise that the Lion had returned directly to the pride. That she was in DC.

Car tires screeched and she whirled around, but it was only an old Cadillac taking a sharp turn, music blaring from its open windows. The driver catcalled her and she ignored him.

She turned on her heel, took one step, and crashed into a large body. "Oh, sor—" Strong hands gripped her biceps to the point of pain, and she looked up into the eyes of Harvey, the enforcer. Just like that, she was twenty-one again. She didn't have to act, not one single bit. She screamed, right in his face, because terror was crawling up her throat. Yes, she'd agreed to this, but it still didn't change the fact that she was scared shitless.

He clapped a dirty hand over her mouth and dragged her into the alcove of a boarded-up shop. "Shut up," he growled into her ear, and even his acidic breath was familiar—like he had persistent heartburn. She flailed, her instinct to get away from him, run, flee this man who only meant bad things for her.

"Knew we'd find you. White is going to be so fucking happy. Party couldn't start until everyone arrived, and I guess you're just fashionably late." He squeezed her breast and she had to bite her tongue so she didn't elbow his gut. This mission required her to be taken by him, which went against her fight instinct.

A car careened to a halt in front of them, an all-black sedan with darkened windows. He pushed her forward, her small stature no match for his considerable bulk. She struggled as the door opened, as he shoved her inside. She rounded on him but he was already in the car, shutting the door behind him. "Fuck you!" she spat. "Let me go!"

"Not a chance." He held up a small needle and the sight of it nearly gave her a heart attack. "Welcome to the party." He stuck the needle into her neck and she fought to stay awake, to keep her eyes open, to *fucking focus*, but in less than a minute the world receded and everything went black.

* * *

When Fiona came to, her skull was being hammered and her stomach flipped and flopped like she'd had too much alcohol. She groaned and rolled over, expecting the feel of her soft sheets and the warm body of Jock. She was in a bed all right, but it wasn't hers, and Jock's arms weren't surrounding her. She opened her eyes, blinking blearily. It took a moment for her vision to clear. She was alone in a bedroom—and it was nearly empty. The only furniture was the bed she lay on. One overhead light cast the room in a yellow glow, and there were no windows.

She tried to sit up, but she couldn't gather her hands under her. Her wrists had been bound together, and a rope tied them to the headboard without much give. She finally managed to bring herself to a sitting position but it was awkward with so little slack in the rope.

She still wore her clothes, which was great, but she wasn't naive enough to think she was getting out of here unscathed. She had no idea where she was or how long she'd been out. All she knew was that she still felt the itch of the tracker. She didn't dare touch her hair, worried there might be a hidden camera somewhere in the room. She couldn't see one, but she wasn't able to adequately study the light fixture above her.

She could hear crying, the sound faint. She knew she wasn't the only one here, and that it must be coming from another bedroom. Another girl. She closed her eyes and wished she could call out to the girl, tell her it would be okay, but Fiona needed to not draw attention to herself.

So she sat, and she thought about Jock. About the moments he'd let the ice wall over his eyes and heart melt so she could see what was underneath. He was wrong. So wrong. She'd dug and dug, and she'd found his hot core. It was warped and red and damaged, but it was there, and even if they couldn't find a future together, she took comfort that he wasn't dead inside like he tried to make everyone believe.

When she'd agreed to this, she'd been prepared to do

whatever it took. She didn't have family. Jock would take care of Sundance. But now...she wasn't so sure. Not with Jock's words ringing in her ear. How would he take it if something happened to her? He had enough anger pulsing through him, and if the woman he loved was hurt...She bit down on the inside of her cheek as the backs of her eyes began to burn.

Then she thought, *fuck it*. She could cry. She *should* cry. It was believable that she'd burst into tears. So she did, thoughts of Jock causing the tears. Life was so fucking unfair. They knew where she was by now; the tracker would be working, but they didn't want to nab the men just on kidnapping charges. They wanted them for everything, and that meant Fiona had to hold out a bit longer.

The door opened, and she hastily wiped her eyes as Harvey entered the room. He stood at the foot of the bed staring at her. She curled her legs under her, instinctively squeezing her thighs together.

He snorted. "Not here to fuck you. You think White would let me get first dibs at his prized pussy?" He shook his head. "Maybe when he's done, though. No shame in sloppy seconds, and I never got some when we first had you."

She shivered, the fear pounding into her skull, and she bit down harder on her cheek until she tasted blood. He held a pill in one hand, and a scrap of black fabric in the other. "Take this," he said, holding up the pill, "so I can untie you, and you can put on this." He tossed the piece of fabric by her side. It was a tiny negligee, and she wanted to throw up just thinking of putting it on.

She tried to look as beaten down as possible. "You can untie me, and I won't struggle. Promise. Just please don't make me take the pill. I'll do...whatever. Quietly."

Maybe that had been a mistake because his brows dipped a minute. "Ten years ago, you didn't do a single thing without kicking and screaming. Now you're sedate and agreeable?"

"I've changed in ten years, and I'm just trying to get this over with and get out alive."

Something else flashed in his eyes, something violent, and it seized her heart. "Whatever. I'll untie you, but swear to God, you fuck with me and I'll fuck you up."

She didn't doubt it. "I promise."

He cut the ropes holding her hands and then stepped back, eyeing her. He jerked his head to the clothing. "I'm locking the door, so don't try any shit. Get dressed, then wait for me." A slick grin crossed his face. "Party starts soon."

He left, and Fiona had her pants down to her ankles when she heard a scream somewhere outside of her room. Screaming, crying, and then a smack. Then silence. She squeezed her eyes shut, vowing to also rip off Harvey's balls.

There was no mirror—smart choice as she would have broken that sucker and gripped a shard from it—but she could see the negligee fit her well. It was a baby doll style—black thong panties and a bra with sheer fabric draping down over her stomach. It wasn't cheap. She could tell by the feel of the fabric and the crystals lining the bra. This wasn't like before. She knew that back then she'd been moved to several locations during the two weeks she was with them, and they'd never cared to put her in anything like this. They'd kept her naked. She still didn't love walking around her house alone naked.

Her nerves were on edge, anxiety spiking. When she undressed, she'd let her fingers brush over the tracker. It was still there, a hard little bump under her hair. That was her tie to Jock, to the crew, and the way she was going to save these girls. And herself, she guessed.

Five minutes later the door re-opened and Harvey entered again. He took one look at her and adjusted himself. She felt her vagina dry up like the goddamn desert. He gripped her biceps—way harder than he had to because she was walking willingly—and dragged her out of the room.

She went on full alert. She didn't want to glance around too much to be obvious, but she took stock of everything. The hallway was long, with heavy wooden doors on each side, and the walls were covered with dark wallpaper in a swirling maroon and gold pattern that she imagined some rich person thought looked expensive. The carpet runner beneath her feet was plush, laid down over dark hardwood. Dark, dark, dark. When she got out, she was painting everything she owned goddamn white.

He tied her hands together again at the end of the hallway, and she suffered through it. Then he tugged on the rope as if she was a dog and led her into another large, high-ceilinged room. She was starting to think she was in some sort of old mansion. This room looked like an old ballroom.

And in this room were a dozen women.

Tall, short, curvy, skinny, all skin-tones, all hair colors. Fiona gazed around the room, her heart breaking at the utter devastation she saw on the faces of these women. They were broken. They'd been here before, and they were here again, and the fight was gone. Despair welled up in Fiona, nearly fucking choking her. She hoped her rescuers came soon.

Harvey shoved her inside and growled. "Don't get comfortable."

"What?" she asked. "How long will we be here?"

"They"—he gestured to the women—"are staying. You"—he smirked—"White has special plans for."

And then he walked out. The door shutting behind him and the lock sliding into place sent a bolt of fear down her spine.

She spun around, taking in the girls, the windowless room. There was nothing in this room to use as defense. All their hands were tied and they were barefoot, wearing practically nothing.

If Harvey'd made a point to say they were leaving then that meant…she was leaving. She was leaving with her tracker and all these women would be left here, helpless. *Fuck.*

One redhead was sobbing, her whole body shaking. "H-H-Harvey told me I wouldn't see my kid again. What did he mean by that? Are they hurting our families?"

Dread slithered down Fiona's spine. No, she didn't think that. She thought it meant they weren't getting out of here. *Shit.* She didn't say that, though; she didn't have to. Because a black woman with long braids said in a tone that was both firm and kind, "Honey, I think it means we're not meant to go home."

The redhead sobbed harder. Fiona met the deep brown eyes of the woman who'd spoken. She stared back at Fiona—the expression of a woman who knew what was coming but hadn't let it break her. Not yet. There were a couple of women around her, others who still had clear eyes, who hadn't yet given up hope.

Fiona glanced around the room and saw another young woman crying. "I'm supposed to get married in six months," she whispered. Yet another said, "I spent thousands in therapy to be able to sleep at night by myself, and now I have to deal with this again?"

Fiona made a decision. A decision she'd known she might have to make, but one she'd hoped to avoid. She hoped Jock understood, she hoped he'd find a way to forgive her.

Mindful of possible microphones and cameras in the room, she stepped toward the black woman with braids. "Hi, I'm Fiona."

The woman stared back at her before her face softened a bit. Fiona couldn't tell her age—she had beautiful high cheekbones and full lips with a bit of red lipstick left over from whatever life she'd been living before she was taken. Again. She also had long black nails filed to points.

"I'm Tianna," she said.

Fiona stepped even closer, right up in Tianna's space. The woman frowned slightly and tried to step back, but Fiona locked eyes with her and got right up in her space again. "I need a favor," she said.

Tianna blinked at her. "I'm thinking now is a time when I'm not able to grant many favors."

"I just…" Fiona screwed up her face, wishing she was a better actress, but she had no other alternative. She crashed her body into Tianna's, sobbing on the woman's shoulder.

Tianna was stiff for a few seconds before trying her best with her bound hands to calm Fiona. "Honey, it's…I know. I know this sucks."

Fiona pressed closer and continued to let her shoulders shake as she shoved her face into Tianna's neck and angled her mouth toward Tianna's ear. She whispered, "I have a tracker in the back of my neck, past my hairline. I need you to dig your nails in and get it out."

Tianna didn't react, didn't do a thing but continue stroking Fiona with her bound hands.

Then she slid down the wall until her butt hit the floor,

and she spread her legs, patting the space between them. "Here, baby. Lay down on my lap. You like your hair played with?"

Fiona nodded vigorously, nearly weeping for real with relief. If that tracker came out, she could leave it there. The crew would find the women. They'd be saved. How was Fiona's life more precious than the lives of twelve other women? It wasn't, and after a lifetime of wondering what the fuck her purpose was, she felt like she'd found it.

She settled herself between Tianna's long legs and rested her head on her thigh, facing out into the room so the back of her head was accessible to Tianna's hands. Thank God for Fiona having a shit-ton of hair, because it hid Tianna's nails moving over her scalp. She called to some of the other women. "Come on, let's all huddle. Kinda cold in here anyway. Could have given us a blanket or turned the fucking heat on. Assholes."

Women surrounded them at once, all of them seeking some sort of heat, some sort of comfort. Fiona met the gaze of a pretty Southeast Asian woman, who smiled at her. Fiona reached out her hand and gripped the woman's fingers and grinned back. The woman squeezed her hands.

They were a shopping list. It was easy to see now. All body types and all ethnicities. Whatever the men ordered, these women were meant to provide. Fiona saw women with stretch marks from their bellies being full of babies, women with wedding rings, women with laugh lines and tattoos. With fucking *lives*.

Tianna was talking to the woman next to her, and Fiona closed her eyes as a fingernail raked over the lump of the tracker. Tianna didn't flinch or make any other sign that she noticed, but she did, because immediately a nail flicked over a tiny stitch. Damn, Fiona had chosen right.

It hurt. The more Tianna dug at the tracker, the more Fiona had to close her eyes and grit her teeth against the pain, but the woman didn't let up. Fiona squeezed the woman's hand she held—her name was Gita, she learned—and tried not to whimper. Tianna brushed the side of Fiona's head and said a soft "I'm sorry" as Fiona felt a trickle of blood leak out of her hairline. It was quickly wiped away.

Tianna was talking about her boyfriend, a retired NFL player who was probably worried sick about her. "He's probably losing his mind and stomping around yelling, aggravating his ACL tear from '06. The year before was when he won the Super Bowl."

Tianna was fucking gorgeous, and her diamond earrings were massive. Fiona was not surprised she had a rich sports-playing boyfriend. Then Tianna started talking about her job—she had her own clothing boutique in Atlanta. From the sound of it, Tianna had plenty of her own money. Fiona comforted herself that Tianna would get back to her store and her customers and her famous boyfriend.

Other girls were talking about their men, and a few talked about their women. She wanted to be fucking normal, not the freak who couldn't bear to be around anyone for ten years.

Tianna's hair stroked her face. "You got someone, honey?"

"Yeah," Fiona said on a whisper. "J. He just told me he loved me, too."

Several *awww*s followed her words, and Tianna's soft voice came after that. "I'm sorry, baby."

"Me too," Fiona said.

Finally, the digging stopped, and Fiona's gut unclenched. Tianna patted her shoulder, and Fiona lifted herself to a sitting position. She was a little lightheaded, but when she looked down, Tianna had her fist tightly closed, a bit of Fiona's blood on the tips of her fingernails.

"Thanks," Fiona said. "I feel much better." She hugged Tianna and whispered in her ear. "Don't let that tracker leave this house. Rescue is on its way, okay?"

"What about you?" Tianna whispered back.

"Don't worry about me."

When Fiona pulled away Tianna didn't look happy with that answer, but she raised her hand and fiddled with one of the braids in her hair. She was tucking the tracker into them.

Just then the door opened and Harvey stomped inside. Fiona rose, lightheaded from the pain in her scalp, to see White standing behind Harvey. The sight of his face pulled her back ten years, and her knees nearly buckled. Then his mouth stretched into a grin. "Show time, my little lion."

CHAPTER NINETEEN

ERICK shook his leg nervously, Roarke muttered to himself, and Wren chewed a nail. Marisol ate five candy bars. Jock...well, Jock sat immobile. His whole body was ice. Was his blood flowing? He didn't know. He'd checked his pulse to make sure, and it was there, steady and strong. His heart was beating, but he couldn't figure out how he was alive with ice in his veins.

He had a reputation for being ice cold but that had never been it. He'd been...nothing. Not warm, not cold, just nothing, because he was unemotional and calculating in his jobs.

This one was unlike any other, though. He was ice cold, and for once in his life so fucking terrified that he had no idea what to do about it. So he didn't move. He only stared at the screen as the red dot made its way to Virginia. Fiona had been nabbed two hours ago, and Marisol was currently barking into the phone with her FBI contact, giving him directions. Meanwhile they all sat in the van, on their way to the location. Because fuck if Jock was going to sit with his thumb up his ass when his woman was in the clutches of sick perverts.

He'd told her he loved her. He'd said that to her face,

and he couldn't remember the last time he'd said that to fucking anyone. Maybe his mom. Or Jonathan, but never a woman he'd had in his bed. He wasn't sure he'd ever fucked a woman other than Fiona who actually knew his real name; that was how much of a secretive bastard he was.

And he'd stayed that way with Fiona for too damn long. He'd held everything close to his damn vest like a stubborn asshole. He closed his eyes for one brief minute as pain sliced through him—hot and sharp, worse than the bullet he'd taken to the hip back when he served.

Then he opened them again and focused on that damn dot.

"They're in some old Virginia neighborhood near the hospital. These houses are old as shit and huge—they call it Doctor's Row," Erick said. "Makes sense because people don't casually stroll through these streets. Some of these houses are renovated and some not. Mostly old money lives there now, not new blood."

"Which means they close their blinds if they see shady shit and don't make a peep," Roarke said.

"Rich white people," Marisol muttered. She'd hung up the phone after shouting at the agent and throwing so much attitude at him that Jock would have been amused on any other mission.

"The tracker hasn't moved for a half hour," Erick said. "She's gotta be there. Has to be it."

"Markham's on it," Marisol said about the agent. "He's calling every fucking judge he knows for a warrant now that we have proof Fiona got nabbed. Not to mention all the digital evidence." That had been a hard sell. The code these assholes used was hard to break—names, locations, sex acts, money exchanged. It was all there, but not in plain speak. Dade had broken it because he had the skills, but convincing the FBI was a whole other thing. These men—Darren's friends—were big players in DC. The FBI couldn't just go storming in and disrupting their lives. But these women had been taken over state lines, and Dade had been able to document this, at least in code.

Jock was still nervous. What if they didn't get to Fiona in time? What condition would he find her in? He remembered when they'd first met, after she shot him, when she'd collapsed in his arms, nearly unconscious. He remembered how long it had taken to earn her trust, for him to get to the point that he could touch her at all. How much would this shit set her back in her own head?

"We're half an hour out," Roarke announced. "Remember we can't go storming in there. All the big players are here; the FBI gets 'em, shit gets shut down. This is over."

Jock had one gun at his back and another shoved in his boot. He'd give the agents about ten minutes to bring out the girls, including Fiona, or he was going in there guns drawn, prepared to shoot some motherfuckers in the face. He'd killed once for Fiona and had no regrets. He'd do it a-fucking-gain in a heartbeat.

And he planned to bury Henry Chamberlain II. Jock wasn't fucking around. That guy wouldn't just be in jail; he'd be so fucking ruined that he'd never lift his head again. Jock had made that man his own personal mission as soon as he'd heard that Chamberlain had a special inclination toward Fiona.

When they drew close to the mansion with the tracking signal coming from it, Roarke—who was driving with Wren in the passenger seat—slowed the van and turned off the headlights. He crept closer, about fifty yards away, at the corner of the block. They could see the house but were far enough away not to draw too much suspicion to their presence.

Jock squinted past the windshield and into the night, able to see dark figures, rifles drawn as they converged on the house.

"Markham and the Feds pulled through," Erick muttered, peering into the darkness along with Jock.

"I'm a tiny terror," Marisol said. "He knew I'd kick his ass."

Screams pierced the night, rich and full of absolute terror. Jock's heart picked up, beating double-time, so damn loud all he could hear was the pounding in his ears. More figures flowed into the house. Soon after he saw the first woman, a tall one with braids, followed by more—all covered in blankets and being led out the front door toward ambulances which were now screeching down the street.

Jock turned, ignored Roarke calling his name and Erick grasping at his arm, and stomped toward the back of the van. He shoved open the doors and hit the ground at a sprint. Fiona, he had to fucking find Fiona. She'd be terrified, and these women...As he drew closer he could see what they were wearing under the blankets. He saw red. Fucking red like a charging bull. Only the terrified faces of the women made him slow down and fix his face so it didn't look like thunder, because he didn't want to scare them any worse than they already were.

There were more FBI agents still inside, but through the open door Jock could also see men in suits, cuffed and lined up on the floor. He looked for Fiona, waiting to catch a glimpse of her blond locks in the moonlight. He spotted a blonde and made a beeline for her, but when she turned around he stopped dead. She wasn't Fiona. He whirled around but everywhere he looked were women in lingerie, huddled under blankets, and none of them were fucking Fiona.

"Fiona!" he yelled like a raving lunatic, but fuck, he'd lost his cool. The ice was melting, and all he felt in his veins was lava, so fucking hot he thought he'd claw his skin off. "Does anyone know where Fiona is!"

The woman with braids padded toward him on the plush grass in her bare feet. She eyed him warily. "Who're you?"

"I'm..." Who was he? What was he to Fiona?

"What's your name?"

"Jock." There, he could answer that.

She cocked her head. "What does she call you, honey?"

He swallowed and said thickly. "J."

Her face immediately changed, sympathy sweeping over her features fast in a way that made his heart slam into the ground. She reached up into her braids and tugged and then pulled out the tracker. "I'm Tianna. She made me take this out of her scalp. Made me keep it. Because they took her somewhere else and she wanted the rest of us to be saved."

He didn't want to believe it. The loss hit him so swiftly that his stomach contracted as if he'd been punched. He couldn't speak, couldn't move, could only stare at that god-damn tracker in her palm.

He slowly lifted his gaze to her. "Where the fuck did they take her?"

She shook her head. "I don't know. Harvey came and got her with some pasty-faced, slicked-hair asshole."

Chamberlain. He knew it.

"Can you get her back?" Tianna was asking. "You have to. She saved us. They were going to kill us, just erase us like we were nothing."

He was going to throw up. His Fiona had done that. So fucking selfless. Now the problem was that if Chamberlain found out there'd been a raid, Fiona would be seriously fucked. Jock looked Tianna in the eye and said the words he felt down to his marrow, the determination sweeping everything in him clean, flushing him out. "I'll get her."

He turned on a heel as the FBI agents began leading the cuffed men out of the mansion. He didn't spare a glance at them. Not fucking one. He walked, then jogged, and then went into an all-out sprint to the van.

The doors opened and Wren peered out with a concerned look. "Where's Fiona?"

Jock leaped into the van, brushing past her, and sat down at his laptop. He had work to do. "Chamberlain took her somewhere else."

"The tracker—" Erick began.

"She had one of the girls rip it out." Jock lifted his head and met the gaze of every single crew member so they understood what Fiona had done. "She ripped it out because she knew Chamberlain was taking her somewhere and she wanted to save the other women."

"No." That came from Marisol. Her eyes immediately glistened in the dark. That was Marisol. Tough as shit, but when you messed with her crew, she got angry and pissed and with that came tears. She'd work through it, though. She always did.

Jock didn't acknowledge her. "I'm sending all of you Chamberlain's file. All his properties, his aliases, everything. We comb through this shit, make calls, find out where the fuck he is. My thought? He took her to one of his places. His turf. We don't fucking rest until we find her."

They all murmured their assent. Marisol was crying softly, angrily, swiping at her cheeks. "I will fucking kill that asshole for touching her," she growled. Yeah, Marisol was protective. Jock knew the feeling.

He focused back on his computer because he couldn't let

the lava in his veins burn him from the inside out. He had to focus, get through this. Get Fiona.

A hand landed on his shoulder. He'd expected Roarke, but instead he saw Erick. "We'll get her back, man. No one else in this crew loses someone."

Pain flashed through Erick's eyes. Jock knew he was thinking about Flynn. Erick covered the pain with a small smile and turned back to his laptop. Jock took a minute to absorb that pain before he began to work.

* * *

Two minutes after Fiona had been shoved in the back of a car and driven away from the mansion, she'd regretted her choice to rip out the tracker. Then she changed her mind and was happy she'd done it, because she knew that right about now the crew would be storming the house with the FBI. The women would be safe. Tianna and Gita and the redhead with a kid. They'd be okay.

Fiona, on the other hand . . . well, her nightmare was just starting. They'd given her a robe but they'd also gagged her. The tinted windows assured no one would see her inside, trussed up and dressed like a lady of the night. Or whatever. God, she fucking hated this. White kept his hand on her thigh the whole time, while he talked on the phone and Harvey drove. Sometimes he'd slide it higher, tease at the hem of her panties. She refused to squirm.

She stared out at the window and tried to think of happy things, like pizza in a hotel with Jock, and Sundance's fur, and Wren's laughter. But that all made her chest get tight, and she didn't want to cry in this car, not in front of White and Harvey.

He ended the call and immediately shifted his weight, pressing close to her side. She closed her eyes so she didn't have to see him. His breath coated her face, and she breathed through her mouth around the gag to avoid the smell. "I wasn't supposed to take you away. To have you to myself. But fuck them. I've waited years for this."

She didn't get it, honest to God. She wasn't that special. Sure, she had blond hair and blue eyes and knew she wasn't ugly, but she couldn't understand what it was about her that drew White to her. She gave him nothing in the car. No tears, no eye contact. Fucking nothing. He wanted to use her? Whatever; she'd lay there like the dead, and no amount of fists would make her do anything else.

"Now I have you back," he whispered as he loosened her gag. "And when I'm done, no one will ever have you again."

He was going to kill her. She'd known this would be a possibility going in, but now she knew for sure. She wasn't getting out of this. White didn't want anyone else to have her.

He was too late, though. Jock had her. He always would.

It hit her then, sitting on the pristine leather seat in the back of this ritzy car, about to sacrifice herself in Henry's hands—she hadn't told Jock she loved him. She hadn't said it back. And Jock fucking deserved to hear it. He *needed* to hear it.

She opened her eyes and looked out the window, ignoring White's breath at her ear, the feel of his hand slipping farther up her thigh. She was going to fight. She'd spent ten years telling herself she'd never be a victim again. That strength and determination welled up inside of her, pumping hot blood into her brain. *Think, Fiona. Think.* She had to get back to Jock. She had to tell him she loved him, and then she'd arm herself with a shovel. She'd dig and dig until she was goddamn bloody and wouldn't rest until Jock was clean inside.

She didn't have her gun, but she'd taken self-defense classes and was strong-ish. Strong enough to take on Henry, who was pasty and thin in a sickly way. He looked like he'd be out of breath running fifty yards. Looks could be deceiving, though, so she had to play this smart.

They were heading toward the coast. Salty air wafted through the vents, and seagulls circled overhead. He must have a beach house. Damn it, she wanted a damn beach house, too, but she wanted to be there in her bikini, drinking a Corona, her only worry deciding which excellent restaurant to order takeout from.

She hadn't wanted to live for ten years. Well, she had wanted to live, but she hadn't wanted to *live*. It'd taken all of this, ending up sitting in the car with fucking White, for her to realize how goddamn badly she wanted to live life to the fullest.

They didn't reach the ocean. They were close; she could tell by the smell seeping through the vents in the car, but she didn't see water. She watched the road, careful to observe how to get back to the main highway.

Finally they pulled down a gravel drive, which led to a small cottage. It had clearly been upgraded from what it originally was, and the additions stood stark and bland against the original quaint house.

Right. Forget about the stupid building. If she played her cards right she'd never have to set foot in it. The car rumbled on gravel which would be hard on her feet, but just beyond that was plush grass and a dense forest. She might cut her feet getting away, but she couldn't let herself be led into that house.

She'd been working to untie the knot on her hands the entire drive, and she was pretty sure she had it loose enough to make it come undone with a solid yank. The men should have used handcuffs, but they must have thought the women were so cowed that they wouldn't try to break knots.

Harvey had to go down first, Fiona concluded. He hit harder and could run faster. This could all go bad, honestly, because if she failed, they'd wreck her. But what did it matter if they planned to kill her anyway?

She'd go down fighting. Fuck this lame bullshit. Jock would want her to fight. Even if he ended up having to identify the defense wounds on her dead body. She shuddered as the car rolled to a stop. She couldn't be that pessimistic. Not yet.

She gathered her wits and waited as Harvey put the car into park and shut off the engine. He withdrew the keys and slipped them into his pocket. As suspected, White reached for the door beside him, and Harvey slid out of the car and opened up her door.

This was it. Now was her time. She placed a foot on the gravel, testing it for sharpness, and was relieved to feel they were smooth paver stones. Then, while White was half in and half out of the car, she pointed over Harvey's shoulder and used the oldest trick in the book. "What's that?"

Harvey turned to look over his shoulder, and she brought her knee up as hard as she could and slammed it into his balls. He didn't even curse, didn't say a word, but followed a pained grunt with a high-pitched whine and bent over. He was on his way to tipping over to his side when she ripped her hands apart, shedding the rope, and took off at a dead sprint. A shout went up behind her—White's—followed by Harvey's breathless, "Fucking cunt!" but she was already in the grass, pulling the gag down to her chin to inhale more oxygen. She made it to the tree line just as a gunshot ricocheted off a trunk near her head.

She didn't even let herself scream, not wanting to waste the air, and kept running, kept going. She took a hard turn as she heard a body crashing after her. She needed to make it out to the road. Someone had to see her there, or there'd be another house…goddamn, she didn't know. This was the only plan she had, and it might suck but she refused to let White touch her, refused to die, damn it. This was not her time. She still had so much to do.

The stupid robe she wore kept snagging on branches and she knew the fabric was ripping, probably leaving a lacy breadcrumb trail, but nothing could be done about it. Then she heard an engine in the distance. Faint but getting closer. A motorcycle. Not a car. But it was something—a person, civilization. She just had to make it to the road to flag them down.

She ran toward the sound, her feet slipping on the roots and rocks. She tripped and fell onto her hands and knees, pain slicing into her somewhere as liquid trickled down her chin, but she ignored it and got back up. She could see a clearing in the trees. It was there, and even though the footsteps behind her were closer, even though she swore she could hear breathing, she kept going, going, going…

She saw the shoulder of the road and had one foot in it, had caught the sight of the motorcycle rounding a bend and threw out her hand to signal the driver, when something viciously tugged her hair and yanked her back.

"Noooooo!" she screamed, and her hands immediately went up to grasp the fingers tangled in her hair.

"Goddamn fucking bitch!" Harvey snarled in her ear as he pulled her back into the woods, away from the road, away from safety. She didn't stop struggling and kicked her feet, but he wasn't letting go this time. Tears burned hot and fresh in her eyes as the motorcycle revved its engine and drew closer. It'd pass them soon. In another few seconds, it'd be out of sight. Harvey dragged her farther and farther from the road like she was nothing, like she was a dead woman walking.

The motorcycle picked up speed and she closed her eyes, not wanting to see it pass. Except it didn't. She saw the sleek black body of the motorcycle for one second before it turned on a screech of the back tire and the smoke of burned rubber and crashed into the trees. *Right. Toward. Them.*

"What the fuck?" Harvey shouted, and shoved her to the ground to draw his gun.

She rolled onto her side, and that was when she saw the driver. He was wearing a black helmet but she'd know those broad shoulders anywhere. He drew a gun from his waistband, aimed it right at Harvey and fired.

Harvey went down like a sack of potatoes. He just collapsed at her feet, a damn hole in his head, eyes and mouth open. She screamed in his dead face, kicking at the leaves, struggling to get away from the body of the man who been dragging her by her hair only seconds ago.

The motorcycle skidded to a halt, the driver ripped off his helmet, and Jock leapt from the bike, running toward her and sweeping her into his arms. Her screams turned into great big, heaving sobs. She clung to him, bawling her eyes out as the adrenaline leaked out of her. She could barely hold her head up, but she didn't have to. Jock was there, lifting her off the cold ground and cradling her in his lap, his big hands taking stock of her body and her limbs while she broke apart in his arms.

"Jesus, fuck, Jesus fuck," he chanted over and over again. His big body rocked, and she curled into him, wanting to be a barnacle on his body for the rest of her life. If Jock was there, no one could hurt her.

"Wh-Whi-White," she managed to say.

He held her tighter. "Crew's got him. You did good, baby. You got away. You did so good."

She let those words soak into her bones. Then she said it, not willing to wait another hour, another minute, another second. She pulled back, gripped his face, and looked him right in the eye. "I had to fight. I had to because I didn't get to tell you that I love you."

His body went solid around her, and his eyes did that melting thing, where they went from glacier to river, but this time, they slipped right into placid. Right into a peace she hadn't been sure she'd ever see. Yeah, all of that, it was worth fighting for. It was worth *living* for.

CHAPTER TWENTY

JOCK heard the shower go off and he was there, rapping the door with his knuckles, not loud but insistent. "Babe, let me know when you're decent."

"Jock, you don't have to come in," Fiona's voice filtered through the door.

He felt heat at his back and knew it was Wren and Marisol. "Babe, your feet are cut to shit. I need to look at them."

"I know how to put cream and Band-Aids on, Jock," she snapped, and he smiled. Fiona already had some of her fire back.

"You don't let me in, I come in."

There was a moment of silence, and then a heavy sigh sounded before she flung open the door. Her pale skin was pinked from the hot water, and her hair was a dripping blond sheet around her shoulders. She had a robe wrapped around her, a big one with long sleeves that covered her hands so only her fingertips poked out.

"Fiona, you want me to look at your feet?" Wren asked from behind him.

"Hey, I'm the one with nurse skills. I stitched Roarke's freaking head." That was Marisol.

"I don't think she needs stitches."

"Still, I'm the one with skills."

Jock turned around with a growl. "Both of you, downstairs. I'll take care of this."

Wren pursed her lips for a moment before rolling her eyes and walking away. "Let me know if you need me, Fi!" she called over her shoulder.

"Don't growl at me, Jock." Of course Marisol was the one who would stay and give him lip.

"You're crowding her," he snapped back.

"Look who's talking, big guy."

"Guys—" Fiona started.

"Go downstairs. I got this," he said to Marisol.

Her eyes flashed. "Look, I just..." Then he saw it. Those flames in her eyes died, and he saw now they were a front for the waterworks that lurked behind. Because tough Marisol was struggling to hold back tears. "I just want to make sure she's okay." Her voice cracked.

Well, now he had to soothe her *and* take care of Fiona. When the fuck did he turn into this guy? "Ah shit." He wrapped his arms around Marisol's shoulders, and she let him hug her for a split second before tugging away. "Don't worry about me. Focus on Fiona. Sorry."

"I'm okay," Fiona said softly. "I mean, I'm not okay, but I'm okay with not being okay. Because of you all. And Jock. I just need some time and some good company and pepperoni pizza. Maybe some brownies."

Marisol smiled, winning the struggle with crying. "Sure, I'll take orders." Then she turned on her heel, obviously happy to have a mission.

"Wings!" He called after her.

She lifted a hand before disappearing down the stairs. "Got it!"

"Hot as fuck!" he hollered.

"Got it!" she yelled again.

He smiled and turned to Fiona. "Ass on the sink counter. I need to see your feet. Why are you even standing?"

She gave him an annoyed sigh but hoisted herself up onto the counter. "Because I thought I was going to have to break up a cat fight between the three of you."

"We weren't going to have a cat fight."

Fiona tried to hide her grin and failed.

He knelt in front of her and lifted up her feet. He had to clench his jaw so he didn't lose it. The soles of her feet were red and raw, and while she didn't need stitches, he worried about infection. Even though she'd just showered, he took a cotton pad and wiped them down with rubbing alcohol. After slathering them with anti-bacterial cream, he bandaged them, taped the bandages so they'd stay on, and covered her feet with thick socks.

She let him, occasionally running her hands through his hair. When he was finished, he pressed a kiss to the inside of a knee and patted her calf before he stood. "Get dressed, babe. Marisol probably threatened the pizza place with all kinds of shit if they didn't make an especially fast delivery for you."

Fiona laughed and it made him smile, the sound worming its way under his skin.

Thirty minutes later Jock sat in the corner of the couch, Fiona burrowed into him so deep that he thought her skin would meld with his. And he didn't give a fuck, not one bit. He liked her there. She'd put on a pair of yoga pants and one of his T-shirts. She hadn't asked, just snatched it out of his drawer. It was so big that it hung off one shoulder, leaving her pale skin exposed. He'd kissed that spot more than once, and each time she sighed and her body relaxed into his more.

The crew was there. They were all together because they wanted to be, and because Fiona asked them to be. He thought she needed to sleep more, but she told him the time she'd slept in the van on the way home was enough. After everything that had happened, it was now early afternoon. Fiona wanted everyone to gorge themselves on pizza and wings and so they did. Now they were done eating and talking quietly, not really wanting to relive the day, but there was no way to avoid the elephant in the room.

Marisol and Wren hadn't left Fiona's side. Which meant Jock had Fiona laying on him, Marisol laying on Fiona, and Wren on the floor, back against the couch, her hand holding Fiona's. He was crowded with women and normally that would make him claustrophobic, but right now he liked having them all there, safe.

"So, you had the wrong house?" Fiona's voice was soft and—he was glad to hear—thoughtful rather than anxious.

"Yeah," Marisol said. "Jock took Wren's motorcycle to get to you faster. Which I'd like to state was Wren's idea, which shocked everyone."

"I would throw my bike into the sea for Fiona," Wren said with irritation.

"How did you know that was where I'd be? I'm sure he owns multiple properties?" Fiona asked.

"He does," Jock said. "Five. One is his primary home, where we'd already set up cameras to watch. Two are apartments and wouldn't be ideal to take a woman he'd kidnapped. One is in Florida, and it was less likely he'd fly there with you. Driving would take too long. The other was that cottage. Gotta be honest, we were all sweating he'd taken you somewhere else, but that was the best lead we'd gotten."

"But the deed we found for Chamberlain matched a different house, which was where we went first," Marisol said. "Township must have messed up a public record or Chamberlain paid someone off *to* fuck it up. No one was there, and we were about to scour the whole area, but that would have taken forever. Jock took off on the bike to check some of the other houses, saw you, saw Chamberlain's car, and phoned us quickly. Then he fucking crashed into the damn forest like an Avenger."

"Call me Chris Evans," he rumbled.

Fiona looked up at him, smiling a smile so damn bright that he wanted to take a picture. She was okay—he was shocked as shit that she was okay after all of this, but she was. And his girl had fought. "For real, baby, if you hadn't run, not sure when we would have found you."

She squeezed his hand and laid her head back on his chest. The crew had made it to Chamberlain, detained him, and waited for the authorities to arrive. Marisol had pulled some strings with her FBI guy to get them to question Jock tomorrow. He'd killed a guy, and although it had been self-defense, it had still taken what felt like an act of God for them not to arrest him right there and ask questions later. Marisol, however, was an act of God.

They'd deal with all that tomorrow. Right now, Jock had his woman laying warm and safe on his chest and everything else could fucking wait.

* * *

Fiona had a gauntlet to go through before she could go to bed. She wanted to be annoyed, but this crew had her back, had saved her life, and she loved them.

First up was Erick, who wrapped her in his arms. One thing she'd learned about Erick was that he gave great hugs.

Even after losing the love of his life, Erick was not stingy with those hugs. He gave them to everyone, mostly his sister. Fiona loved that Wren had that sibling bond because Fiona had never had a sibling.

"Glad you're back home," he said.

"Me too."

"You need anything, I'm close, okay?"

She nodded. "Thanks, Erick."

Then came Roarke, who patted her cheek in his manly, thoughtful way and brushed his lips across her temple. Wren gave her a gentle hug—good hugs ran in the Lee family. "Love you, Fi."

"Love you too, Wren." Fiona was warm, inside and out, for the first time in a long time.

Then it was Marisol's turn and this woman didn't hug so much as squeeze the life out of Fiona. "Brave, beautiful girl. I got your back always."

"I'll return the favor sometime."

Marisol pulled back with a grin. "Knowing me, I'll need it."

Then they were gone, all of them, and it was just Jock and Fiona in the townhouse. He locked the door and reached for her hand. "Tomorrow, we move. Don't want to put you through that trauma now so Erick is watching the house overnight. But tomorrow, we gotta get gone."

The way he said it was matter of fact, not that soft voice he'd been giving her since she got home. She swallowed and couldn't stop the tremble in her voice. "We? As in—?"

He stepped into her space, right up against her with his hand wrapped around her neck, fingers brushing where the tracker had been embedded in her skin. "We as in you and me. As in I'm by your side, holding your hand. As in we live together, you're in my bed, by my side. We as in I fucking love you, Fiona. I got you back, and I'm ready to do what I gotta do to keep you with me." Then something like vulnerability flashed in his eyes, clear in the sunlight streaking through the windows. "Unless you don't want me there."

He was giving this to her. He was giving her a future, a life, something to do rather than just exist and live in fear. Something other than surviving. It would be a tough road with Jock; she knew that because she wasn't stupid. He'd fall silent, he'd hide his emotions, but she was confident they could work on it.

"You really want to be there?"

"I want to be there so bad, I'm willing to bare what soul I got left." He answered quickly, with no hesitation. "I'll do it, then you can decide if that's what you want to take on. But warning, it's not pretty."

She shook her head and lifted her hand to Jock's cheek, swiping her thumb across his lower lip. "I saw enough to know I want it."

His hand tightened on her hip. "Babe."

"Kiss me."

"That fucker get his mouth on you?"

That made her pause and not in a good way. "You need to know that before you kiss me?"

"Need to know how hard I gotta work to erase every memory of him."

Now that made her smile. "No, Jock, he didn't get his mouth on me. I sat in that car with his hand on my thigh, and I thought about you. Your voice and—"

"Stop, Fiona."

"—Your touch and—"

"Got it."

"—And everything that was you. Because it gave me reason to get back to you."

His mouth crashed onto hers at the same time he cupped her ass and lifted. He didn't give her time to jump, not on the balls of her injured feet. He lifted her off the ground so she could wrap her legs around his waist. His mouth licked into hers, claiming her over again, and she loved it, every single beat of his heart against her chest, every soft moan of his into her mouth—fucking loved it.

"You too tired?" he asked against her lips as he moved them upstairs to the bedroom. "We can take a rain check."

"No." She squirmed against him. Sure she was tired, but she'd already napped.

He wasted no time crashing into the bedroom with zero grace. He was gentle about placing her on the bed, though, but then his clothes were shed in little time, along with the sounds of fabric tearing.

She shimmied out of her yoga pants and had her shirt pulled over her head and tossed to the side when his body covered hers. "I still have my underwear on," she whispered as his lips went to her neck.

"I know," he said.

"Don't you want them off?"

"Sure do, but I want to take them off myself when I'm down there. Give me time."

Her belly dipped. Jock's hands felt amazing—they always did—rough and calloused, yet he knew just how to touch her to make her writhe on the sheets with need.

"I'm so damn lucky to be here with you," he murmured, and she wondered if he was saying that because he felt compelled, or because he knew she needed to hear the words. She didn't care which was the answer because she did need to hear it. She needed to know she was loved and wanted after feeling like a piece of trash.

Jock held her like precious cargo, his big hand cupping

her breast as he sucked a nipple into his mouth. She arched off the bed, gripping his hair tightly as he played her body like an instrument, using his tongue and hands.

She didn't even have time to register that her panties were off because then her legs were thrown over his shoulders, his big hands gripped her ass, and then he pulled her to his mouth.

Jock's tongue could work goddamn miracles. He licked her like a cone, like he was tracing the alphabet, making small humming noises that vibrated her clit better than anything battery-operated. She was soaked. She could feel it in his stubble as it brushed her inner thighs, and she could smell her own arousal as he added two fingers and plunged them inside.

She clamped her thighs around his head and shouted, "Fuck, J!" and came like a rocket. A sneak-attack orgasm she hadn't seen coming hit her like a goddamn freight train.

Jock was over her before she finished and he kissed her, sliding his hands over her skin, caressing her like she was a diamond. "Please," she murmured, feeling the hard heat of him against her stomach. "Come inside, J."

After rolling on a condom he entered her, his eyes heavy-lidded as he slowly inched his way into her body. She moaned softly at the feeling of fullness as he began to slowly thrust in and out of her, his big muscular body over top, protecting her, while his hands stroked her hair at her temples. He began to say her name, just a soft chant, mostly just a movement of his lips, and it was beautiful, powerful, flowing into her and washing her clean.

She came again as he kissed her, and her contracting around him must have sent him over the edge because he thrust inside on a long moan and his dick pulsed as he came. She felt the tension leave his body, and she didn't mind when he gave her some of his weight; she wasn't ready for him to leave her body yet.

He panted harshly in her ear before he finally pressed a kiss there and said, "About ready to sleep."

"It's mid-day," she said.

"Don't care. You only slept in the car on the way home."

That was true. "Okay, well how about we talk a bit first, then sleep?"

He pulled back to look at her. "You wanna talk?"

She nodded and bit her lip. "Got some digging to do."

"Babe, we got time."

"I want to start now," she whispered. "I wasted ten years, and I don't want to waste any more."

He closed his eyes like it hurt, and when he opened them, she saw a placid lake, right there. He was at peace. "'Kay, babe, then we'll talk."

She grinned.

CHAPTER TWENTY-ONE

"ARE you mad at me for doing what I did with the tracker?" Fiona asked softly.

They hadn't talked much about what had happened because she'd slept on the drive. When they'd gotten home, she'd showered and ate with the crew before falling into bed. He didn't mind that sequence of events.

"I wasn't mad," he said. "I was worried and a little freaked out. What you did...that was fucking selfless." They were lying on the bed, the sheets covering them haphazardly. Jock was on his back, Fiona laying on top of him, her fingers stroking the hair on his chest. Her tits were pressed to him, and he could reach her round ass anytime he wanted. Fucking heaven.

"I never thought I'd make a decision like that." She sighed, and her breath coasted over his skin. "But I did, and I don't regret it. Not one bit."

"We should find Tianna."

She jerked up. "What?"

"Tianna. She was the one who told me who took you."

"Really?"

"Yeah, I was walking around the front of the mansion looking at the women and calling your name. She walked up to me and asked who I was. I told her I was Jock, and she asked me what you called me." Her body went still in his arms. "I told her you called me J, and that was when she showed me the tracker."

Fiona pressed closer to him. "They had us in this room, and I knew they were going to separate us. While Tianna was scratching the tracker out, everyone was talking about their significant others. I mentioned you. So damn glad I did."

"Me too."

"I want that."

"Want what?"

"I want to find her. She said her boyfriend is a retired NFL player."

"No shit?"

"No shit."

"Maybe he'll give me some memorabilia," Jock muttered. "For saving his woman."

Fiona laughed. "According to Tianna, that man is into her, like way into her. He'll probably give you his freaking Super Bowl ring."

Jock craned his neck to look at her. "Does her man have a freaking Super Bowl ring?"

"I don't know. They hard to get?"

Jock threw back his head and laughed. When he stopped, he held her gaze with a grin. "Yeah, they're kinda hard to get."

"I knew that," she said. "I just wanted to make you laugh."

"Succeeded."

"I wasn't sure I'd get to see you laugh again."

And there it was, leading right to the talk he knew they'd been heading for. "Wasn't sure I was going to laugh again, to tell you the truth."

She propped her chin up with her fist on his chest. "I'm glad you said what you did, before I left. I wanted to save the other girls and get back to you. I wasn't quite sure how I was going to manage, and for some time, I wasn't sure I could. But then I couldn't imagine you having to learn about something happening to me. Not after our talk."

"Not sure there'd be much left of me if something happened to you."

"Tell me," she said quietly, and he knew what she was asking. Still she explained. "I don't know about your family, or what you did before you became...this. You didn't come out of the womb six-foot-whatever-you-are with a scowl and a beard, did you?"

"No."

"Tell me," she whispered.

So he did. He told her about his mom, how she'd raised him and his brother on her own. How they'd been forced to be adults before they should have been. How Jock joined the Army at eighteen, and his brother got himself a scholarship for journalism because he was nosy and could write like a demon.

"Got deployed to Iraq and got in deep with a local terrorist cell. Dismantled them, but not enough. There were stragglers. My brother came over on his fucking own—freelance—to get the story of what my men and I did. Remaining terrorists of this cell figured out who he was, what he was to me, and they executed him."

She gasped, and her face went white as snow. Jerking to a kneeling position, she held the sheet to her chest and placed a hand on his. "Jamison, my God, I'm so sorry. I'm so, so sorry."

"That's how I met Roarke. I left the service, found some private contractors—ex-military—who were working off the grid. I was hired by them to take down the rest of these terrorists, and Roarke had been hired, too. We met, killed them all, and after that, I got drunk one night, told Roarke everything. It's why he asked me to help him with his brother. He knew."

Her hand was so warm on his chest, and for the first time, when he thought about it all, he didn't want to carve out his heart with a knife. It hurt, it fucking hurt so bad to spew those words, but he welcomed the pain because it was so much better than the numbness. How had he thought numb felt good? It wasn't good. Not at all.

So he placed his hand over Fiona's and said more. "Not the greatest man. Also spent some time as a hired hitman."

Her eyes bugged out. "I'm sorry?"

"I only took certain jobs, men who were shit criminals who slipped through the system, but it still wasn't good what I did—playing judge and jury. Did that for a few years then went back to freelance hacking. That's what I do now." His hacker name—Jock—along with Roarke's and Erick's—had been floating around the Dark Web for years. They were known as gray hat hackers, which meant they were willing to flirt with the law with their hacking if it resulted in the greater good.

Fiona's fingers curled into the hair on his chest, and her eyes shifted beyond his shoulder. He didn't panic, but he felt the anger rise. She'd fucking asked, hadn't she? He'd warned her…

"I told you," he said through clenched teeth, and her gaze shot to him. "Told you not to go digging. So if this is too much for you, then I fucking warned you. You wanna look at me now like I'm—"

She didn't let him finish, didn't let him work himself up into a rant. She pressed her lips to his. Then her other hand came up and brushed through the coarse hair on his face. "Stop," she whispered against his lips. She didn't have to say that. He was done. "I was processing. That's all. You said you're done with that?"

"Done," he answered swiftly.

"It's past," she said softly. She pulled back, and he noticed the sheet had dropped and pooled around her waist. Her gorgeous tits were on display, pink nipples begging for him to touch.

"J," she called softly.

He jerked his face back to hers. He wrapped his hands around her hips, picked her up, and settled her onto his lap. She squealed but didn't protest as her legs straddled him. She gave him a look that was a cross between an eye roll and a flirty side-eye. "I love you," he announced.

Her expression immediately warmed. "J..."

"I told you that shit, and I'm glad I did, but it's still there, still inside me, and it always will be. And that's something I guess we'll deal with over time. I don't know when it will happen, that something reminds me of him or the pictures I had to see of how he died, because straight up, it was ugly. And that's guilt I live with every day, that I'm the reason they took him."

"Jock—"

"I don't want to hear different because it doesn't matter. I'll feel guilt always. I feel guilt now having a woman like you in bed with me when what's left of my brother was cremated so I could scatter him in our hometown lake."

"You don't deserve to be miserable just because that happened to your brother. You don't deserve to live like a cyborg. You can be happy and still mourn him. The guilt and grief makes you human. And for a while there, I wasn't so sure you were human."

He laughed softly. "I wasn't so sure I was either."

"But you are," she leaned into him, so soft and so sweet, that blond hair all around them, blue eyes shining. "And I love you."

He kissed her again because he wasn't sure when he'd ever tire of it. Not ever. That kiss turned into more, where he worshipped her body until they both came.

After a dinner that they ate sprawled in bed, he tucked her into his side. She fell asleep first, but Jock stayed awake staring at the ceiling. There was something bothering him, something he was missing. He couldn't figure it out. He scrolled through his phone, checked all his contacts. He even texted Tarr, who didn't respond, so he figured he was out on a job.

Then Fiona burrowed further into his side. So he didn't bother her with the light of his cell, he turned it off and rolled into her. He slept, but he didn't sleep easy. Even though Chamberlain and all the men were in FBI custody, Jock wasn't taking any chances that Maximus would get word and issue another threat. Jock had an uneasy feeling the war had started, and it wouldn't be done until Maximus had touched every one of their crew. Tomorrow, Jock and Fiona needed to pack and get the fuck out, somewhere away from all of this. Then, maybe then, he'd relax.

* * *

Erick Lee sipped his coffee and set the travel mug down in the cup holder of his Challenger. He'd been on duty all night, watching Jock and Fiona's townhouse. Roarke had been worried about him when Erick volunteered to pull night duty, but Roarke didn't know Erick averaged three hours of sleep every night. He was fueled on coffee and a burning fire in his gut that he hadn't been able to extinguish ever since Flynn was killed. The hot anger was just there, flaming constantly, keeping Erick awake but riding a knife's edge of pain night and day.

So really, Jock and Fiona were doing him a favor letting him watch their townhouse, giving him something to do. He had his radio on, Princess Nokia's "G.O.A.T." playing softly.

Parked on their side of the street a few houses down, he kept his eyes on the house, constantly scanning. He knew Jock wasn't settled. Erick wasn't either. All online chatter showed that Maximus knew what had happened with Fiona and the FBI. Would Maximus retaliate? Erick had no fucking doubt. But for now, maybe they'd all get a reprieve. Still, he wasn't taking chances, which was why he was watching Fiona and Jock until they could get out of town.

Movement caught his eye in his side mirror. Something small was slinking across the road. The crouched prowl of the four-legged animal let him know it was a cat. Then it stopped suddenly and craned its neck over its shoulder, into the bushes alongside the townhouse beside Jock's.

Erick tensed and followed the cat's line of sight. He always listened to animals, goddamn always. They knew shit, could see and hear better than humans, and had a sixth sense. If that cat heard something in the bushes, then Erick was watching, too. Of course it could be a squirrel, a rat, another goddamn cat, but the more the feline in the road stared and hunched, the more Erick felt the hair rise on the back of his neck. Then the cat took off, running away at a dead sprint.

Fuck. Fuck him. He pulled his ball cap low over his eyes, grabbed his gun, and shoved it into the back of his jeans.

He'd parked where he did for a reason—he could duck out of the passenger side and immediately be surrounded by a line of trees that would lead him down to a backyard, where he could then sprint along the backs of a few houses until he reached Jock's. First, he'd check out what was moving in the bushes in the townhouse beside Jock's.

So with a deep breath—that was what he did—Erick scooted to the passenger side and opened the door enough for his wiry frame to slither out. He ran in a crouched position down the line of trees and across a few backyards, using more trees as his cover. When he reached the townhouse next to Jock's, he drew his gun.

The lights were off in this house. No sound, no nothing. Same with Jock's. This had probably been stupid. He glanced back at his car. No movement there either. He took a deep breath and raced to the corner of the townhouse. There he plastered himself against the wall, gun at the ready. He heard it then, the breathing. A human was breathing. What fucker was hiding in the bushes? What kind of low-rate shit was this?

Erick counted to three in his head and turned on his heel, gun drawn, voice firm. "Hands up."

The bushes moved. No human emerged. "Look motherfucker—"

He didn't get the rest of his threat out because a body crashed into his from the side. He swung his gun around, ready to fight, but he never got the chance. A face loomed over him, and all he caught were high cheekbones, full lips, and red hair curling out from around the edges of a baseball hat. Then something smashed into the side of his head and he wasn't seeing anything anymore.

CHAPTER TWENTY-TWO

JOCK opened his eyes with a start. Something was wrong. He felt it deep in his bones even as Fiona lay next to him, her head on his chest. He'd insisted she get dressed before she fell asleep, and now he was so damn glad he did.

He heard it then, a creak, one soft footfall somewhere in the house. Sundance was in the bedroom with them and perked his ears. Jock made two decisions. Save his woman and dog. While Sundance would defend them, he knew whoever was in that house knew what they were doing. They'd kill Sundance, and if Fiona saw her dog die in front of her she'd lose her mind. He slipped out from under the sheets, guided a confused Sundance into the adjoining bathroom, and locked the door. There. Done. Next was Fiona.

He heard another creak. The stairs. *Motherfucker*. He tugged his jeans on and shoved his gun in his back waistband. He shook Fiona, and her eyes blinked at him, a smile creeping across her face until she got a good look at his body language. Then she stilled, instantly alert. Yeah, she'd been through some shit and knew when it was going down.

"Someone's in the house. Gonna hide you. Do what I say."

She nodded. He picked her up and walked over to the

closet. The top shelf was narrow but sturdy enough to hold her. Crazy, because it wasn't as safe as he'd like but short of throwing her out the window, he had no choice. He pulled down a blanket, helped her climb onto the shelf, and shoved the blanket in front of her. She didn't say a word the whole time. "Hold that in front of you to cover yourself. Whatever you do, no matter fucking what, do not say a word. You hear me?"

"Jock," she finally whispered, her eyes shining wet and bright in the moonlight.

"Don't, Fiona."

She pressed her lips together and nodded.

"Trust me, baby."

"I do."

"Love you."

She choked out an, "I love you too," and then he closed the door. She'd be able to see through the downward angled slats through the closet door. If Jock went down, he wasn't confident she was hidden well enough. So he texted Roarke: *Got trouble, come quiet and armed.*

Jock didn't know how many were in the house or who'd sent them. All he knew was he felt bad intentions, as weird as that was to think. He took a moment to worry about Erick but couldn't dwell because he had to focus on himself. Still, he hoped to hell his buddy was okay.

He drew his gun and wrapped his palm around the grip, finger on the trigger. He stood with his back beside the bedroom door. And he waited.

Whoever was in his house was good. Not as good as him, or other men he'd worked with, but good. Anyone else wouldn't have heard a thing, wouldn't have felt what Jock felt. But Jock wasn't anyone else, and those two footfalls had given him a heads-up.

He went to that mental place where he'd been before Fiona, when he'd had to work, to kill, to hurt. He didn't want Fiona to see him like that but he had no choice, not if he wanted to keep them both alive. He kept his breathing steady and let his veins freeze over with the numbness he'd welcomed for so long.

The bedroom door didn't open. Jock watched the doorknob and waited. Based on his estimation from the sounds on the stairs, whoever was in the house should be at the door by now. Why weren't they opening it?

He stayed put, but his heart began racing, the ice not working like it used to, not when he had so much on the line, not when he knew Fiona's warm and very much alive body was in the room, counting on him to protect her.

Just when he considered walking out of the bedroom himself—something he didn't really want to do because then he'd be exposed at all angles, rather than here in the bedroom where he knew his back was safe, the doorknob began to turn. Slowly, ever so slowly. He hadn't locked it because it wasn't fucking normal to sleep with a locked bedroom door. He wanted this guy to think he and Fiona were still in bed. Easy hits.

Jock wasn't going to be a fucking easy hit. The door began to swing inward and still Jock waited, his gaze waiting for a body part, any fucking body part.

A foot came through first, clad in a big black boot. Jock took aim and fired right at the toe. Blood sprayed and a man screamed, "Mothershit!"

Jock flung the door open the rest of the way, pulling the body through and onto the ground. He brought his gun around, ready to finish off the job, when something cold pressed against his temple. "Don't, motherfucker."

Jock froze. The man on the ground writhed in pain, knee

pressed to his chest, dark liquid oozing out of his boot. Jock didn't move his gun, which was still trained on the guy's head, but he slowly looked out of the corner of his eye to see another man, watching him with cold, dark eyes.

As much as Jock wanted to finish off the guy on the floor, he couldn't. Then he'd get shot, and Fiona would be vulnerable. This, he knew, was about him—his hit leftover from his enemies after he'd taken out the terrorist cell that killed his brother. This was his past rearing up, big and ugly, and now it was putting Fiona at risk, too. He hoped they didn't know about her, and they kept their focus on their target—him.

Except Jock couldn't understand why the man with the gun trained on him hadn't pulled the trigger yet. If this was a hit, why wasn't Jock dead already? He didn't recognize either guy but that wasn't new. They all hid their faces to keep their identities a secret. Getting made meant getting dead. Still, the man on the ground smelled new, fresh, damn near amniotic. The man with his gun trained on Jock had the dead eyes of someone with experience. That made Jock happy because that meant the man wasn't going to be sloppy. But that made Jock not happy because that meant the man was good.

Sundance was losing his fucking mind in the bathroom, barking his damn head off, scratching at the door and throwing his body into it.

"Tell that dog to shut it, or I shoot it," the man with the gun announced.

"Sundance, enough!" Jock shouted.

Sundance stopped but continued to whine in a low tone. It seemed that was okay because the man didn't give another order.

"Fucking shoot him already!" the guy on the ground hollered. "He put a bullet in my foot!"

"Shut up," Dead Eyes said, not taking his eyes off Jock. "You'll be fine, and if you whine about it one more time, I'll put a bullet somewhere you won't whine about at all."

That shut up the injured guy fast.

"Now get the fuck up."

The man slowly stumbled to his feet and then with a sneer, reared back his fist and slammed it into Jock's stomach.

He saw it coming so he didn't tense. He absorbed the blow, and to be honest, it wasn't that bad. It took the breath out of him, but he could take a punch. He could take a lot.

Jock knew two things—one, he could maybe take these guys right now. If he failed he'd fuck up big. They'd find Fiona because her hiding place wasn't that great. So two, he had to let them do what they wanted to do. He had to let them draw it out, and he just hoped he was still breathing with all his limbs by the time Roarke came.

Dead Eyes cocked his head. "I know who you are, and you're not a dumb fuck. There a reason you're not fighting me in an effort to get dead quicker?"

Jock didn't say anything. He'd learned a long time ago that silence was best. Silence made people uncomfortable. Silence made people talk. Silence prevented Jock from saying anything they could interpret. Silence was hard to read, especially Jock's brand of cold, emotionless silence.

Dead Eyes was a professional, though. He held Jock's gaze for a long time before he shrugged and stepped back, gun still aimed at Jock's head. He wouldn't miss. Jock knew that as much as he knew he'd do anything for Fiona. Dead Eyes would not fucking miss.

"Get that chair," the man said, tossing his accomplice a rope. "Tie him to it, rope around his chest and the back of the chair. Rope holding his arms down on the arms. Don't fuck it up or he'll fuck *you* up. And I'll let him, before I put a bullet in his brain."

The man sneered at both of them and limped over to a plush armchair in the corner. He pushed it to the center of the room, and that's when it hit Jock that he should have left the bedroom. He should have kept them downstairs because now Fiona was going to see all of this. Jock hadn't thought about that, confident he could take on the intruder. Now Fiona would watch while they worked him over. And he worried she'd make a sound or worse—she'd climb out and yell at them to stop.

Jock let himself be pushed into the chair, and he rested his hands on the arms while the injured guy tied the rope around him, knotting it at the back with curses and mutters and promises of retribution.

Dead Eyes pulled a bundle out of his jacket pocket and laid it at the foot of the bed, the same bed Jock had just been in, holding Fiona tight to him. Dead Eyes unrolled the bundle to reveal a whole lotta knives and other instruments of pain. Jock stopped watching. He stared straight ahead, just as the injured man came around the front of him and clocked him hard in the temple. Pain exploded behind his eyes, but he didn't get close to losing consciousness. They wanted him awake for this, probably.

He heard the whisper of a knife leaving its pocket. He continued to stare straight ahead. He shut everything off. Everything. He had to. He couldn't focus on Fiona in the closet or anxiety over the pain to come. He had to get where he needed to be to get through this. He focused on one thing, and one thing only, and that was staying alive as long as possible.

Then Dead Eyes leaned into him with his hands clasping Jock's bound forearms on the arms of the chair. "Wondering why you're not dead yet?" He didn't wait for an answer, which was great, because Jock didn't intend to talk. "You're not dead yet," Dead Eyes said, "because when we took the hit on you, we were told to make a statement."

Jock didn't react. A statement meant they'd work him over, leave him a mess so whoever found his body— namely, his crew—would be scared shitless. Jock stared over the man's shoulder, refusing to make eye contact. Jock was starting to suspect the man behind his hit had changed from his old enemies to a more recent one, and that was enough to numb his body as ice froze in his veins.

"So, I was told to make a statement of you, and gotta be honest, I'm going to enjoy the fuck out of this. I also know the blond is somewhere in this house. I was told to make hers quick, but I'm not sure I'm too keen on this order after they showed me what she looks like. So I'm thinking I'll play with you for a bit, go find her, take her on this bed in front of you, and then finish both of you. Like that plan?"

They knew about Fiona. Jock fought not to show the fear he felt flooding his nerves.

"I just like everyone on the same page and to know what's going on." Dead Eyes leaned back and twirled the knife in his hand. He gripped the hilt and slammed it into the back of Jock's left hand.

Jock bit down on his cheeks so hard that he tasted blood. He didn't scream because that wasn't how Jock processed pain. His whole hand was a burning ball of agony, and it was traveling up his arm like it'd been ignited. But he went to that place in his head, the place where he separated his body from himself, where he was just as dead as the man who stabbed him. He didn't make a sound, but his chest strained against the ropes as he sought to inhale oxygen, his nostrils flaring.

"Ohhh, you're going to be one of those," Dead Eyes said, gingerly holding another knife, this one slightly curved. "You're going to be one I have to break."

Jock didn't bother to tell him there was nothing to break. He wouldn't scream ever. He'd just retreat further and further into himself until he couldn't remember his own name, until he was just flesh to poke.

This time, the knife went into his side. The man knew what he was doing. None of these were kill shots, and with the knives still plunged into his skin, he wouldn't bleed out either. There'd be fatal wounds later, but for now, the guy was playing. Just like he'd said he would.

The next one flicked at his nipple, enough to draw blood. The wet bead trickled down his ribs to pool in the waistband of his jeans. "You know what this is, right?" Dead Eyes asked as he perused Jock's body for his next cut.

Jock didn't answer.

"No one wanted to take your hit. It was about to expire, and then a whale came in and snatched it, re-upped the bounty. Wanna know who that whale is?"

Jock could guess. He didn't.

"Maximus," Dead Eyes said. He placed the knife at the corner of Jock's left eye and sliced right down his cheek.

Jock flared his nostrils at the pain and at that damn name. Maximus had told them he'd make them pay. Jock worried for the crew—Roarke and Erick, Marisol and Dade.

"Don't know what you fuckers did to him, didn't ask. Took the job because I'm out after this. Need a lotta cake to set me up for life. Thinking of moving to Sweden. Ever been there?"

Jock had. He didn't answer. He was having trouble breathing now. The knife in his side was leaking too much blood.

"I've never been." The other guy was all glee and friendship now that he was getting to watch Jock being worked over.

"Heard it's peaceful. I like peace," Dead Eyes said, picking up another curved knife. He stuck it into Jock's thigh, and for the first time, Jock wanted to howl in pain. There was nowhere that didn't hurt on his body. He felt his head list and had to focus through the haze of pain to stare straight ahead. Dead Eyes leaned in again and wiggled the knife in Jock's hand. "Heard the women there are fine as fuck. Your piece would fit right in. Maybe I'll change the plan and take her with me."

Jock fought to stay conscious as Dead Eyes tossed a knife in his gloved hand. He flicked a tip on Jock's ear, the part that was missing because Fiona had shot him. "Oh, see here? Ear is already damaged. Should we throw the whole ear away?"

"Absolutely," said the other man, who was standing too close to the closet doors for Jock's comfort. He shifted his gaze to the man for a brief moment, and the pain swamped in. The place he relied on to protect him wasn't working because Fiona had reminded him he had a heart, he had a core. He wasn't all ice like he tried to make himself believe.

Dead Eyes laid the knife at the top rim of his ear, where it connected to his head, but Jock was watching the other guy, who was now craning his neck to peer at the closet doors.

No. He didn't give a fuck about his ear, but they couldn't find Fiona. But if he gave anything away, they'd know. They'd fucking know. Helplessness swamped him, because this would be worse when Fiona was taken. It would be playing out in front of him, right here, and he wouldn't be able to do a goddamn thing about it. The man gripped the door of the closet and opened it.

A lot happened at once. Dead Eyes whirled around. "What the fuck?"

Something hard crashed to the ground from the closet, a form wrapped in a blanket, and Fiona emerged, gun in hand—where the fuck had she gotten a gun?—feet braced apart, eyes wild, hair a static mess sticking up at all angles.

"No!" Jock finally screamed, and her gaze came to him. Pain was etched there. Pain and anger and so much fucking fire that the look nearly incinerated him. Jock wasn't seeing so well, but he saw enough to know he'd love that woman for the rest of his life, whether the rest of his life lasted only the next ten minutes or the next fifty years.

Fiona was brave as fuck, but she was one person, and there were two men in the room, both armed.

"Don't move!" she shouted, but like they were going to fucking listen. Jock surged against the ropes binding him, the knives holding him in place to the chair. But he couldn't do anything. Fiona fired at the injured guy, but her aim sucked, even from close up, because she was shaking so goddamn bad. He knocked the gun out of her hand and wrapped her up in his arms. She fought, kicking and screeching, setting Sundance off a-fucking-gain. Dead Eyes stalked toward the bathroom just as the other man threw Fiona on the bed with a gleam in his eye that had Jock's stomach sinking into the floorboards.

Except Dead Eyes never reached the bathroom door. The other guy never even got to unzip his pants as he intended.

A nearly silent *zrip* sounded near Jock's head, and the man standing over Fiona jerked, the back of his head exploding in blood and bone as he collapsed. Fiona screamed, Jock jerked. Another *zrip* rent the air, and Dead Eyes went down, a hole in the back of his head, forehead blown out. He was dead before he hit the floor.

Jock's muscles weren't working well, but he turned his head to see Tarr standing in the doorway, holding a gun with a silencer at his side. His eyes were in shadow from his ball cap rim, but Jock knew that mouth, those wide shoulders, that red hair curling a bit beneath his hat. "Fuck," was all the man uttered. He went to a knee at Jock's side and slashed through the ropes with one of Dead Eyes's knives. "Jock, you with me? You okay?"

"Fiona," he murmured, and then she was there at his side, crying hysterically, her hands shaking as she kept reaching out to touch him before pulling back. Finally she cradled his face, the side Dead Eyes hadn't carved up. The sobs wracked her body so hard she couldn't speak. "You okay?" he asked, and her head bobbed until finally she choked out, "Jock."

"I'm all right," he muttered. His body felt warm, kinda soft. He wasn't so sure he was all right, but he had to reassure her. Tarr was on the phone, rasping out a couple of short words.

"How did you...how?" Jock mumbled.

"Told you I'd keep an eye on you. By the way, the guy in the Challenger? Lured him from his car and knocked him out because they were going to kill him. Apologies for that, but he's got a lump instead of a toe tag, so maybe he'll find it in him to forgive me."

"Erick's okay?" Fiona asked.

"Fine. I laid him out downstairs on the couch on my way in. He'll wake up soon. Called your crew. They know what happened. Now I gotta go."

"Go?" Fiona shrieked.

"Oh yeah, called 911 too. Don't care how you explain this, that's on you. I kept you alive."

"We're even," Jock mumbled. "Debt paid."

"Never paid," Tarr said on a near-silent whisper. He didn't touch Jock but instead gave him a salute. "You'll be okay. Help's coming." He pointed to Jock's face. "Scar will look badass." Then he shoved up the bedroom window and stuck a foot through and disappeared.

Jock tried to focus on Fiona but there were two of her. Maybe three? He was floating now. Were they on vacation? Yeah, that was it. He was in a swimming pool, Fiona was walking toward him in a bikini, holding drinks with umbrellas that he planned to gulp down like shots, not caring they were girly.

"Like that bikini, baby," he muttered.

"What?" She was sobbing, her hands fluttering over him like butterflies. Why was she crying? Where did the drinks go?

"I'll get next drinks," he said, but the words didn't sound right, slurred.

"Jock!" she screamed, but he was underwater and he couldn't hear a thing.

CHAPTER TWENTY-THREE

THE two minutes and thirty seconds she spent in that bedroom with two dead men, a frantic dog, and an unconscious Jock were the longest of Fiona's life. There was blood everywhere... so much blood. She stripped the sheets, tearing them with her teeth and pressing them to all the places where Jock was leaking blood. Sometimes he'd stir and his lips would move, but other than that he sat with his head hung between his shoulders.

She barely kept her shit together. She talked to him, assuring him he was going to be okay because, if she didn't keep busy, keep talking, she knew she'd be catatonic in the corner in the fetal position. She had to be strong for Jock. If it was her in the chair, he wouldn't give up, and he wouldn't break down.

Thank God that Jock had insisted she keep her feet bandaged with heavy socks because she was walking in a mixture of blood...

She shivered and pressed a strip of sheet to his face. His beautiful, proud, Viking face that that fucker had carved. If she'd wanted to leave Jock's side, she would have gone over to that sick fucker and kicked him.

She stroked Jock's hair just as the rumble of a muscle

car sounded on the street. She knew that engine—it was Roarke's. The car shut off just as sirens sounded in the distance. She took Jock's pulse but didn't know enough to tell if it was weak or strong. All she knew was that it was there, his heart was beating, and he was breathing.

Roarke and Wren were at the door in less than thirty seconds. Roarke skidded to a halt, hands on the doorframe, while Wren ran into the back of him and peered into the room.

Roarke's eyes were huge, and Fiona wondered what the fuck he was thinking. "Help" was all she said, one ragged word that sliced up her throat like razor blades.

"Oh, Fi." Wren's hand covered her mouth as Roarke stepped to Jock's side, checking his pulse and running his hands over his friend's body. "Fuck, fuck, fuck. Erick is downstairs laid out on the couch like he's taking a nap, but he's got a massive lump on his head. What the fuck happened here?"

"Someone Jock knows…" Fiona wrung her hands, staring at the blood on them, so much blood, so fucking red.

"Fi." Wren's voice brought her back to focus.

"Someone he knows knocked Erick out so these two men didn't kill him, then he came up here in the middle of…this." She gestured to Jock's body as another sob rocked her. "He killed them both, then jumped out the window. Gone."

"Jesus," Roarke said. "We'll deal with that later."

The sirens were screaming now, sounding like they were right outside the house, thank fuck. Roarke took off downstairs and returned with two paramedics who took one look at the room and swore. They immediately tended to Jock, but just the sight of them touching his body was enough to cause Fiona's heart to beat out of her chest. Jock would hate that, fucking hate strange people touching him, handling him, talking to him. Oh God, he'd hate this so much.

He'd done this for her. He'd stayed silent and let them stick knives in him because he'd been stalling. She had enough presence of mind to know that. Her J.

The paramedics stayed calm as they worked on extricating him from the chair. The knives were embedded in the wood, and they had to pull them out in order to get Jock's body loose. But the jostling was causing more bleeding, and as each second ticked by Fiona felt more out of control.

They wrapped a cuff around his arm, and then one paramedic looked the other in the eye, communicating something that Fiona could tell was not good. "What?" she screeched, surging off the bed where Wren had been holding her. "Is he okay?"

"Ma'am, I know this is hard, but we need you to calm down so we can do our jobs."

"He has to be okay!" she screamed, knowing she had to shut up but not able to. "He has to be, he has to be!"

Roarke was at her side now, trying to get her to sit down, but she fought him. Kicked and scratched as she saw them lower Jock's body onto a gurney. What if they took him away and this was the last time she saw him? What if...

She fought harder and didn't calm until she felt a slight pinprick in her arm, and then her body was heavier...was she floating? She was floating. She sank into a cloud and she slept.

* * *

Fiona sat in a chair with her knees hugged to her chest and kept her eyes on Jock, where he lay in the hospital bed. She hated seeing him like this, but she'd also seen him with multiple knives sticking out of him. Hooked up to an IV, clean and bandaged, was preferable. He was breathing, heart beating, sleeping. He was alive.

She'd heard he'd woken up briefly when they'd first got him to the hospital and pumped him full of blood. His only word had been *Fiona*, and Roarke had assured him that Fiona was fine, just sleeping off a sedative. Jock had stayed conscious long enough to answer a few questions, and then passed right back out.

Watching Jock sit in that chair while those men hurt him, absorbing the pain with a blank face, would forever be one of the worst things Fiona would ever witness. He'd been so strong, and part of her had wanted him to cry out, let it go, rage and thrash and be angry. But he hadn't; he'd sat there like he was a pincushion made to bleed. It had nearly killed her.

She'd remembered that he'd shoved her purse on the shelf, the one with her gun. So as silently as she could, she'd pulled out the gun. Of course the one guy had heard her so she'd had no choice but to draw the gun on them, although it hadn't been effective. She didn't want to think about how badly it could have ended.

Jock's hand twitched and she reached out, lacing her fingers with his. "J," she called. His eyes worked beneath his closed eyelids, and his forehead creased. She didn't want to wake him up before he was ready, but damn she wanted to see those eyes.

She untucked her knees, dropped her feet to the floor, and pressed a kiss to his hand, the one they'd stabbed, right below his bandage so her lips touched skin.

When she lifted her head his eyes were open. His one cheek was covered in a bandage where that freak had cut him, but his eyes were uncovered and open, just slightly swollen. His gaze roamed her face, and as he tracked her body, squeezing her fingers as he did so, his eyes warmed, that peace returning, the one they'd had for a brief moment the night before, before everything had gone to hell.

"Baby," he murmured.

She'd told herself she wouldn't cry, that she'd done enough, that she was tired of hysterical Fiona, but damn, the tears burned in the back of her eyes and she couldn't help it. At least they rolled down her cheeks silently and she wasn't sobbing.

He tugged on her hand and winced.

"Don't," she said, sliding her chair closer. "Don't move. You have…lots of bandages, and stitches." She reached out to touch his face but drew her hand back.

Something flickered in his eyes, a wave of uncertainty. "Not gonna be pretty anymore."

Seriously? He was worried about that? She narrowed her eyes. "You were never pretty and I still fell in love with you," she shot back.

He tried to grin despite the bandage on his face. "There's the fire."

"Damn right, saying stupid shit like that. You took stab wounds for me, you dumbass. You're never getting rid of me now. Not ever."

"Don't wanna get rid of you."

Then the tears burned again. "I was so scared," she whispered, and just like that the humor fled his face.

"Fiona…"

"You didn't move, didn't make a sound. Hell, I thought you were dead already."

He shook his head. "Checked out. Had to do it. Didn't do so well because I was worried about you the whole time."

"That was horrible." She wasn't whispering anymore.

Now she was halfway to anger. "I don't ever want to go through that again."

"Baby, my job..."

"I know, I know. And I'm not telling you not to do...whatever it is you do. But I need a vacation from this for now. Somewhere we can go, just the two of us, and forget about rapists and hit men, and all this other shit, and just be us. An us without the drama."

"Beach," he said firmly.

"What?"

"Beach. Drinks with umbrellas. Hot as fuck. You in a string bikini. Hotel with one of those balcony curtains that blows in the breeze while we fuck on a big bed."

She wanted that. Goddamn she wanted that. "You need to rest..."

"I'll fucking rest," he griped. "You think that I won't heal like a motherfucker if I know I get you in a bikini at the end?"

"You're not a superhero. You can't speed up the healing process." She glared at him.

And just like that, he gave her a gift she hadn't been sure she'd ever get again. He laughed. His long, loud Jock laugh that tapered off quickly because he grimaced with pain. "Don't make me laugh."

"Don't act like you're Wolverine then, Jock."

"You promise I get you in a bikini?"

"I'll wear any goddamn thing you want if you heal and take me to a beach, feed me, and fuck me."

"Done," he announced.

She pressed her lips together so she wouldn't cry again. After so many years of only existing...she was living again. Looking forward to a future with a man who she could barely believe was real.

"Black." His voice cut through her thoughts.

"Sorry?"

"Black bikini. Just plain black. But it's gotta be strings. The kind you tie at the sides that makes every man imagine slipping his fingers through the loop and watching it come undone."

She couldn't breathe. He'd been stabbed for her and nearly died, and he was talking about damn bikinis. "Jock."

"But none of them are gonna be thinking it, or at least they won't be doing much looking because I'm going to be next to you, and once these bandages come off I'm going to look even scarier."

She pressed her lips together and tried not to laugh. "This is true. You're scary on a good day."

"Great. Scars will up my cred."

"I love you," she said abruptly.

His gaze swung to her and held. "Baby."

"I can't wait to live life with you."

"Can't wait to live life with you either."

She leaned in and pressed a kiss to his lips. When he whispered, "Love you," a single tear of hers fell onto his bandage. It was a happy tear.

* * *

Jock stood in Marisol's kitchen while she flew around the room making enough *carnitas*, rice, and beans to feed an army. When he told her that, she snapped, "We are practically an army!" And he couldn't disagree so he shut up.

Fiona stood tucked into his side, something she didn't do because she felt like she couldn't be without him. She did it because he liked her there and she liked to be there. They were leaving the next day to go to an all-inclusive resort in Barbados, and he couldn't fucking wait. Neither of them had wanted to return to that damn townhouse so they'd been renting a hotel room since he'd been released from the hospital. Roarke, Wren, Marisol, and Erick had moved everything from the townhouse into storage. After Barbados...well, they hadn't gotten that far yet. They'd come back, maybe get a place in DC. Neither were in a rush because Jock still hadn't stopped talking about Fiona in a bikini.

He'd seen her luggage—she'd packed ten bikinis and seven of them were all black.

Erick waltzed into the kitchen, gave Marisol a squeeze, and grabbed a beer out of the fridge. He no longer had a lump on his head from being knocked out by Tarr, but he was no less pissed. Even now he leaned against the counter and eyed Jock. "Heard from your friend?"

Jock shook his head. Tarr had gone underground. Unsurprising, as they'd gotten word Maximus had bought Jock's hit and hired the men Tarr had killed. Maximus had also gone silent, and Jock was sure the silence wouldn't last. But Jock would take advantage of it now, and get the fuck out of town. The rest of the crew was going to do the same. Jock didn't expect Maximus would send someone after them right now. He'd lick his wounds and prepare another attack. This was definitely the start of a war.

Erick scrunched up his nose in irritation. "I still want to know what the fuck that was about. Why knock me out? Why not give me a chance to help him? Two against one? Shitty odds."

"You don't know Tarr," Jock explained. "Works alone. Always. While I don't necessarily agree with what he did, he did keep you alive."

"He gave me a concussion."

"You're alive," Jock repeated. Erick still looked pissed. He also looked like he was scheming, and Jock didn't like that look. "Erick, do not dig."

Erick tried to appear jovial, but Jock could see something lurking under that. "Dig? Me? Nah, I'm cool."

"Erick, you do not want Tarr's attention."

He took a long sip of his beer. "I'm thinking it's a little late for that."

Jock watched him for a beat. "Why do you say that?"

Erick grinned. "Nothing, just saying, we've already met."

"That's not what you meant."

"Sure it is."

"Erick!"

"Can't wait for dinner, Marisol." Erick took another sip of beer and walked out of the kitchen whistling.

Jock looked to the ceiling and closed his eyes. "Jesus fucking Christ. I just want a vacation."

Fiona laid her hand on his chest. "You'll get one."

"I fucking better."

"The flight leaves tomorrow, and that plane is in the air even if I have to fly it myself."

"Can you fly a plane, baby?"

"They're all automatic now, right? I'm sure I can figure it out." She grinned up at him, and he'd just lowered his head to kiss her when Marisol clapped, startling him.

"No making out in the kitchen," she announced. "It's unsanitary, and I also don't want to look at it. Shoo!"

She waved them out of the kitchen, and they wandered out where Wren and Roarke were sitting on the couch playing *Call of Duty*. Erick sat nearby, cheering them on.

The doorbell rang and Jock frowned.

"Can someone get that?" Marisol called from the kitchen. "Or you're all gonna stuff down burned rice."

"Who is it?" Jock asked.

"Answer it and you'll see!" Marisol shouted back.

Fiona left his side to sit next to Wren, and Jock looked through the peephole. Dade stood on the doorstep. He opened the door and leaned against the frame. "Kelly."

Dade looked up and his face was clear of bruises, but his hair was dyed a dark brown, nearly black. "Jock."

"Joining us for dinner?"

"Marisol invited me." He stepped inside so Jock had no choice but to step back. "Heard about what happened. Glad to see you're healing."

"Taking a vacation with Fiona tomorrow," Jock offered, but he wasn't sure why. Maybe because he just couldn't stop talking about it.

Dade grinned, but same as Erick, that grin was covering something else. "Good, glad to hear it."

He made to walk past Jock, but Jock stopped him, his fingers on Dade's biceps. Dade looked at his hand and lifted narrowed eyes to Jock. "What?" he bit out.

"You have something to do with Tarr showing up?"

Dade was a good actor, but he was a little off his game. He was in a friend's home and so his armor wasn't all in place. Which was why Jock saw surprise register on Dade's face. Surprise and a bit of satisfaction before he shut it down. "Don't know what you're talking about."

"You're telling me Tarr figured all of that out on his own? How many men, their plans, the time and place?"

"Tarr's a smart guy."

"Sure he is, but he's not that smart. Doesn't have all that access."

"Guess he's got some friends, then. Friends with access." Dade held Jock's gaze but said nothing more. That was all Jock was getting, but it was all he needed. He didn't know why Dade had decided to continue to tie himself to this crew, but Jock wasn't going to complain. Dade, along with Tarr, had most likely saved his life.

"All right, if that's how you want to play it," Jock said quietly.

"Not playing anything," Dade snapped. "Can you let go of my arm now?"

His tone amused Jock, but Jock tried not to let it show. He dropped Dade's arm. "Sure. Everyone's in the living room."

Dade's eyes slid over Jock, and he walked past him into the living room. When Jock hit the room, Dade was standing next to Fiona. She was smiling up at him, turning all the fire and sweet that was Fiona onto Dade.

Dade was smiling back, a warm smile Jock hadn't known Dade was capable of. And it hit Jock that women were a bit of weakness for Dade. He loved them, and not in a way that meant he wanted to own them, control them, or fuck them—at least not these women in his life—but he loved them in a way that meant he wanted them safe and protected. Dade took care of Wren, and now he'd take care of Fiona. The men in the crew—he'd help them, too, but probably only because it made the women happy.

Filing that information away, Jock moved to take the seat next to Roarke. He'd stopped playing, letting the controller dangle from his hand to take a sip of his beer. "How's the body doing?" he asked.

"Stiff sometimes," Jock answered. Fiona insisted he massage his scars to prevent scar tissue buildup and had him lather them with scar cream. He couldn't understand what the big deal was. What did scars matter? He'd asked her that recently and explained that he thought chicks dug scars. And she'd glared at him and then told him that was exactly why she was so adamant. "No chicks will be digging your scars except me!" she'd snapped at him, eyes flaming.

He'd stopped complaining after that and practically bathed in the scar cream because it made her happy.

He met her eyes on the other side of the room. She grinned, he grinned back, and he leaned against the sofa, closed his eyes, and enjoyed the quiet murmur of his friends' chatter until Marisol's voice cut through it all. "Asses at the table. Food's coming up!"

EPILOGUE

AN hour into the vacation Jock decided he was buying a beach house somewhere hot as fuck just so he could see Fiona in a bikini more often.

He'd thought his presence would deter assholes from looking at her but it did not, and therefore he also decided that this future house he planned to purchase would be on a private beach. He glared at an older man who looked like an attorney, who had his eyes on Fiona's ass while she walked toward Jock. Jock had his arms on the edge of the pool, body in the water, watching his girlfriend walk toward him. She held two drinks with pink liquid, both with umbrellas.

Tarr was on the phone, bitching into Jock's ear. "Tell Erick to back off."

Jock sighed. "I did."

"He's not listening."

"I'm not his keeper."

"Jock—"

"Erick doesn't wish you harm, but he's curious. He's nosey. That's what he does for a living, and to be honest, he might play with you for a bit. He likes pranks."

"I fucking don't," Tarr said.

"Just ignore him," Jock advised, not sure if that would work or not.

"Fucking ridiculous."

"Look, I got Fiona about to hand me a pink drink with an umbrella in it, and so I'm done with this conversation."

Tarr spoke again, and when he did, there was a smile in his voice. "Pink drink with an umbrella, huh?"

"Yup."

"Looks like you're living the high life."

"You bet."

"I'll let you go." And then Tarr was gone.

Fiona stood above him grinning, probably because the drink was pink and she'd probably flashed the bartender a smile to make the umbrellas pink, too.

She dropped to a crouch and sipped one and then closed her eyes. "Oh my God, this is good."

He took the other drink from her. "What is it?"

"I don't know. I told him to make me something pink and fruity."

He took a sip. It was definitely pink and fruity, and rum-based. It was also fucking good. He ditched the straw and took a gulp, crunching a cube of ice between his teeth. He set his drink down and beckoned to Fiona. "Sit."

She took a seat at the edge of the pool, and he immediately slipped between her legs where they dangled in the water. He snaked his hands around and cupped her ass. She widened her eyes at him and choked mid-sip. "J."

"Don't."

"We are in public."

"Yeah, and that guy behind you is liking your bikini too much. Rethinking my request on these bikinis, babe."

She rolled her eyes. "You didn't complain an hour ago when I put it on. You immediately took it off, and now I finally have it back on again."

He grinned. "True."

She leaned down and pressed a kiss to his forehead, right at the edge of his healed cut that would in fact scar like fuck. "Every woman in this resort looks at you, and I don't get all macho."

"They do not."

"Do too. You're just too busy scowling at their men to notice."

"Then their men shouldn't look at you."

"Jock."

"Fiona."

They went into a stare down, but amusement glittered in Fiona's eyes. God, she was beautiful. He pressed a kiss to the inside of her knee and watched her eyelids dip, even though he'd just been between her legs an hour ago. "J," she breathed, and he kissed her other knee.

"Stop, I want to finish my drink, not have you drag me back to the room caveman-style." She huffed and closed her lips around her straw.

She was right. He drank more, and when she was finished, he coaxed her into the pool with him. She came, heated wet skin, legs wrapped around his waist, arms clutching his shoulders. He spun them, and she made a small squeal as the water lapped at their bodies. He kissed her shoulder. He kissed a lot of places because he could.

"Who was that on the phone?"

"Tarr."

She blinked, not expecting that, and for a moment he

saw the pain flash, the memory of what had happened, before she shut it down. "So he's okay?"

"Wouldn't have picked up his call because I'm here with you, but I wanted to make sure he was okay. He is, and he's pissed."

"Why?"

"Because Erick is sniffing around."

Her mouth formed an O.

"I told him to relax. Erick likes to know who pulls one over on him."

"What's your history with Tarr?" she asked.

He hadn't told her yet. "It's a long story. I'll tell you sometime when I don't have you happy and drinking and in a bikini. But short story is that I took a bullet for his sister, and he loves his sister. She's alive and happy and now making him an uncle for the third time, and so he thinks he owes me."

"J," she said, voice full of wonder and admiration, and it made him hard. In the pool. In public.

"Don't say my name like that unless you want to leave this pool and lock the door to our room."

She pursed her lips and gave him a look.

He changed the subject. "Texted Wren, let her know we made it down okay."

"Oh, I forgot. Thanks for doing that." Her hands played with his hair at his nape, hair that was too long. He was thinking of finding a barber on the resort to take care of it for him.

"When we get back, do you want to be near your girl?"

"I thought Roarke and Wren weren't in DC much."

"They're not, but that's where they're based. When they come home, they do it there. Marisol also stays there now, and she's kind of fond of you."

MEGAN ERICKSON

"I love her," Fiona said. "And watching you two fight is entertaining."

"Bicker."

"What?"

"We don't fight, we bicker."

"Whatever," Fiona laughed.

"We'll stay in DC then," he decided.

She didn't say anything, just made a happy sound.

"And we'll travel a lot," he said.

That earned him a, "I'd like that. Maybe Indiana."

He froze. "What?"

"Visit your mom."

"Fi—"

"I'd like to meet her." She wasn't backing down. "We don't have to stay. We can pass on through, but we should stop in and say hi. She lost one son, don't make yourself lost to her, too."

"You don't know her," he said tersely.

"No, I don't. But sounds like you two don't know each other so well either. People change, J. Our mistakes, our decisions, everything in our past changes us, and you and I know that more than most."

She was right, damn it. "Fine, we'll visit."

That earned him Fiona's tits pressed tight against his chest and her breath in his ear. "Love you, J."

"Love you too."

"And I love this vacation."

Jock didn't say anything because yes, this vacation was the shit, and there wasn't a lot not to love.

Then she went and did it. "Thank you, J," she said into his ear.

He lasted another fifteen minutes before he got them drinks to go and dragged her back to the hotel room. Then he proceeded to take off the bikini, and they didn't put clothes back on for the rest of the day.

When she was asleep in his arms that night, he stared at the ceiling. He did it grinning, and then he said to her closed eyelids, "No, thank *you*."

DID YOU MISS THE FIRST NAIL-BITING MISSION IN
THE WIRED & DANGEROUS SERIES?

HACKER EXTRAORDINAIRE ROARKE BRENNAN LIVES EACH
HOUR—EACH BREATH—TO AVENGE HIS BROTHER'S
MURDER. ONLY NOW WREN LEE WANTS IN TOO...AND
SHE'S THE WILD CARD HE CAN'T CONTROL.

PLEASE SEE THE NEXT PAGE FOR
AN EXCERPT FROM *ZERO HOUR*.

ROARKE stared at his orange juice, wishing there was vodka in it. Anything to calm his trembling hands. He'd slept like shit last night and was paying for it this morning with frayed nerves.

His apartment in Northeast DC was his safe haven. One thirty-foot room on the first floor of an old warehouse with a kitchen on one side, a sitting area in the middle, his bedroom at the far end, and his bathroom with a shower stall behind a curtain. Normally he came here to clear his head, to forget about the last mission he'd completed before he had to focus on the next one. But now everything about this place made him think of his brother. So he wanted to burn it all to the ground.

Flynn's laptop sat on the scarred wooden table. On the lid was a peeling Green Day sticker and a scratch along the side where he'd dropped it on the sidewalk outside his apartment. Roarke remembered that day because he'd been juggling his Italian sub along with Flynn's pastrami on rye while Flynn fretted over his laptop.

Growing up, they'd always had each other's backs. Their parents died in a car accident when they were kids, and so their legal guardian was Uncle Frank, their mother's brother, who worked at a local factory. Frank made it clear from the first curl of his lip while he blew cigarette smoke in their faces that their presence wasn't wanted in his home, but he was happy to *hold on* to the money left to Roarke and Erick by their parents.

It was a mindfuck to go through the formative years of your life feeling like a burden. Flynn had been so young, and while he understood more than Frank probably thought he did, Roarke made it his life mission to be his brother's shield. All of Frank's hissed words, his derision, his utter contempt at having to provide their basic needs—Roarke stayed on the front lines of it all. He'd covered the inner scars with the ink on his outer skin, but it hadn't helped much.

When Roarke was old enough, he'd thrown himself into the Web—fandoms, chat rooms, any place where he could feel like he fit in. When he found a coding tutorial, he felt like he'd found a home. Within a year, he was doing minor hacks for pranks. As a teen, he did everything from hack into radio show phone lines to ensure he was the fifth caller for Pearl Jam tickets to writing open source code for other hackers to use. Of course, he'd gone too far once, and ever since he'd done his best to stay within the law.

He'd been so proud when he'd shown Flynn some basic programming skills and Flynn showed natural talent. It gave them something to bond over, something that shut out the outside world. Roarke had scored a pair of old laptops for cheap when his school sold them because they'd upgraded the staff's equipment. So he and Flynn sat huddled in the bedroom they shared, threadbare carpet beneath their toes and paint peeling around their heads. And they'd learned how to be a couple of the most elite hackers on the eastern seaboard. They'd been just kids, and it'd all been fun and games at the time, until it wasn't.

Roarke downed the rest of his orange juice and juggled the glass between his palms. Flynn's face flashed in front of his eyes, and Roarke swore he could feel the heat of Flynn's arms as he gave him one of his famous Flynn hugs.

He cocked his hand and threw his glass at the brick wall opposite him.

The crash and subsequent rain of glass shattered the silence. Juice and pulp dripped from the bricks as Roarke stood there, clenching and unclenching his fists as the anger burned through him, hot, bright, and sharp.

Roarke was a fixer. Flynn had called him that. If there was a problem, he fixed it. He wasn't about empty promises or platitudes. But he couldn't fix Flynn. He couldn't bring him back, and the helplessness was nearly crippling. Flynn, his little brother, with his big, white grin and lanky limbs and infectious laugh, was dead. He'd failed to protect him, and the way to get revenge was to place in danger another person he cared about—Wren.

He closed his eyes and pictured how she looked last night, lavender hair framing her face, those bright red lips, that fucking body he couldn't help but touch.

He'd crushed on her as a teen, but as an adult, he fucking *wanted* her, like he'd never wanted anyone before, and wasn't sure he'd ever want anyone else in his life. When all he'd had of her was links and lines of code, he could handle it, but now that she was back, in the flesh, all the rules he'd set for himself regarding her were breaking apart.

Roarke had seen Darren Saltner a couple of times. He was a smarmy bastard. His touching her, flirting with her, thinking he was worthy of her attention was like a vice in

Roarke's chest. He'd wanted that to be his touch, his hands between her legs.

Fuck, he was an asshole.

As a teenager, he'd tried to ignore the gorgeous, charming younger sister of his best friend. He'd practiced his scowling in the mirror, as if it would ward off everything he was feeling for her, but it never worked. She'd tagged along with him and Erick, asking questions about programming. She smiled and laughed and always smelled like a dream—*how did women always smell so good?*

So he did what a fuckhead teenage techie who was crushing hard on a girl did. He hacked into her online journal. Total dick move. He squirmed every time he thought about it.

He didn't know what he was looking for, maybe a poem where she professed her love for him? He sure as fuck didn't find that. He found a whole manifesto about what she wanted for her future—a husband and three kids and a happy domestic life with a house in the suburbs and a dogwood in the front yard.

That wasn't him. Even at sixteen, he knew that was never going to be him. Erick and their parents placed her on a pedestal, and he didn't want to be the person who dragged her off it.

So he'd turned off the part of him that wanted Wren. That hadn't stopped him from tracking her life as best as he could from behind a monitor. So maybe he'd done a little puppet mastering behind the scenes and made sure Wren never saw the strings. Watching her life for ten years through a web of links was not satisfying, but it'd been all he had.

Which was why it burned him that he hadn't known what she'd been up to with Dade. Dade Fucking Kelly.

With a frustrated growl, he turned away from the mess he'd made and sagged against the wall until his jean-clad ass touched the floor. He stared at his bare feet, a roaring lion inked on the top of one and a sleeping lion on the other.

So Wren was back, and she'd changed, but he hadn't. He'd known since he was thirteen that he'd never have a normal life with a nine-to-five job. He'd always wanted to travel and play a little fast and loose with his profession. Hell, he paid taxes on only about a third of his income. The government thought he was a landlord. They had no idea his main source of income was from hacking. *Hacktivism* was the term he preferred, or white hat hacking. He wasn't a criminal. He maybe did criminal *things*, but it was all in an effort to defeat the real bad motherfuckers.

Flynn had been his sidekick, along with Erick, since they were teenagers. A couple of years ago, Flynn had said he wanted to get straight, have a family, and be an active member of society. So he got a job at Saltner Defense—a computer security software company—where he'd planned to work and pay taxes and fit into the general population.

Until he uncovered something he wasn't supposed to and paid for it with his life.

Roarke stared at his hands, where GAME OVER was tattooed on his knuckles. He cracked them, deep breathing to get himself under control before the hot rush of anger took over and he *did* actually burn his apartment down.

After glancing at his watch, he rose to his feet. He had a half hour to cross town to where his team was meeting in the basement of a warehouse he owned.

He finished getting ready, grabbed a can of his ever-present addiction, Diet Coke, for the road, and was in his vintage Mustang within five minutes.

Roarke owned an old warehouse in Southeast near the Anacostia waterfront. When he arrived, he tossed his empty soda can into the dumpster and entered the code to the door. The keypad beeped, and he opened the heavy metal door. It latched shut behind him as he descended the stairs that would lead him underground. After another code and another door, he entered the room where the team was gathering. There he found Jock, their best programmer, hunched over his computer at the single conference-style table in the corner of the room.

Jock glanced up, his blue eyes taking in Roarke's appearance before he nodded and resumed whatever he was working on. The man had earned the name Jock long before Roarke met him; it was a hacking term that meant using brute force tactics. One look at the six-four, two-hundred-fifty-pound Jock and anyone could see the name fit.

Roarke met Jock—real name Jamison Bosh—on a job a couple of years ago when they were hired to hack into a terrorist cell's network. Jock was a silent mastermind, stoically dismantling the cell's communications until the leader lost contact with his team. It wasn't until later that Roarke learned Jock's brother—while on deployment—had been killed by the cell. He'd shown zero emotion, and when the task was done, he'd walked away.

He knew Jock would understand why this was so important, to avenge the loss of his brother just like Jock had done. When Roarke asked the man to participate, he hadn't hesitated.

Marisol Rosa was the next to show up, the buckles on her black boots rattling as she stomped her way across the concrete floor. She blew a bubble of pink gum and popped it with a click of her teeth as she tilted her head. Her purple hair was shaved on one side and long on the other, so it draped over an eye as she took him in with purple contact-colored eyes. "What's good, Brennan?"

He could never figure out if she was coming on to him or punking him. Gender didn't matter to Marisol when it came to loving and fucking, so it was anyone's guess. "Pissed off."

She grinned at him. "Wouldn't want you any other way." After winking, she sauntered over to where Jock sat. She hopped onto the desk beside his computer, where she perched with her legs swinging. "Can I touch your beard?"

He didn't acknowledge her presence. She shrugged and smacked her gum. "Guess that's a no."

Marisol was a little unpredictable, but she was loyal and crafty. She grew up in the Bronx surrounded by her Puerto Rican family, who had no idea they had a social-engineering mastermind in their midst. Marisol had an uncanny ability to ferret out information from anyone and could change her appearance and personality easily to slip into situations. Hacking wasn't just coding, it involved using people skills. The greatest security threat was human stupidity, and Marisol had a lock on finding the weakest links. That wasn't even getting into her coding skills, for which she'd served three years in the New Jersey prison system. She operated legally now, mostly, and Roarke had worked with her recently on a server's security breach. She'd outsmarted every offense the hackers had thrown at her, smiling the whole time. It was all a game to her. But it was a game she played to win.

Voices drew Roarke's attention, and he turned to see Erick trudge inside, dark circles under his eyes. He glanced at Roarke and jerked a thumb behind him. "So she wore you down, huh?"

Roarke shifted his gaze to the door as Wren walked inside. This morning, he'd wondered if he'd imagined the whole thing, the heat of her soft skin on his palm, the sound of her breath catching in her throat, the rise and fall of her chest.

This was going to be a fucking disaster. He wasn't impartial with Wren. She was a wild card he couldn't control, and he couldn't keep a handle on the emotions surging through his blood.

And of course, she was looking as hot as ever. She wore tight jeans, a blue shirt that hugged her curves, and heeled brown boots. Her hair was pulled up onto the top of her head, and her nails were tipped with hot pink polish.

Her eyes didn't leave his as she made her way to where he was standing. Roarke had to force himself not to look at her breasts, which were close to spilling out of her shirt. He swallowed and looked at a random point over her shoulder.

A wolf whistle sounded in the cavernous space, and he whipped his head around to see Marisol wiggling her eyebrows. "No one told me there'd be pretty eye candy on the team," she said.

There was a beat of silence before Wren started giggling. He narrowed his eyes at Marisol. "No fraternizing with other members of the team."

She rolled her eyes at the empty threat. "You're a buzzkill." She beckoned to Wren. "Come on over, sweet cheeks. I don't bite, and I'm really good with my hands."

Roarke dropped his chin to his chest. "Fuck me."

Wren's hand brushed his arm as she passed. When he glanced up at her, he saw the old Wren for a moment. The one with the innocent smile, who saw *him* and noticed his inner turmoil when no one else did. Then, in a moment, it was gone, lost beneath the click of her boots as she made her way over to Marisol.

He thought belatedly he should have complimented Wren. Told her she looked nice. Smelled nice. Did something new with her hair. Wasn't that how to treat women? He'd never been good at it. Lately, he relied on his tattoos and moderately attractive face to get women into bed. Wooing one? Fuck if he knew how to do that.

Wait, there'd be no wooing. None at all. He shook his head. Enough with the distractions. It was time to rally the troops.

He walked over to the table and stood at the end, drawing his laptop from his bag and placing it gently in front of him. Everyone took a seat except for Marisol, who still sat on the table, watching him.

He took a deep breath. "So—"

A door banged open, the sound like a shot, and every person in the room flinched. Roarke's heart leaped into his throat as he whirled around to see Dade swagger into the room.

Roarke's shoulders dropped in relief. It was just this fucker. He resisted punching Dade in his perfect face. "Nice of you to join us."

Dade shrugged, and as he drew closer, Roarke spotted another cut on his eyebrow. What the fuck was this guy doing? He gestured to Dade's face. "Is whatever you're doing that's making you bleed going to interfere with this mission?"

Dade leaned against the wall beside the table, purposefully not taking a seat. "Nope." His eyes scanned the table before landing on Wren, and then his lips split into a grin. "Hey there, Wren."

Marisol straightened. "Roarke said no frater—"

"Everyone just shut up, for fuck's sake," Roarke growled. "Swear to God, this is like herding cats."

"Well," Erick pointed out, "we're your cats. That you handpicked from the shelter. So that's on you. I prefer wet food by the way."

"My catnip is for medicinal purposes," Marisol piped up.

Roarke breathed in through his nose and out through his mouth before he committed multiple homicide. "All right, enough. I gotta go over why I got you all together. Some of you know the basics, and some of you know next to nothing." He glanced at Dade, who stared back impassively. "So listen the fuck up, okay?"

Roarke knew talking about this was going to be like ripping off a Band-Aid, one that took skin with it. He opened the laptop in front of him and tapped some buttons. An image projected onto the far wall. He ignored the *ooh*s and *ahh*s as he focused on a picture of the graying, skinny, sallow-skinned motherfucker who killed Flynn.

"This is Arden Saltner, owner of the computer security software company Saltner Defense. Two years ago, my brother, Flynn Brennan, decided he wanted out of hacking and was hired at SD in their research department."

He flashed the company logo. "His job was to analyze possible viruses and malware so SD could protect their clients from those threats. Everything was fine until he discovered a previously unknown zero-day vulnerability in the latest release of the QuartzSoft Operating System."

He glanced around and found most people nodding, but he needed to explain everything so there were no team members left behind. "A zero-day is a weakness that is unknown until after a product launches, which gives developers zero days to fix it." He tapped another button. "Some companies, like the developer of the operating system Flynn found, offer bounties for a zero-day. Flynn took his findings to Saltner—as he was supposed to do based on the rules in his department—who said he'd taken care of it and notify QuartzSoft. This was important because this vulnerability allowed a hacker to access personal information from OS users, like credit card numbers."

He took a deep breath. "All of this we know because Flynn told Erick. The rest of what we know is based on what I pulled from Flynn's hard drive after he died." He tapped away again, pulling up several screenshots. "Flynn inquired about the result of his zero-day findings with Saltner in an e-mail dated December 18, two months before his death. The response was from Saltner himself, who said QS had been notified. A month went by, and Flynn did some checking on his own, discovering the vulnerability hadn't been fixed. He contacted a friend, Matthew Dominguez, who is an employee at QS, and he informed Flynn that QS was never told about this vulnerability. They dug deeper and found that the zero-day was being sold on the black market for three million dollars."

The room filled with whispered curses. Even Dade winced and rubbed his face with his hand. The black market for hackers was infamous. Anything and everything was up for sale—credit card information, IDs, and zero-day vulnerabilities that even a low-level hacker could exploit for financial gain.

Jock spoke up, his voice gruff. "So Saltner put the zero-day up for sale rather than taking it to QuartzSoft and collecting their paltry bounty."

"QS offers like...maybe five figures for their zero-days," Erick said.

He pulled up a picture of a young man with glasses. "That's Matthew Dominguez. During his last conversation with Flynn, my brother informed him that the seller was

Saltner. Their code name for Saltner was Evelyn, after the Angelina Jolie character in *Salt*."

Roarke pressed another button, swallowing around the lump in his throat and breathing through the tightness in his chest. The images on the wall went dark. "That was the last communication from either of them. Three hours later, Matthew was killed in a single-car crash. And approximately six hours after that, Flynn was found with a bullet in his head."

Marisol shook her head while Dade stared at the blank wall. Wren was crying silently, her shoulders shaking. Erick stood behind her, biting his lip while rubbing her shoulder. And Jock looked... Well, his face never really changed, but there was something like anger simmering beneath his tanned complexion.

Roarke wanted to take his computer and throw it against the wall. Instead he quickly deleted the files permanently from his hard drive.

He took a minute to get himself under control while his team processed this information. Then he raised his head and spoke around gritted teeth. "I brought you all together because you are the most talented hackers I know. Whether I trust you with my life"—he glanced at Dade, who kicked up his lips into a smirk—"is another story, but it doesn't matter, because I trust you with code. When I recruited you to this team, you all agreed you wanted revenge for Flynn, and that's what we're doing.

"The mission is twofold. First, we need to find out if the zero-day sold, because if it has, we have a lot of vulnerable people. Then we get dirt on Saltner and take him down." Just saying the guy's name tightened Roarke's chest. "This is dangerous, possibly deadly, and I understand if you want to walk out that door right now. This is your chance, no judgment, to back out and go on with your life."

He closed his eyes slowly and opened them to level a look at Wren. Part of him wanted her to stand up and walk out. She didn't have to get in deeper with Darren. This could all go away for her. She could be safe.

But the other part of him, the part he wished he could delete off his hard drive, was the bit of him that wanted her to stay because, now that she was back in his life, he didn't want to let her go.

She met his gaze steadily, and he wondered if she could see his emotions swirling in his head like a two-toned tornado. Her eyes were dry now, staring back at him with that same defiance she'd shown in the parking lot. She stood up, jerked her chin into the air, and mashed a fist into the table. "I'm in for Flynn."

His emotions warred in his heart—having Wren stand up for Flynn was a beautiful thing to see, but knowing this would put her at risk made him want to slam his head into a brick wall. Instead, he nodded at her, and she nodded back, flashing him a brief smile.

One by one, the rest of the team stood up, echoing her and saying, "I'm in for Flynn."

Dade hadn't moved from where he stood, still staring at that spot on the wall where Roarke had projected images to plead his case.

As his team waited silently in the underground room, their fists on the table and their words reverberating off the bare walls, Dade strode over to the table. He licked his lips and brought his fist onto the table with a crash. "In for Flynn, too. So when can we get this motherfucker?"

Roarke smiled.

* * *

Gathering the team was the easy part. Formulating a plan? Not easy.

It really was like herding cats. Roarke hadn't chosen the team members for their cooperation skills. Hackers were notoriously solitary, egotistical, and resistant to authority. He quickly reworked his leadership strategy because lording over them like a master coder was only going to piss them all off.

He had a tentative plan to reach Saltner, but the inclusion of Wren made their job easier, as much as he didn't want to admit it.

"So lemme get this straight," Marisol said, tapping her long nails on the table where they all sat. "Pretty bird here is our foot soldier. She's gonna peddle her ass to Darren—"

"There'll be no ass peddling," Roarke growled.

Marisol lifted her eyebrows but kept talking. "And get dirt to use against Saltner."

Erick cleared his throat. "We want to ruin the fucker. Wren getting in with the family will give us access to information we can't get remotely."

Roarke watched Wren carefully, scanning her body for any sign of nerves. When he saw her fingers shake a little before she clasped them and shoved them into her lap, he was relieved. Nerves were good; it meant she understood what this meant, that it wasn't some game.

It still didn't ease his conscience over her being involved though.

Dade leaned back in his chair and laced his hands behind his head. "Is the ultimate goal to make Saltner disappear or to turn him over to the police?"

"Police," Roarke said quickly. "As much as I want to tie

cement blocks around his ankles and throw him in the middle of the fucking Atlantic, I care more about watching him go down for a computer crime or homicide."

"So we're going to gather information on him, showing he committed a crime, and hand it over to the police?"

"That's the plan." Dade knew of Roarke's refusal to kill anyone. Roarke had been close once, so close to doing it, and he wondered all the time whether he would have regretted it if Mother Nature hadn't taken care of it for him first.

Dade narrowed his eyes. "You're willing to trust the justice system to get revenge for your brother?"

Roarke clenched his teeth. After what he'd done in his teens, he'd vowed to be as lawful as possible. Killing Saltner was pretty far off that vow. "I have to. I just have to."

Dade was silent for a long moment. "And what if we can't pin anything on him?"

Roarke rapped his knuckles on the table. He'd deal with his morals if that was the only way they could take Saltner. "Then we figure something else out."

Dade smiled, his evil grin sending chills down Roarke's spine.

Marisol was watching Dade with raised eyebrows. "Well, aren't you a scary mofo."

Dade blew her a kiss, and Marisol ran her tongue over her lip seductively.

"Christ," Roarke said. "You all need to get laid, then come back. The hormones in here are making me antsy."

"You're just mad Korean Princess over there has a date with your sworn enemy." Marisol looked at her nails, refusing to make eye contact.

"Okaaaay," Erick interrupted, which was good, because Roarke wanted to throttle Marisol with his bare hands.

"Let's all go home, get some rest, and come back tomorrow same time."

Jock was the first to get up, probably over the shit show that was forcing him to be around people. Marisol shrugged and hopped off the table, linking arms with Wren as they walked to the door. Wren glanced back at Roarke, but he couldn't read her face, and within seconds she was out the door.

He blew out a breath and tugged on his hair. Across the table, Dade was watching him intently. "This could be bigger than Saltner, you know."

Roarke nodded. "I realize that."

Dade opened his mouth like he was going to say more but then closed it. "All right then."

"I don't have the answers. And I don't even have a solid plan," Roarke said. "I know that's fucked up, but Flynn is dead, I have a trail, and I'm going to fucking follow it until I can't anymore."

Dade chewed his lip before standing. "I understand. See you tomorrow." He nodded at Erick before opening the door and letting it slam shut behind him.

Roarke steepled his fingers and squinted at his best friend. "Why do I have this sinking feeling in my stomach?"

Erick kicked a chair leg in front of him. "Because this is a clusterfuck."

"You were supposed to say, 'Gee, Roarke, this is all going according to plan.'"

Erick snorted and glanced up, blinking through his bangs. "You know I'm not happy about this Wren thing either, right?"

"I know."

"But this is her choice."

"I know that, too."

Erick was quiet for a moment. "We can protect her. But I think...she's gotta do this. For herself. No matter the outcome."

Nothing made Roarke as bitter as when he wasn't in the know. "What exactly has happened with Wren the past ten years?"

Erick eyed him. "Man, that's her business."

Right, and so it wasn't Roarke's.

"Look, we have a good team." Erick said the words like he was trying to convince both of them. "A team and an underground bunker. What else do we need, really?"

Roarke leveled Erick with a glare. "A well-developed plan would be nice."

Erick's lips shifted to the side. "Oh yeah, well, that."

COUNDON